The

WEDDING

of the

TWO-HEADED

WOMAN

❧

ALSO BY ALICE MATTISON

The Book Borrower: A Novel

Men Giving Money, Women Yelling: Intersecting Stories

Hilda and Pearl: A Novel

The Flight of Andy Burns: Stories

Field of Stars: A Novel

Great Wits: Stories

Animals: Poems

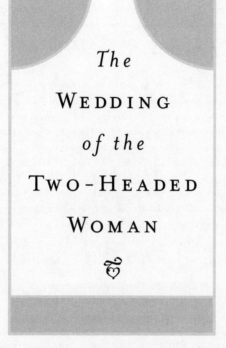

The
WEDDING
of the
TWO-HEADED
WOMAN

ALICE MATTISON

WILLIAM MORROW
An Imprint of HarperCollinsPublishers

THE WEDDING OF THE TWO-HEADED WOMAN. Copyright © 2004 by Alice Mattison. All rights reserved. Printed in the United States of America. No part of this book may be used or reproduced in any manner whatsoever without written permission except in the case of brief quotations embodied in critical articles and reviews. For information address HarperCollins Publishers Inc., 10 East 53rd Street, New York, NY 10022.

HarperCollins books may be purchased for educational, business, or sales promotional use. For information please write: Special Markets Department, HarperCollins Publishers Inc., 10 East 53rd Street, New York, NY 10022.

FIRST EDITION

Designed by Stephanie Huntwork

Printed on acid-free paper

Library of Congress Cataloging-in-Publication Data

Mattison, Alice.
    The wedding of the two-headed woman : a novel / by Alice Mattison.—1st ed.
        p. cm.
    ISBN 0-06-621378-9 (acid-free paper)
    1. Women—Connecticut—Fiction. 2. Community theater—Fiction. 3. Middle-aged women—Fiction. 4. New Haven (Conn.)—Fiction. 5. Murderers—Fiction. I. Title.
PS3563.A8598W44 2004
    813'.54—dc22
                                                                2003044295

04 05 06 07 08 WBC/QW 10 9 8 7 6 5 4 3 2 1

For Edward always

The

WEDDING

of the

TWO-HEADED

WOMAN

Nothing distracts me for long from sex. A friendly, intelligent man makes a funny remark, almost for his private benefit. He thinks nobody hears, but I laugh. For a moment shared understanding exhilarates us both; then I go further. I feel a yen to place my hand on his bare thigh, to see what he's like with no clothes on. I was single for decades, after a brief early marriage, and there were many men like that.

What interests me about sex is nothing dangerous, nothing life-changing. It's like the impulse that sends some women into stores that sell colored floss and kits for making stained-glass pendants—and of course I know that sometimes those women can't refrain, even when pendants hang in every window, twisting together on their dirty strings, falling and breaking into the shards they once were, maybe killing the cat. Sex has mostly, for me, been less threatening than that, a reasonably healthy pastime, a form of arts and crafts that uses people instead of glass or thread.

At length, though, even so delightful a practice as sex begins to feel airlessly limited, a means of expression made clumsy by the need to include bodies as well as talk. At such times, I can be diverted by a different kind of activity: I like to put on conferences. Like patches of plain fabric in a quilt, unremarkable people look better in contact with others, and I look for chances to arrange them. In the seventies I ran something called Women's Weekend. Later I persuaded the community college where I taught to host a colloquium, What Do We Really Think About Race? Most recently, along with my mother, Roz Garber, I ran a conference on mothers and adult daughters. Along comes an idea—ideas come while I'm driving—that requires multitudes (at least groups) arguing and laughing. I start making calls in the car, on my cell phone, then continue at home, buoyant over subject matter, forgetting that by the time my conference takes place, I'll have to think of bodies after all, bodies with their stodgy requirements for food, bathrooms, directions, and unlocked, lighted rooms, bodies that may miss the afternoon session because they're in bed with other bodies, even mine.

I am in my mid-fifties, and I have long, blond hair, possibly too long or too blond for my age. I bear the last name, Andalusia, of a man I no longer know and scarcely remember, with whom I moved to New Haven, Connecticut, thirty years ago so he could go to Yale Medical School while I supported him. When Dr. Andalusia left, I stayed. I'm not the only Yale divorcée who has liked New Haven, to the puzzlement of a departing ex. I liked East Rock and West Rock—red, striated traprock cliffs that bracket this city—and I liked the dirty harbor full of oyster boats and oil tankers, and the

Quinnipiac River emptying rather grandly if messily under Interstate 95 and into Long Island Sound. I liked the decorous, well-proportioned New Haven green with its three old-fashioned churches—two brick, one reddish stone—its bag ladies and black teenagers; and I was amused by the way each man I slept with connected to someone else I knew: he'd gone to school with the last man I slept with, or his sister cleaned my teeth. The story I'm going to write down had to happen in a small city. Here, you're never quite sure you're done with a person; you never know how many ways the two of you will touch.

Someone I stopped knowing many times was the man I eventually married, Pekko Roberts. Pekko is a New Haven native, a noticeable man in his sixties: sturdy, white-haired, with a big, white beard he brushes daily and a tidy but prominent belly. More often than not, I broke up with him when we had dated for a few months and were talking about living together. I don't know why I kept leaving him, since I claimed to be tired of being single, and pointed out to myself that a variety of partners isn't inherent to the pleasures of sex. Pekko was in love with me, which made me a little restless, but he wasn't so in love that he couldn't see my faults, about which he was frank. "Daisy, you're not making sense," he'd say when I wasn't; I'd get angry. He wasn't imaginative in bed, but sex with Pekko made me happy; with him, I didn't experience what often took place after sex with other men: a half hour of dismay, even loathing, about my middle-aged body, my habits, my friends, the way I lived my life. I could talk myself out of that unexplained despair, but with Pekko it didn't come. He was moody and often silent, gruff but not unkind; he knew himself well enough not to blame others for his bad days. His caring—about me, about others—

might be expressed in grunts, but I never doubted it. He was a lake I could swim in, in which the drop-offs and rocks were what they were, but the water was clean and not too cold, and there was intense pleasure to be found by swimming out to the center, turning on my back, and closing my eyes in the sun, whatever that means in terms of a guy.

Four years ago, in 1998, Pekko and I bought a house together in Goatville, a nineteenth-century New Haven neighborhood of small houses with steep roofs and long, skinny backyards, where dogs bark through chain-link fences. (We also bought a dog, a standard poodle called Arthur: a dog should be able to pronounce his own name.) The narrow two- and three-story houses on our block look like kindergarten drawings. It's a cityscape best seen in winter twilight, when the peaked roofs of different heights are scribbled over by the bare branches of maples, oaks, and sycamores. Our house isn't covered with ugly aluminum siding, like some, and after many discussions, we had it painted light gray with dark and light blue trim. Pekko said the color scheme was fussy.

So we lived together, and even held an offhand wedding. We tried to control our exuberant young dog, and we talked about our house, Arthur, our experiment in not breaking up, more than we talked about what we each did when we weren't together. I didn't mind Pekko's moods as much as I'd expected to. Sometimes I'd suddenly feel alone again, but I'd never minded being alone; it was restful. I established moods of my own.

What I did when we were apart was teach, with decreasing interest. Then one day, I stopped my car at a traffic light next to a red Audi driven by a young woman. The entire backseat and front passenger seat were filled with paper—old newspapers and mail from the look of it—all the way to the bottoms of the windows. I couldn't stop thinking about that car, and a week later, when I saw the Audi parked not far from where I live, I taped a note to the windshield. "I'm expensive," I wrote, as if I'd done this before, "but I can help." The clutter stopped at the windows: the owner liked light, not darkness, and was cautious and disciplined enough to observe some limits. She called me, I figured out what to do, and it worked.

This was work I couldn't stop talking about at home. I was non-threatening, I explained to Pekko. Neither the owner of the Audi nor I had a driveway, so we moved the car to a parking lot and surrounded it with cartons. Only one was labeled "Keep." Then we undertook a long process of sorting and deciding. I was so conservative, so hesitant, that after a while she became impatient—and nervous because I charged by the hour—and she threw away armloads.

"You like this," said Pekko. "Quit your job and start a business."

"How will I live?" I said, but I had stopped what I was doing— glancing at the paper in our kitchen—to think how much I'd like to have such a business.

"I make enough for both of us," he said.

I was incredulous. "If you support me, you'll start ordering me around. You'll expect me to cook."

"It's an investment," he said. "I don't care if you cook. When you get rich, I'll do something new, and you'll support me." Pekko had enough money, I was pretty sure, that he could do whatever he liked, whether I was rich or not. He's had many businesses over the years. Now he buys and manages real estate in New Haven's inner city.

("You're a slumlord?" I had said, when we got together after one of our gaps, and he described his new work.

"Without me they'd be homeless.")

I liked teaching, but I'd had that job for decades—I was tired of it. Still, I'd never considered letting a man support me. "I'd be like a whore," I said.

"What?"

"You're offering me money for sex. You pay, I go to bed with you."

Pekko sighed. "It's different when you're married," he said. Then he added, "I won't make fun of you if you fail," and I understood what I'd been afraid of.

To my mother's consternation—"As a teacher, you had clean hands!"—I became someone who sorted and organized clutter. I want to manage not just people, it seems, but their belongings, and they seem to want me to do it. I've been doing it ever since—two or three years.

༃

Pekko cooks well, several times a week. Single for a long time, he learned to fix a few good meals to impress women. "Chicken is the best," he used to say. "Women claim to like fish, but they're easier to seduce after chicken." One day in February, about a year ago—2001—Pekko broiled chicken breasts ("You want to say 'breasts' early in the evening") spread with Dijon and sour cream. He'd found thin asparagus and strawberries at an Italian market a few blocks away. So we ate a spring meal, but it had started to snow in the afternoon, and now it was snowing hard.

Snow made us want to stay in our warm house and take each other's clothes off, and Pekko's cooking works on me. The winter strawberries weren't quite sweet, so we dipped them in sugar. After eating them, we might have licked the juice from our fingers and gone to bed, but the phone rang. My mother—who moved to New Haven from New York when she retired—was calling from a soup kitchen in a downtown parish house, where she helped serve supper on Thursday evenings. The volunteers had locked their coats and purses in a closet, she explained with some zest, but now the lock was broken and nobody could open the door. The only locksmith they could reach had had a minor car accident in the slippery snow and refused to come until morning. "Pekko could fix the lock," she said. "Also, I could take a cab home, but my house keys are locked in the closet." She no longer drives at night and had gone to the soup kitchen by taxi.

I love to drive in snow, and I had a key to my mother's house. Pekko doesn't mind driving in snow, he likes my mother, and the story of the lock interested him, but by the time he'd taken off his apron—Pekko cooks in an apron—I was leading the way to my car, with an extra coat for Roz over my arm. I hate being a passenger in any weather. Pekko stumped along behind me in the light, gritty snow.

So I drove, and it was a little slippery. At the soup kitchen, the eaters had departed and the trays had been washed and replaced in the church kitchen. The place smelled of tomato sauce. I'd picked up or delivered my mother there a few times, and once I had stayed to serve dessert, wearing plastic gloves to offer assorted day-old pastries to men and women who thoughtfully chose a cherry Danish, an apple turnover, or an iced cruller. It's a surprisingly appealing place, whether because a significant number of the guests are experiencing chemically induced euphoria or because black, Hispanic, and white people order one another around with jocularity and no fuss.

Now, the director—a big, cheerful woman with a loud voice—was organizing attempts to open the closet. The key went in, but the cylinder flipped over and over without resistance, without catching. So many people were sure they'd know just how to turn the key that Pekko couldn't get near the door. The soup kitchen is staffed partly by volunteers, partly by people doing community service who are sent by the courts, and partly by kids from some kind of reform school. One of those—nobody was asking how he'd acquired his experience—moved forward now, and we joined the group watching him.

"I *never* put my things in that closet!" said a woman in a coat, with self-satisfaction. She could have left but didn't. The rest, a coatless group of four or five, stood around my mother, who looked out from under white curls like a wise woman, good-naturedly razzing the young man at the door. I joined the crowd. Pekko watched quietly while the young man worked a length of wire coat hanger into the disabled lock. He bent it so it surrounded the bolt inside and came out the bottom, but it didn't dislodge the bolt. "This is a good lock," he said respectfully. The sexton arrived. He explained loudly that the door was specially braced and wouldn't come off even if the hinges were removed.

"Pekko!" said one of the coatless women—a thin white woman, maybe in her forties.

"Hey." Pekko shook her hand solemnly. "How are you, Daphne?"

My mother got interested. "You two know each other?"

"Do you know Gabby?" said Daphne. For some reason they call my mother Gabby at the soup kitchen.

Pekko introduced me, and Daphne said to him, "I heard you got married." Then to me, "I worked for Pekko when he had the restaurant." That would have been twelve or fifteen years ago. When we met, he owned a frozen yogurt store.

Daphne said she was working at the soup kitchen because of a traffic violation, and I wondered if that was true. I didn't think you had to do community service for a speeding ticket.

"What are you doing these days?" Pekko said. Daphne's face was jumpy, lined by too much smoking. Light brown hair fell close to her eyes, and a skittish teenage face was visible beneath her present one.

"Waitressing, still. Whatever I can get my hands on, but that pays the best. I'm working lunches now, so I can come here in the evening."

Finally the sexton shooed us all out. The director's car keys were in her pants pocket. Coatless, she led two people with neither coats nor keys to her car. Pekko offered Daphne a ride, and she followed us, hugging herself in the cold, while my mother came along, diminutive in my extra coat. I'm tall. Pekko hadn't had a turn at the lock.

Daphne lived in Hamden, so I took Roz home first. Pekko and I sat silently in the front seat while Roz and Daphne chattered in the back like our children. Daphne talked about her kids, and Roz volunteered facts about my two older brothers and me, as if we were Daphne's kids' counterparts, and as if I wasn't there. "Oh, Daisy had excellent teeth."

Roz lives in a small brick house on Prospect Street. "It's too much work for me," she told Daphne as we approached it. "It's supposedly low maintenance, but it's not low enough." She had a contract for snow removal, but keeping up the yard was difficult. "No help from my daughter," Roz said. "*She's* no gardener."

"I like to garden," Daphne said, after a pause. We had reached Roz's as yet unplowed driveway, and I drove up it. I didn't get out to help her. My mother, firm on her legs, was wearing state-of-the-art boots. "I could do your yard work," Daphne continued, as Roz opened her door.

"You could?" she said, climbing out. She took my key to her house, and said, "I'll keep this coat for a while. I like it." She made her way through the snow, and as she let herself in, I backed carefully down the driveway. Then I took Daphne, who became quiet, to Hamden.

On the drive home, I asked Pekko, "What's Daphne's trouble?"

"She's had plenty of troubles," he said. He reflected for a while. "No fractures that I know of."

"Healthy."

"Well, I think she once had cancer."

"That's why you shook her hand that way?"

"No, no. It was a long time ago."

"What else?"

"Nothing else."

"Is it all right if she does yard work for my mother?"

"I suppose. She's a nice woman."

At home, there was a message for me on the answering machine. The last time I'd had the urge to put together a talking event, I'd gone on the radio instead of assembling a group. I'd become interested in a small, homey radio station not far from New Haven, run mostly by volunteers. I worked in their office for a while, then persuaded someone to let me substitute on her low-key, casual show when she went on vacation. So I'd done a few shows, playing music and reading poems aloud, and apparently people liked them. The message, that February evening, asked if I'd be interested in doing five programs on "a topic of public interest."

"I could talk about hunger and homelessness," I said to Pekko. "Or prostitution. Do they let you talk about whores on the radio?"

"Like daytime television?" He was stamping snow off his shoes. "What makes you think of that?"

"More like oral history. Sociology. Are some of your tenants prostitutes?" I asked.

He didn't answer. I wrote down the name and phone number of the woman who'd called. Then I started washing the dishes. As I stood at the sink, still cold from being outdoors, Pekko came and stood behind me, putting his hands on my waist, then drawing them down the sides of my hips. Then he pressed his body into my back and moved his hands to my chest. I left the broiler pan to soak and turned toward him, my breasts throbbing. I didn't reach under his clothes with my wet hands. Arthur squeezed his head between us, so Pekko put him in the yard. We went to bed at last, hurrying under the comforter once we were undressed. Pekko's solid body was confident and warm as it moved above me. We came at the same time, and lay quietly afterward. I reached to stroke the side of his body, and he took my hand, held it, then let it go.

It was early for bedtime, and I'd left the dishes in the sink, but I thought I'd get up only to brush my teeth, then read in bed before sleep. Pekko now snored lightly beside me, but when I sat up, he roused himself, slapped his bare thighs as he swung out of bed, and said, "I'll take Arthur for a walk."

Arthur likes an evening walk, but he'd been outside for forty minutes, barking now and then at the other Goatville dogs. "It's snowing," I said.

"I think it stopped."

I wanted to stay near him. "Shall I come?"

"No." He got dressed, and after a while I heard the jingle of the choke collar, and then Pekko let himself out, locking the door behind him. In the old days, a man I'd brought home would sometimes leave after sex when I expected him to spend the night. I'd be disappointed, then relieved. Now Pekko and Arthur took a long walk. I brushed my teeth and was asleep before they returned.

❦

I like serious clutter. I'm not stimulated by messy closets but by rooms piled to the ceiling. And I do *like* it, though it makes me slightly ill with anxiety. I like dismantling it, but I am sad, which might be why hoarders trust me. I can find what's worth keeping: love letters from the First World War, usable furniture for the homeless shelter. I don't like garbage—smelly clutter—and sometimes the distinction is subtle. If everything is wet or otherwise disgusting, I call in a firm that empties and fumigates, but if possible I work myself, salvaging what I can—most often ceramics and glassware, which doesn't crumble, rust, or become permanently stained or greasy. Of course the usual problem is dust. A mask offends some gatherers. I carry a small battery-powered vacuum cleaner. I don't mind bugs, but I'm afraid of snakes.

The recalcitrant hoarders I like best are the divided souls, like me, not the single-minded accumulators who've been prodded to call me by a horrified acquaintance. My favorite clients have had a partial conversion: a vision of a bare room, a vision they're resisting. One man hired me when the immense accumulation of trash in his apartment was what he called "complete."

"Now," he said, "it's time to go the other way."

"How do you know?"

"It's what I imagine." I join a client's inner life. I view and handle its embodiment. What could be better? Secrets please me—learning them, telling them—especially when revelation confirms separation. When I'm alone with my oldest friend, a social worker named Charlotte LoPresti, I don't tell secrets easily. "What are you afraid of?" Charlotte would say, if she read what I just wrote. I don't know what I'm afraid of, but I know I like the edge of secrecy, the nearly public edge.

When I began volunteering at that local station, radio wasn't entirely new to me. Years ago, at the time of the conference on women, I was interviewed at a small radio station full of unwieldy equipment with the mechanical look of the thirties or forties: metal poles swung in our faces; nothing flickered electronically or kept discreetly to itself. As far as I remember, nobody was present except the interviewer and me, and between the contraptions holding microphones aloft, I could hardly see her. I thought nobody was listening. First we talked about standard women's issues. Soon we began telling personal stories, and I forgot the possible radio audience. It was a call-in show, but the phone didn't ring. When it did, and a listener asked me to repeat the conference schedule, I looked at the interviewer, startled. She laughed lightly, and I complied.

Then we returned to our conversation. See, she seemed to say, listeners make it *more* private.

Those more recent evenings—playing Billie Holiday and Bessie Smith, reading poems—felt similar. It was late at night, and I seemed to be alone. The last time I did a show, I read parts of Wallace Stevens's long, difficult poem "An Ordinary Evening in New Haven"—because I always thought it should be heard on some ordinary New Haven evening. Like others in this town, I imagine, I'd come upon it first in a table of contents, and read a little because it seemed to promise to describe my life. It didn't. I had no idea what it was describing. It has thirty-one sections, each almost a page long. Somebody's in a hotel room, and then he's walking around among the Yale colleges and New Haven's churches. He imagines New Haven, and he tries to work out the relation between the city he sees—"the eye's plain version" and the city he imagines, "an impalpable town, full of impalpable bells." Out loud, I read,

> *The point of vision and desire are the same.*
> *It is to the hero of midnight that we pray*
> *On a hill of stones to make beau mont thereof.*

> *If it is misery that infuriates our love,*
> *If the black of night stands glistening on beau mont,*
> *Then, ancientest saint ablaze with ancientest truth,*

> *Say next to holiness is the will thereto,*
> *And next to love is the desire for love,*
> *The desire for its celestial ease in the heart.*

"Next to love is the desire for love," I repeated firmly—talking, perhaps, to nobody. I think Pekko and I had just gotten married then, or maybe we were planning our casual little wedding. I wasn't certain I loved Pekko, but I knew I desired to love him, and I was glad when this poem I didn't understand—but liked—seemed to tell me that was almost as good.

Then someone called the station, as someone had called that first station, all those years ago—breaking into solitude, proving I wasn't alone. A man who identified himself as Isaac said, "The poem was written in 1949, so the hotel at the beginning is the Taft. The hill of stones could be East Rock. East Rock is certainly visible from the high windows of the Taft."

꽃

Maybe I finally married Pekko because he'd become a slum-lord—because in his screwy way he was demonstrating his love for the city of his birth, which is a city I've become quite fond of myself. New Haven is turbulent, multiethnic, industrial—formerly specializing in the manufacture of guns—and somewhat but not quite dominated by Yale. If you lingered in some literate nook here—say the Foundry Bookstore—and talked to the people you saw, many would report that they, or their parents or grandparents, moved here to study or teach at Yale. Not Pekko; he's a townie. His sexy name comes from an immigrant great-grandfather, but most of his people have lived in New England for generations. His grand-parents moved to New Haven from Rutland, Vermont, so his grand-father could work as a police officer.

"Yale!" Pekko says impatiently. In New Haven, Yale employs, Yale owns, Yale operates, Yale pronounces—and because of Yale, crimes here are national news, so we who live here find ourselves defending the place, even defending homelessness, poverty, and criminals. Pekko says, "Those professors think New Haven is Yale plus blight. They've never looked around." My mother would tell me to point out that New Haven has many thriving neighborhoods with well-kept old houses, including some big, fancy ones still inhabited by single families. Our mansions are not funeral homes.

"I'm a realist," Pekko says. He'd acknowledge that New Haven has plenty of blight, though much of it, these days, is being replaced with public housing developments so pretty they look like sets for *Our Town*. Drug dealers live in Pekko's properties. If they pay the rent, he doesn't bother them. If they don't, he says something to somebody—he knows everybody—and the police hold a raid. "It's faster than eviction," he says.

From the time I began talking about my radio series on prostitution, which was arranged within a few days, Pekko seemed uncomfortable. It was one thing to be a realist; another, apparently, to be a realist on the radio. I'd agreed to put together five one-hour programs, once a week, starting in a month. I was somewhat alarmed that the people in charge believed I was a radio interviewer who could lure former prostitutes and knowledgeable professionals to the station, but I seem to run my life by pretending I already am what I want to be.

"You must know prostitutes," I said, the day after I'd made the agreement. "Or former prostitutes. Poor women have no choice." I told him about a discussion of homelessness I'd attended once at which a powerful, attractive woman looked steadily at the audience and said, "Well, a woman can always find a place to stay."

He shrugged and looked at me as if to say, Of course. As if I'd said, "You must eat fruit," which comes to mind because he was eating an orange. Every year he orders a box from Florida.

Pekko didn't want to talk about whores, but I did, and I described a fellow teacher who made extra money modeling bathing suits whenever a local manufacturer entertained out-of-town buyers—and even more money going to their hotel rooms. I recounted two occasions in my twenties when I myself was approached by potential johns, both as I looked into a shop window at the wares displayed, which for all I know is a signal. I was frightened when a man outside a bakery said quietly, "If you come home with me, I'll give you twenty dollars," but a few years later, when a similar man—in a well-pressed, conservative raincoat—lingered beside me before a display of Marimekko dresses, then said, "Would you like one of those?" I was not scared or angry but fascinated.

I said, "I'm waiting for my husband," who was Bruce Andalusia, and I was even more fascinated when the man apologized and thanked me—as if I was warning him that Bruce might beat him up, though I was merely refusing his offer politely. I couldn't help imagining what might have happened, titillating or terrifying, if Bruce hadn't been on his way, and if I had said I would like one of those richly dyed dresses.

"Is prostitution always appalling?" I asked Pekko, who had listened to what I'd said without comment. "Is fantasizing about it inherently disrespectful—like glamorizing rape?"

He shrugged and shook his head, gathering his orange peel and emptying his hand into the garbage pail on his way out of the room.

☙

I did put on five radio programs about prostitution: they happened, people heard them—or didn't—they were over. They weren't important, but in one way or another, they determined the next half year. They are the beginning of the story I seem to be telling. The first show, in March, was on another night when wet snow made driving difficult. I was afraid my guest, a social worker who counseled drug-addicted women, wouldn't show up, but she did. "Do prostitutes want our pity or our respect?" I asked her; in a raspy voice with a Brooklyn accent she said, "Nobody *ever* wants *anybody's* pity." She talked matter-of-factly about her clients' lives, how they might turn to prostitution now and then, yet insist they weren't pros, how some of them *were* pros. Yet again, I'd agreed to a call-in show, but this time I knew people were listening. A producer sat behind a glass partition screening calls. I was nervous that callers would condemn prostitutes, but the first person I talked to was a man who'd patronized prostitutes and had discovered how decent they were; the second was a woman whose sister, a prostitute, had been killed by a man she'd picked up. "If prostitution is a victimless crime, I don't know what a victim is," she said.

The last person we had time for was Mary, who sounded just like my mother until the strange moment, thirty seconds into her contribution, when I realized Mary *was* my mother. "Wait a second," I said, then quieted myself. Roz or Mary was saying, "My cousin turned tricks during the Depression. She was a classy whore—an escort for businessmen. A call girl. She looked as if she didn't have a brain in her head, but she was a college graduate. She'd gone to Hunter, like me, and we couldn't get jobs. Even to be a salesgirl at

Macy's, you had to be Vassar or Smith. And I have to say, she was a nice person, but not that nice. Let's not start thinking these women are saints."

I thanked my mother for her contribution—wondering which of my relatives she meant—and soon the show was over. As I drove home, alert for slippery spots, my hands trembled on the steering wheel. I was tired, and giddy with relief from a tension I hadn't known I felt. And happy. I parked just down the block from our house, fitted my key into the lock, and crouched to forestall Arthur's joyful leap at my chest with his front paws. He led me to Pekko, who was stretched out on our bed with *The New York Times* (he takes the *New Haven Register* at his office) and still another orange. By March he has used up the oranges from Florida and is buying them from Stop & Shop. Pekko said my mother had called to say she'd forgotten to listen until it was too late. "Oh, sure," I said. "Did you hear Mary?"

"I forgot to listen, too," Pekko said.

"You did?" It had not occurred to me that Pekko might not be listening. I wasn't sure if I minded or not.

Arthur sprang onto the bed and stood over Pekko, licking his lips and cheeks above the beard, celebrating my arrival with Pekko, then returning to celebrate their celebration with me. I sat down on the floor so as not to be jumped on and pinched Arthur's bony neck through his black curls. The dog settled beside me while Pekko peeled the orange with his thumb, making a yellow pile of peel on our puffy green comforter. Then he ate it, section after section. When Arthur vaulted onto the bed again, he received an orange section.

"You forgot?" I said. I reached over and took a piece of the orange so as not to have to wonder whether I'd get any.

The penetrating smell of the orange peel narrowed my scope from the southern Connecticut listening public to the bedroom I sat in, while juice stung a paper cut on my finger. I should wear gloves to clean up trash, but I never bother. Leaning on the wall, still stroking the dog—who had returned to me—and looking up at Pekko, I said, "You really don't think it's a good idea to go on the radio talking about whores."

"I forgot. Oh, I suppose I was afraid you'd get calls from my friends, confessing to being pimps."

"I used to think you might be a pimp."

"I've done everything," he said. "But not that."

"I thought that after one of our breakups," I said. Our many separations were abrupt and surprising, each precipitated by a trivial disagreement. I'd drive away from the argument, stunned. Now my date book would be wrong and my days lopsided, skewed by absence. A few days later, I'd convince myself that the disagreement had indeed been significant; something was truly amiss. Once, I believed he despised me because he was incorruptible while I was amoral and irresponsible. Another time, I was afraid he was a crook. Sometimes a year or two passed before he called me again, or I called him, or we met by chance, falling into each other's arms as if the other had been lost all that time, beyond the reach of e-mail, regular mail, phone.

The orange was gone. I said I needed a glass of wine, because I did need it, or because I was mildly taunting Pekko, who hasn't drunk alcohol for decades, after heaven knows what before that. He doesn't do drugs, either, possibly so as to look down on people who do. I started refusing joints (I'd never had my own supply) when I decided to marry him, so I wouldn't be one of those people.

"Who's Mary?" he said eventually.

"Am I supposed to call my mother?"

"She said, 'Tell her don't bother.' Who's Mary?"

I fetched a glass of Merlot and sat on the edge of the bed while I told him about the show.

"I should have listened," he said. "Are you sure it was Roz?"

"She did go to Hunter. I've never heard the story of the cousin who was a call girl. Maybe she didn't want me to know."

"Maybe it's not true," said Pekko. He and Roz and I, I thought. There's not one of us you can trust. "Maybe *she* was the call girl," Pekko said.

Next day the snow was less of a presence than it might have been, but the weather was damp and cloudy, and I slipped when I ventured down the steps, in my bathrobe, for the *Times*. I spent the morning at home, working on my coming radio shows and printing out clients' bills. The phone rang as I left, at last, to keep an appointment with someone who didn't interest me, Ellen Arlington. Ellen's immense quantities of junk consisted not of objects she'd chosen to keep but of what had been imposed upon her: given, forcibly lent, or abandoned. Her accumulation concealed rather than revealed her, and working with her taught me nothing. I turned back to the ringing phone, hoping she was calling to cancel, but the voice was a man's.

"Daisy Andalusia," he said quickly. "I'm a listener. Love that station." He talked fast but didn't sound peremptory or bureaucratically self-important. This speed seemed to claim, with a childlike guilelessness, that the speaker talked fast to have enough time for extra remarks, since he was unendingly fascinating. So I pictured a man in a house, a man in a tan sweater with his back to a kitchen window.

He sounded friendly, but it occurred to me for the first time that a listener could call to be rude, or to hurt. "You didn't say your name," I said.

"Gordon Skeetling, the Yale Small Cities Project." Office after all—Yale office: a large, glossy brown desk. "You work on messes," he continued. "I've meant to call you for weeks, but I didn't know if you'd do. Then, there you were on the radio. I assume you're the same Daisy Andalusia. I've got a mess."

A client of mine had recommended me. "I was afraid you might not be intellectually up to the job," he said, "but you're smart, which is what I need: someone with brains, not just someone with a feather duster."

"I know people who clean to earn their living but are smart," I said.

"Of course. I apologize. I'm a snob. Come see my mess." I pictured him walking back and forth, stretching the phone cord—a man in his late thirties, not quite as good-looking as he wanted to be. I made an appointment to visit his office in a row house on Temple Street, a downtown street at the edge of the Yale campus.

As soon as we'd settled on a day and time, Gordon Skeetling said, "That social worker didn't know what she was talking about," changing subjects so fast I had to think what social worker he could mean.

"On my program?"

"She was advertising despair as tolerance. You don't know how to keep a girl from turning tricks, so you decide it's her right to do it. Tell me if I'm wrong."

"Isn't it her right?"

"It's her right to step in front of a speeding truck, but if I see her, I'm going to grab her and pull her back," he said. "Do you know about the Soul Patrol? A possibly simplistic solution to the moral problem, but intriguing, especially if you want to focus on local stuff. Which is the advantage of regional radio—you can do that."

"What's the Soul Patrol?"

"Back in the seventies. Probably you'd rather keep your show current. Black women mysteriously murdered—quite a number of them, mostly prostitutes. In those days hookers walked on Chapel Street near Howe. You could see them there any evening."

"I remember."

"You go back, like me." He was older than I'd thought. "So the brothers from Dwight decided they'd just keep the hookers company, a brother walking behind each woman. Of course business went way down. Those white guys from the suburbs figured they'd look somewhere else."

"Were the murders ever solved?" I asked.

"I don't know. Maybe we could find some guy who was in the patrol, for the show."

We? I thought. I said, "Are you black?"

"White."

I'd never asked such a question. He seemed to offer permission of one sort or another. I got off the phone and hurried to my appointment.

When I saw Gordon Skeetling a few days later, he did not wear the sweater I'd pictured. His hair was gray, thick, and straight—floppy—but his face was young, with inquiring, surprised blue eyes under black eyebrows that came to points. He was fifty, I guessed, a thin, rangy guy in a striped shirt and no tie, with long arms that often stretched sideways—toward a light switch, a coat hanger, a chair. He wore no wedding ring. Two desks stood in his big office—the main room of an old brownstone—but he was alone.

"I'm one of those Yale people who doesn't get tenure and doesn't get fired," he said, showing me around. "I got a grant and talked myself into an office, more than twenty years ago, and I'm good at finding money, so I've been here ever since. They're a little ashamed of me because cities mean grubby, but they keep me because I locate my own funding. Mostly, I work on small cities, humdrum problems. I'm a researcher. I find things out for people who want to know them."

"New Haven?"

"Sometimes New Haven. When Yale is accused of ignoring the inner city, they trot me out and I talk about research I did on public schools, or a study of prenatal care in low-income areas. That one, I worked with the medical school."

I felt the sense of permission I'd had on the phone—Gordon Skeetling gave it and had it—which surely is the opposite of arrogance, though he'd called himself a snob. I liked the thought of this man with long arms, unintimidated by Yale, who casually grabbed money and used it for some slightly confusing purpose. Gordon Skeetling found himself funny but wasn't bitter, though he'd kept a job into middle age that probably wasn't the one he'd imagined. Enjoying the permission, I said, "Did you think you'd do something else, twenty years ago?"

"I don't remember!" he said, waving his right arm, with apparent pleasure in his capacity to forget. "I have a law degree," he said, "but I never practiced."

He led me to his archive—the mess that had brought us together—which was behind French doors, in a side room that had

windows, because this row house was at the end of the row. The archive had once been a dining room or library. When I saw it, I sighed happily and stretched out my own arms as if to claim it, exaggerating the gesture to show that I too could make fun of my enthusiasms, that I had enthusiasms as remarkable as his.

It was a colorful mess. Color matters. It was orderly but not too orderly. Extremely straight piles of accumulated artifacts make me uneasy, but these were rough piles in red, blue, green, yellow, and purple folders. There were heaps of folded maps, and the walls were covered with maps pasted to poster board in a nice, amateurish way: maps of Waterbury, Connecticut; Waterville, Maine; Worcester, Massachusetts; New Brunswick, New Jersey. New Haven. I said, "I'm glad New Haven counts."

"New Haven counts. You like New Haven?"

"I do."

"So do I," he said.

Some maps were framed and properly hung. Others were propped against the wall, with still others behind them.

"What's in the folders?" I said.

He shrugged. "Clippings, pamphlets, studies, offprints. Rules and regulations. Statutes and ordinances. No person shall keep a goat in the city of . . ."

One wall held books and shelves of black boxes. On a table I saw posters and placards that Gordon Skeetling probably stole, warnings not to park because of construction, parades, street sweeping, leaf sweeping, snow plowing. A long table was covered with stacks of newspapers. Although he now worked alone, he said, over the years he'd sometimes had interns or assistants. He'd kept anything that excited somebody, and maybe that was why the room had tautness

despite the conglomeration. It didn't smell of exhaustion, like heaps
and piles that have become routine.

"You just like cities?" I said.

"That's why I'm here."

The man was respectable. People in expensive offices with central air-conditioning took him seriously. But he was quirky, like me
and my friends. I thought people like him had to run antiques shops
or used bookstores in Vermont, but he'd found a way to impress people in charge. I wanted him to be impressed with me.

He perched on the edge of a table, and I did the same. "So," I
said, drawing out my notebook, "you want me to work along with
you, and make decisions about what to keep?"

"I'm too busy. Work by yourself. That's why you had to be smart."

"I do this *with* my clients," I said. "Unless they're dead. Then
they can't complain about what I throw away."

Gordon Skeetling shrugged. "Pretend it's yours. Figure out what
you want. If I yell, yell back."

"Then why?" I said, interested but wary.

"I would like the archive to be smaller," he said, reaching his
arms in both directions, as if to measure the room. "But primarily I
want it used. Make something."

"What sort of something?"

"I don't know. We'll talk."

I looked to see what I was sitting near. Stacks of tabloid newspapers, big old stacks of *The National Enquirer*, the *Star*. "You like
these papers?" I said.

"Not as much as I used to, before they were all about celebrities,"
he said. "I used to buy them for the headlines. 'Fisherman Kisses

Loch Ness Monster. His Wife Divorces Him.' Wonderful headlines and then wonderful subheads."

"They don't particularly have to do with cities."

"I guess not," he said, unperturbed. "Let me show you a good one."

He knew where it was. Others had taken this tour. The headline was maybe twenty years old. It read, TWO-HEADED WOMAN WEDS TWO MEN, and the subhead was DOC SAYS SHE'S TWINS.

"I *love* that," said Gordon Skeetling, stretching his arms wide, and I loved hearing him sing the word *love*. "Twins!" This man wasn't afraid of himself.

❦

Of course I wanted a rich, glamorous call girl for my show. In my imagination, she'd come to the station in a fur coat, murmuring, "I hated them all, but they didn't guess." One morning at Lulu's—my neighborhood coffee shop—a journalist I knew handed me a scrap of paper with a phone number on it. "She's a psychologist in Boston," she said. "She used to be a call girl. She's willing to be interviewed by phone."

"I *liked* it," the former call girl said, in an educated voice, on my third show. She'd been a graduate student in psychology, and she claimed that she'd practiced on the men she visited in their hotel rooms. "I learned more than I did in the placements they made me do for school. I felt sorry for them, and I helped them—for plenty of money. I lied to my friends about where I got my good clothes."

"You're still talking about it," I said. "People might recognize your voice."

"Maybe I want to be found out," she said amiably. "I don't think much of psychologists who don't have a little pathology of their own. How do they sympathize with the lure of the irrational?"

I too, in my youth, was bold, smart, sexy, and in need of money. "But wasn't it humiliating?" I said.

"Assuming it's humiliating," she said, "depends on giving sex a certain weighty symbolism. You could feel that way about sharing food with someone, or shaking hands..."

"Yes!" I said.

She went on, "It's not sex for money that makes prostitution disgusting. It's the opportunity for blackmail, for disease, for cruelty. It's dangerous because it's a secret."

"I guess the secrecy is inherent," I said. But I was mistaken. Our city held one former prostitute who cared nothing for secrecy, but I hadn't found her. She called the station. "I have something to say about whores," said her message. "My name is Muriel Peck."

Muriel Peck worked in a health program for poor people and in her spare time was an activist for prostitutes. She was willing to come to the station and discuss her history and views, so I canceled the criminologist I'd scheduled for the last session. A dark-skinned black woman wearing blue jeans, a purple corduroy jacket with a hood, and hiking boots, Muriel Peck arrived carrying a large blue-and-green bag, which turned out to contain rag dolls about two feet tall: one pink, one brown, and one green. She propped them on chairs. They were whore dolls, she explained. She'd made them. One doll was dressed in a short, sequined skirt and a bra top, another wore overalls, and the third—the green one—a long, old-fashioned skirt with a bustle. There was no way to know they were prostitutes, except that they wore cardboard labels: "Lady of the

Night," "Woman of Ill Repute." The point was that women of all sorts have become prostitutes.

"Being a whore did not make me somebody who was only fit to die," Muriel said confidently on the air. Her graying hair stuck out from her head a few inches in all directions, which made her head look big and led the eye to rest on her face, which was still but intense, with prominent nose and cheekbones, and hooded eyes; you looked to make sure she wasn't angry. "That's how people thought for centuries, you know—not just about whores but about any poor girl who went to bed when she wasn't married. Italian girls, Jewish girls. I am part Italian and part Jewish. Black skin is like chocolate ice cream. Any flavor the factory messes up, they add chocolate and everybody says it's chocolate. That's why you sometimes find a strawberry in chocolate ice cream."

"Oh, that can't be right," I said.

"Oh, yes. One fourth Jew and one eighth Italian. I can show you the family tree."

"That's not what I was doubting!" I said. "I'm one fourth Italian, too."

"There you go."

"Three quarters Jewish." We seemed to have changed the subject. Listeners probably thought they'd somehow tuned in to two ladies in a living room.

"Why did I start?" Muriel said, though I hadn't asked. "I was poor. Times were bad. The factories seemed worse."

"But wasn't it dreary, being a whore?"

"Yes."

She now worked in organizations that fought to decriminalize prostitution. "Some of us want to make it legal," she said. "Some just want to take away the criminal penalties, so a girl can go to the doctor without thinking next stop is the jail."

She'd quit being a prostitute after two years. "I was lucky. My pimp died." Eventually she'd gone to a community college, and later she'd studied nursing. She wanted to talk about the dolls, and I tried to describe them. "All sorts of women," she said again. "Shakes up your preconceptions."

"Even green women," I said.

"Even green. I make baby dolls too, for kids. Some kids love the green dolls, the lavender dolls. Some scream if you show them a green doll."

"The babies are not whore dolls," I said.

"No indeed. No baby whores. Child prostitution is one hundred percent evil. Because no child chooses that. Even if they think they choose, they don't choose."

"So adult prostitutes choose?" I said.

"Some choose," Muriel said sadly. "And those are the ones you're talking about on this show, am I right? The dead ones, the ones in jail, the ones somebody won't *allow* to talk. You don't have *them* on your radio show."

"No," I admitted.

☙

I liked Muriel Peck. After the show she stuffed her dolls into the blue-and-green bag, and reached to shake hands. I was sorry I wouldn't see her again. The radio series had just ended, and I drove home, pleased with myself but sad. I didn't know who'd heard me. I didn't know if Pekko had; he'd listened to one or two of the earlier shows. My mother admitted to hearing all but the first, and my friend Charlotte and her husband, Philip, had been carefully faithful, leaving enthusiastic phone or e-mail messages, but Pekko had said little, though I thought he'd heard at least one show. I wished I could gather my listeners into a room and look at them.

At home I was greeted by Arthur and poured myself a glass of wine while Pekko, who had been reading the *Times,* watched me from the kitchen table. "Tired, sweetie?" he said, and I nodded. Our kitchen is big, and at one end there's an old sofa, a faded greenish, comfortable thing, from the beach house where Pekko used to live. I sat down on it. "I caught part of that," he said.

"Was it all right?"

"I know Muriel Peck."

"She lives in New Haven."

"The crafts are a sideline," he said. "She works at Hill Health. That's her real name."

"I know."

"For years and years," Pekko said, "New Haven had visible hookers on Chapel and Howe. I guess they all died of AIDS."

"I remember them."

He gathered the newspaper sections. "Oh, Daisy."

"What? You hated the program?" I drank all my wine in a rush and stood up to pour some more.

"I didn't hate it. It was good. You're funny on the radio. Your voice goes up and down. It's nice."

"But?"

"If you were going to talk about New Haven, you couldn't find any other topic?"

"Pekko, there's nothing wrong with talking about prostitution," I said.

He gestured with the newspaper sections, as if they contained relevant evidence. "Look," he said. "I'm not going to tell you this is some picture-perfect New England village where the big event of the week is the minister's wife baking cookies."

"Those places have prostitutes, too," I said. The phone rang.

"But don't you see what you're doing? So many people are already afraid of this city."

"It wasn't just about New Haven. Wait a second."

"Well—"

I picked up the phone, thinking I should tell him about the Soul Patrol and Gordon Skeetling. He hadn't heard the show on which I mentioned it, and so far, I hadn't told him about my newest client. "Hello?" I said, my mind on Pekko, who left the room.

"I got the right number," said a woman. "I recognize your voice. Muriel told me to listen, and I just heard the show. I called her and got your number." I put my hand over the receiver and called to Pekko, but he'd turned on the TV. The call was the third one that mattered arising from the radio show. The first was Gordon Skeetling, the second Muriel Peck, and the third was the woman on the phone. I was too unsettled and tired to take in her name that night, but I listened when she said she wanted to put on a play.

☙

Her name turned out to be Katya, and she had some sort of theater-related degree and a grant to put together community theater. Ordinary people would make up a play and produce it.

"I want you," she said. "You say what you think, and you don't mumble." The cast was about to meet for the first time, and Muriel had already agreed to join. I wanted to see Muriel Peck again, and I was sad about an ending and looking for a beginning. So I found myself, a few days later, in a big, drafty room at a downtown parish house (not the one that housed the soup kitchen; much of New Haven's communal life takes place in parish houses) with Muriel, two other women, a man, and Katya, thinking up a play. We sat on mats on the floor, though chairs were piled in a corner, and Muriel brought one for herself, saying, "The floor is for dogs, cats, and babies." Katya—a big, white woman with glasses and long, light brown hair over her shoulders like a cloak—began with mindless physical exercises. Then we talked briefly about who we were. After that Katya asked us to say the most outrageous, the most unspeakable things we could think of. I was unimpressed, but I joined in. Oddly enough, or maybe not so oddly, we began with obscenity and profanity, and worked our way backwards to phrases of some interest, remarks that we'd heard or that had been said to us, remarks we could imagine someone making at a tough moment. It was true that one of these statements might conceivably be the basis for a play, or a moment around which a play could be constructed.

"I never loved you, not even the night we robbed the bank!" said the man, who was young and Asian—Korean American, I found out later. This project had self-conscious ethnic diversity, like a photograph in a college view book. Katya and I were the only white people, and I liked that.

"Bank is predictable," said Katya. "I never loved you, not even the night we robbed the natural foods store!"

"Your ugliness is beautiful," Muriel said now.

"His ugliness, her ugliness . . . ," Katya mumbled.

"Buy me a snake, honey," one of the other two women said. One was black and one was Hispanic.

"Buy me a car, buy me a rake, buy me a gun, buy me a man, buy me a . . ."

I said, "It's a headline." Everybody turned toward me as I sat cross-legged on my mat. They nodded, as if to say they knew what a headline was. "Two-Headed Woman Weds Two Men," I said. "Subhead: Doc Says She's Twins."

They laughed, beginning to be comfortable, this little group, mussed and sweaty from the exercises. I can work up a sense of competition in any situation, and my skepticism about this undertaking disappeared temporarily when they liked my suggestion. There were other ideas, but we came back to Gordon Skeetling's favorite headline. We could imagine a play about the Two-Headed Woman. We could begin to imagine her life.

"At first, she's a baby," Muriel said. "I can make a two-headed doll."

"That sounds horrible, a two-headed baby," said the man.

"You want a two-headed woman," Muriel said slowly from her lone folding chair, turning her big head in his direction, "you got a former two-headed baby."

When my friends the LoPrestis take a trip, Philip keeps a journal that he later copies and gives to people he knows, recording not private insecurities or arguments with Charlotte but discoveries of painters and architects, praiseworthy restaurants, hotels worth the money. He must like to imagine being asked for advice; so do I. I'm no journal keeper, and I began writing this narrative without knowing why, but as I proceed, the reader I think of wants a guidebook. A voice—maybe Philip's, maybe my brother Stephen's—asks, "What's it *like* to live the way you do?"

"The way I do?"

"Heedlessly. Is it a choice, or is this the best you can do? Is it worth it?"

"Heedlessly? Is that how I live?"

The client I described to myself as Irritating Ellen, who couldn't reject what nobody wanted, was in her late forties, with too many light brown curls on her shoulders and fluttery arms, accustomed to shrugs and hugs. Though she'd given me a key, trusting me instantly, she seemed able to leave her job at any hour to meet me. Ellen had grown up in a big house, all cupolas and porches, on East Rock Road. When her husband left her, she and her two children returned there to live with her parents. Now one parent had died and the other was in Florida, while Ellen and her kids lived on with their own possessions, her parents', and everybody else's. We had an appointment on a sunny morning in March—around the time of the first meeting about the play—but when I rang the doorbell, I heard no footsteps. It was the first day warm enough that waiting wasn't uncomfortable, and Ellen's old-fashioned street was pretty even in the dull season between snow and buds. Each ample, intricately trimmed house had its own variation: carved balusters, curved front steps, a widow's walk. As I stood there, my mind went not to Ellen's mess but to Gordon Skeetling's, and I tried to think where I'd sit in that side room so he couldn't see me through the wide glass doors. When Ellen still didn't come, I let myself into her crowded foyer and big, crowded, dusty living room, planning what I might do in her absence, noting that in Ellen's house windows were obscured with junk. I was about to find the kitchen and fix myself a cup of coffee when Ellen came toward me. Not every window in this house was blocked, and sun lit her solicitous face. She held something in her arms.

"I'm sorry," she said. "I'm here."

I thought she carried a pile of old clothes, but it was a baby.

"You didn't let somebody give you that!" I said. Her children were school age.

"Just for a few hours." The baby, a tense creature with hard fists and a swirl of light hair, was soon screaming.

"Why didn't you say no?" I said, as if my work with Ellen entitled me to candor. I don't have children, and other people's instigate too many feelings in me: a wish both to protect them and to shake off encroaching protection, and helplessness, and also a frightening wish to hurt. Apparently I am both the one who might be harmed, rescued, or stymied by good intentions and the one who'd do the hurting, the saving, the encroaching. Soon I was carrying this girl around, my arms itchy with conflict while her fingers clutched my hair. Later, I couldn't remember why Ellen suddenly wanted to show me something she had to retrieve, kneeling, from a basket on the floor—or exactly when she handed me the child. "At least she doesn't have two heads," I said nervously, so then I had to explain.

"I did theater in college," Ellen said.

"This may not qualify as theater."

"Mostly I was a director," she said. "Sometimes I acted. I wish I had time for it now."

I might have said she'd have time if she didn't let other people rule her life, but the one-headed baby was making too much noise. I didn't want to prolong the conversation anyway, lest Ellen try to join our cast. If she did, I'd drop out, I thought. If Ellen was even slightly interested in our play, it must be too obliging. The baby's sobs quieted as I held her.

"We can make lists," I said. "Get paper." I demonstrated surprising patience with other clients, watching myself in disbelief as their tedium just made me smile like a cartoon Buddha, or a stereotype of a cloistered nun. With Ellen, I was my cranky self.

She went for paper. As I waited, I noted that she or someone else had once woven baskets, or people had taken to giving her baskets. Tall hampers and wicker urns held dusty dried flowers or fabric scraps that would never make a quilt. She might have carried baskets of goodies to her grandmother through the wood: she had that look. When she returned, she stood in the dust motes under her high ceiling, holding paper and pen ready. Even scrap paper in this house had been donated: this was the stationery of an oil company.

I didn't know what to say while holding a baby. When I pretended to sympathize with other clients' acquisitiveness I was not pretending—though I wasn't a gatherer myself—but I couldn't seem to join Ellen in her acquiescence, even temporarily. The baby wouldn't settle into my arms but stiffened and arched. She and Ellen were in cahoots, preferring discomfort. Ellen had reasons I was too bored to refute for refusing to take any single load to Goodwill. "I thought we'd just arrange it more efficiently," she always said.

"Could I have a cup of coffee?" I asked now.

"Of course!" I followed her into the kitchen, a big room with old-fashioned appliances. I stood where the baby could see over my shoulder, out the window, and she calmed enough that I gingerly sat down. Ellen measured coffee into a coffeemaker that stood on a tiny open space at the corner of a cabinet whose surface was filled with stacks of bowls, vases, and carafes. Glass doors in cupboards revealed shelves crowded with china and glasses.

Ellen served me coffee in a mug in which magenta and blue glaze splashed over speckled gray horizontal ridges, and my mood shifting, I curved my fingers around it to feel the warmth. "Hold the baby well away from the mug," Ellen said, and I looked at her, startled by authority in her voice. I never yearn for the objects I see when I work. I alternate between wanting my clients to keep their elaborate constructions of junk and wanting to destroy and banish their possessions any way at all, ignoring civic-minded strictures about recycling, toxic waste disposal, and charity, scoffing at the supposed obligation to avoid waste by providing simple good people in simple good places used tires to make sandals of, used paper to turn into new paper. At home, after a day of work, I consider throwing out everything I touch, and Pekko and I don't have a lot of objects. But in Ellen's kitchen, I liked the mug I drank from, and then I desired something else: a fat white pitcher, possibly Italian pottery. It was about the size of the baby, with painted yellow flowers. Next to the sink, it took up counter space. "Let's start by getting rid of that pitcher," I said.

"My cousin . . . ," she began. "And I think it's nice."

"Everything's nice, but let's decimate this collection, for a start. Let's put every tenth object in the garbage can."

"You said you had ideas," Ellen said.

"Oh, you hate everything here."

Ellen stood and stepped backwards, leaning against her sink as if to insert herself between me and everything in the room. She stretched her arms out and put a protective hand on the yellow-and-white pitcher. Then the baby wriggled, and for a second it seemed she'd fall. I started, and she did slip through my grasp, but I caught her with my other hand. In the meantime, Ellen's arms swept toward us, and the pitcher crashed to the floor as my client cried out in grief and anger. Its interior was red clay, with the potter's coils still visible. Ellen took the baby and carried her upstairs, shaking her head when I offered to clean up the shards. "Next week," she said as she left the room, her coffee untouched. Not "Never."

༄

The play began with the pregnancy of the two-headed baby's mother, who didn't yet know about the two heads. The first time we tried making up a scene, I played the father. Feeling helpless, I stood in the middle of an open floor next to the young black woman, Chantal, who stared at me through rimless glasses. She had rolled up a sweater and stuffed it under her shirt. "Are you worried about your wife?" Katya prompted. She kept a tape recorder running.

So the father of the two-headed baby would be a worrier. "Did you sign up for childbirth preparation classes?" I asked my wife, remembering a friend's account of this phenomenon.

"Shut up, I'm cooking!" she said. "Shut up! I'm dancing!" Chantal mimed cooking and dancing. She'd once been in an improvisation troupe. She had a quick way of moving, turning her head swiftly in response to what others said, so her glasses flashed.

"Did you ask the doctor if it's all right to dance around like that?" I said, again after silence.

"Doctor, may I dance? May I eat? May I fool around with men?"

"*Men?*" I said. It was embarrassing. Why was I doing this?

The doctor sat on the floor, cross-legged, giggling. She was Denise, a Hispanic woman of about forty. Now she seemed to realize she had to talk. "None of that stuff. Certainly no sex," she said as the doctor. "And don't eat."

"But I'm hungry," said my wife. "I'm horny."

The childbirth preparation teacher, who was Muriel Peck, organized two pregnant women and their husbands (everybody including Katya), and made the women lie on the floor and breathe deeply. After a while she stopped and said, "This isn't a play."

"It doesn't matter," said Katya from the floor. "We'll settle on a script later."

I tried to be the husband. "My wife can't lie on her back," I said. "Her belly is too big."

"I'm fine," my wife contradicted me. "Leave me alone. I want to suffer."

The other father—the Korean American kid, David—turned to me. "Are you glad your wife is pregnant? I'm scared."

"I'm scared, too," I said. "I'm scared the baby will die. I'm scared I'll kill the baby."

"How would you do that?"

"Oh, there are plenty of ways to kill a baby."

In labor, Chantal kicked rapidly, then got up and ran around in circles. "In the improv troupe," she said, "we looked for the large, surprising gesture." Then she sat down on the floor and said, "I don't want to be a mother! I can't get this baby out because I don't love it!"

"Oh, you'll love it," said the doctor. "But this is a difficult birth. I'd better do a cesarean."

Chantal said, as herself, "Doctors call it a C-section."

"A C-section."

Katya stepped in as a nurse. "Here's a knife!"

"Did you wash it?" said the doctor. I was surprised, and I laughed. I hadn't expected Denise to surprise me.

With a swoop of the imaginary knife, the doctor slashed Chantal's belly. She reached forward. "I know how they pull it out, because I had one," she said. She grunted and held up an imaginary baby.

"Oh, my God," the doctor shouted. "The baby has two heads!"

All of us except Chantal rushed around, clutching our heads. I was astonished to be doing this.

Chantal shouted, "It's my fault!" and we stopped. "I slept with another man when I was pregnant. Each head looks like one of them."

"Unfaithful?" I said. "How could you do that to me?"

"Well, I'm the one who slept with your wife," David said. "But I didn't make her pregnant. I'm Asian, and neither of these heads looks Asian."

"It's too soon to tell," Denise the doctor said firmly. "Stop yelling, all of you. Nobody can live with two heads. Don't look at the baby. She's going to die. She has too much brain."

Chantal had been lying on the floor, but now she sat up and said firmly, "Let me see my baby!" After the boisterousness, this was somewhat impressive. Obediently, as her husband I took an imaginary child from Denise and carried it toward my wife. "I love the baby," she said, taking the child in her arms.

"Better not love the baby," said the doctor.

"But I want to love the baby!"

"Give it a name," said the doctor. "Name the baby before she dies."

"I'll name her TheaDora," said Chantal. "That way, we don't have to decide if she's one person or two people. She's Thea and Dora, or she's TheaDora."

Katya stopped being the nurse and withdrew to her place beside the tape recorder. "I'm the baby," she said, and wailed. David joined in as the rest of the baby. This play was full of shouting.

🍂

Pekko's back reveals more than his face. A thick man, he experiences feeling with his shoulders. He thinks his face conceals him, and maybe it does, but his back is less circumspect. Walking into the kitchen one evening, I saw his back first as he sat at the kitchen table, talking on the phone, and I guessed we wouldn't be making love for a while. He was elsewhere and needed to be retrieved, but I don't know how to do that. I'd come home tired and was in the bathtub when I heard him come in, greet Arthur, and then answer the phone. From the rise and fall of his voice, the pauses, I knew he was talking to my mother.

Pekko was the landlord of several apartment houses and one of the last SROs in New Haven—that's a single-room-occupancy building, in which people with meager resources have a room with a hot plate and use a bathroom in the hall. At the time I'm recalling, he was having the hallway fixed up and painted, and uncharacteristically, he'd hired a contractor who was a former drug addict and who'd put together a company of ex-users. They were competent, but they wanted to be watched and praised as they worked. "I'm not a kindergarten teacher," Pekko had been saying. He hates standing around. He's incapable even of waiting while I finish playing solitaire on the computer (and he thinks playing solitaire is addictive behavior). Pekko looks like the king of spades, by the way.

Walking into the kitchen behind him, I sat down, half listening and looking over the mail, assuming Pekko would soon hand me the phone, but he didn't. It had grown dark, and he hadn't bothered to stand up and turn on the light.

"You buy these things ready-made," Pekko was saying. "She doesn't have to be an old world cabinetmaker." At last he hung up.

I was too tired to talk to Roz, but I said, "She didn't want to talk to me?"

"She called to ask my advice."

"I gather, but usually that's just an excuse."

"Not this time."

"What did she want?"

"She wants to hire Daphne to install kitchen cabinets."

"But she already has kitchen cabinets," I said. "Not that she cooks."

"She doesn't like them. Daphne claims what she's really good at is carpentry. She says she took a job training course in carpentry for women."

"Is that true?"

"I don't know. Your mother seems to think I'm an expert on carpentry and an expert on Daphne."

"She thinks you're an expert in everything, but you like that. How did they get from raking leaves to carpentry this fast?"

"How should I know?"

"She had her in for coffee," I said, picturing the two of them in the kitchen. "She was so happy with Daphne's raking that she offered her a cup of coffee." This image annoyed me, as if my mother was allowed to have coffee only with me, although I didn't visit her often. "There were the old cabinets," I continued. Then I said, "I wish she wouldn't make friends with people like that."

"Like what? There's nothing wrong with Daphne."

"Pekko, *you're* obviously wary of Daphne. And she's doing community service. Doesn't that mean she committed a crime?" I stood up and turned on the light.

"I don't know anything about it. We're old friends," said Pekko. "I ought to fire those druggies and hire her to paint that staircase."

"Did you sleep with her when she worked for you?" I said.

"I didn't even know you then."

"I don't *care*." But now he picked up the newspaper. So I went back to reading the catalog I'd glanced at before, and time passed, and the mood changed. I for one was too hungry to think about what my mother and Daphne did, or even what Daphne and Pekko did.

I was too hungry to think and too hungry to cook, too tired even to take on the minor responsibility of suggesting dinner out. I knew Pekko wanted me to take charge, and I thought he might know I wanted him to. So we continued to sit. This sort of impasse led to bad times in our dating days. We'd finally eat at ten o'clock and be so hungry we'd quarrel. Now, Arthur pressed his head onto my lap and under my hands, making me stroke his hard, narrow skull. Then he thrust his nose into the crotch of my pants. I rose to feed him and broke the tension in the room. Pekko stood too, slapped his thighs, and watched me feed the dog. "Basement Thai," he said. The Thai restaurant we like best, where there's usually room for us, is in a basement on Chapel Street.

"It's Tuesday, so I have time," I said.

"No radio."

"Radio's finished. No play." Both were on Wednesdays.

But that made me think about the radio series, and I wanted to ask, "Was Daphne ever a prostitute?" Of course I wouldn't get an actual answer.

"So what you're saying," said Pekko, "is that if you had something to do, you'd skip dinner with me and do it."

"I'm hungry," I said.

※

"Why the fascination with prostitutes?" Gordon Skeetling asked a few days later, as we walked down Temple Street, where the sycamores weren't green yet. He'd proposed lunch so he could explain what he wanted of me. "Not that you can't develop your own ideas." He had a way of whooshing aside objections that hadn't yet been made, by claiming not to disagree with them. The objections were bold, so within a sentence or two he might make fair conversational progress on my behalf. Now he added, after "fascination with prostitutes," "Not that there's anything illegitimate about the subject of prostitution."

"That's right, there isn't!" I said, instead of claiming I wasn't fascinated.

We crossed a parking lot and entered Clark's Pizza—which is Greek despite its name—through the back door. It's an old-fashioned lunch place with red upholstered booths and a menu including gyros and moussaka. Gordon had a light, tenor voice— the voice of a younger man—and as we sat down in a booth near the windows, I looked around to see if anyone was listening.

"Prostitutes are just one sort of needy person," I continued. "They're usually poor. They may be homeless. They may have AIDS."

I ordered a Greek salad, and he asked for spanakopita. I didn't feel rushed with Gordon Skeetling, so after my outburst I tried to answer his question truthfully. Of course I didn't know *why* I'd wanted to do a series about prostitution, only that I did. "I'm not a prostitute," I began again, in a different tone.

"Were you ever offered money for sex?" he said. "It never happened to me. I guess I'm not attractive enough."

"Twice," I said and told him the stories I couldn't get Pekko to listen to—the man outside the bakery, the man outside the dress shop. I remembered another occasion I didn't mention.

"Were you tempted?" he said quickly, sounding not as if he was trying to get personal but as if he was such a curious person he couldn't keep from asking. Then he answered his own question. "Well, you were tempted as I would be—by the chance to learn something. Not by the money or the sex itself."

Then he added, "What did you do, when the first man asked you?"

"I think I pretended I hadn't heard. I hurried away. I was afraid he might follow me."

He nodded, and shrugged off his raincoat, and he was wearing a tan sweater, the way I'd first imagined him. He was narrower than I thought when I saw him in a jacket. He took up room when he spread his arms, and now he stretched one arm along the back of the booth. Behind us, a small child stood up and patted Gordon's arm vigorously. He ignored her.

"Yes," I said slowly. "It's the idea of doing something with a stranger that you'd ordinarily do only with someone you cared about. Or at least knew."

"Something about eliminating distance?"

"No. I think prostitutes and their clients must be lonely. They don't make a connection."

"With me they do," he said.

"You patronize whores?"

"No, but I buy them drinks, or cups of coffee. I don't want to sleep with them, but I like to talk to them. Like you, but I've never gone on the radio."

The child in the next booth had been coaxed to sit down, but now she turned and patted Gordon's arm once more. He glanced at her as if at a woman who tapped his arm in the street. "What you do for a living is perfectly respectable, of course," he said then. "This poking in attics and cellars. But I wonder— Don't be insulted."

"I'm never insulted."

"You go to people's houses, and they take you to a private room and show you something they don't show anybody else."

"Yes," I said. "The locked door. It's true."

Our lunches were brought. "Maybe trash is the new genitalia," said Gordon.

There was one more interruption by the child, and I asked him if he had kids. "Nieces, nephews," he said.

"Me too. You're married?"

"Twice," he said. "Not now. You?" So I told him about marrying Pekko after years of being single.

"I know Pekko Roberts," he said. "We were on a board together."

He ate spanakopita in silence, concentrating on cutting layers of phyllo dough and spinach and feta cheese, and then told me more about the Small Cities Project. He was a paid researcher; small cities paid him for studies, and in the course of his research, he often found a magazine piece he wanted to write. "The archive is leftovers," he said. "My thought is, if you show up, read, throw away the trash—well, what's left will have an emphasis, just because I do, because the people who've worked with me do, maybe because you do. Maybe everything you look at will have to do with prostitution. The process could lead to something—another radio series, a paper, a book. I can pay you for a while, but if you hit on something big, you'll have to find somebody to fund it."

I considered mentioning what I'd already come up with, after my single look at his archive—the play about the two-headed woman—but I didn't.

On April 1, Muriel brought the two-headed doll to rehearsal. She was bigger than a baby, a tan rag doll with something inside to stiffen her a bit. Her arms were slightly bent, and her legs were straight and fat. She wore a yellow nightgown with broad shoulders and two neck openings, and out of each opening rose a head. One had a dark brown face, short, black yarn hair, and black button eyes, while the other's face was peach-colored. It had short, yellow hair and blue eyes. The doll was startling, and it silenced me; I stopped feeling, at least for now, as if I'd wandered into something beneath me. I was the first to take it from Muriel, and I held it gingerly. Both faces had appliquéd circles of red felt for mouths. They silently screamed. "You sewed each strand of hair, one at a time," I said.

"You make loops, then you cut them. It makes that cute baby fuzz." Muriel's placid pride did not quite acknowledge the doll's strangeness. It was numinous, and nobody ever picked it up casually.

When we began rehearsing, David and Muriel played the baby's parents, because Katya said it was too soon to decide on roles. As the mother, Muriel stroked the baby and walked with it. Muriel's body was muscular and efficient, and she walked fast. She always wore jeans. She made dolls, but she looked as if she'd wear a hard hat and drive a bulldozer.

"There's something I have to tell you, dear," said her husband. "I want a divorce."

Muriel turned her still, intent face in his direction. "You're going to leave me alone with TheaDora?"

"April fool!" said David. "I don't want a divorce. April fool!"

"Lover boy," Muriel said slowly, "I have to tell you something."

"What's that?"

"Our baby has two heads. Not April fool. Not April fool." Muriel was bigger than David, and when she stared at him, he seemed to grow smaller. He'd gone to Yale and was barely out of college. He had told us he worked with computers.

When David and I left together after the rehearsal, I asked, "What made you say that?"

"The April fool joke? I felt mean. That doll is so weird."

❦

The next time I saw Ellen she had no spare children in her arms, and we tried to make a plan for her kitchen. She still wanted to keep everything, just rearrange it, and I forced myself to agree. She didn't mention the broken pitcher. Sitting on the floor, we gathered pots and pans and crockery from her many pantries and cabinets and shelves, and then we grouped everything in categories: baking pans in a pile, sugar bowls in one corner, stacks of plates in another. Ellen's children came home from school, and each watched us briefly before turning away. One was a rather mature-looking girl with long hair, who looked around critically but didn't speak. The other I took to be a boy—stubby, plump, with a practical look—but she later turned out to be another girl. For the rest of the afternoon I heard footsteps or music, occasionally, from upstairs. The children played sad folk music, not what I'd have expected. Ellen and I had made matters worse, but as we worked she said, "This was a good idea."

"What about supper?"

"We'll order in."

"What about breakfast?"

"Breakfast is easy."

At least she didn't have a dog running around. "Why don't you have animals?" I said, surprised by that thought. "Where are every-body's unwanted cats and dogs?"

"I got rid of them. Three cats and a dog. Justine's allergic."

"What did you do, kill them?"

"No, I didn't kill them!" She sat up. She'd been lying on her stomach, pulling dusty bowls out from a deep shelf, getting dust on her skirt. Ellen wore wide cotton skirts in pale, swirling prints. "I bought cute things for them—leashes, little beds. Then I lined them up outside a supermarket and looked pathetic until people took them." We stopped working and began discussing animals. Ellen had missed those pets. We had a conversation new friends have, beginning with childhood dogs, but I grew bored with her undifferentiated grief for the pets of her life. I didn't want to be her friend, but I kept listening, and narrowly missed eating Chinese takeout with her and the children. I promised to come the next day. When she was out of the room for a moment, I dealt with my feelings by pocketing a sugar bowl—a rather nice one, blue ceramic—and later I threw it in the garbage.

❦

As my mother told Daphne, I am no gardener, but on a windy but sunny Saturday I raked the mucky dead leaves of the previous autumn—leaves we hadn't bothered with when they fell—into piles. Arthur sniffed the fecund stuff my rake was exposing and sometimes rolled in it. I was cold, but activity warmed me. Inside, the phone rang. Pekko wasn't home, but the machine would pick up the call. When Arthur barked, I followed him down the alley between houses and found my mother ringing our doorbell. She came into the yard.

"Daphne did that for me," she said, after watching me for a while. "She took a long time, and she charged me by the hour."

"It's a big job," I said. I leaned the rake on a tree.

"I'm not complaining," my mother said. "It's important to know how to charge. I hope you charge your customers enough."

I offered her coffee, and as she explained that she'd come with another question for Pekko, I heard him thumping around inside. Roz isn't shy about visiting, but she doesn't want me to think she moved to New Haven to bother me, so she always gives a reason. When we came into the kitchen, he'd discovered the blinking light on the answering machine and was listening to a rapid, friendly message from Gordon Skeetling. "Hi, Daisy, it's Gordon," and his 432 number—which always means Yale—spoken in the hasty manner of someone who knows you already have it.

"Who's that?" he said. "Hi, Roz."

"A client."

"Gordon who?"

"Skeetling. The Small Cities Project. He says he knows you."

"You're working for *him*? Why didn't you tell me?"

"Who is he?" said Roz. "A big shot?"

"He says Yale barely tolerates him," I said to Pekko. "He sounds like your sort—inner city and all that."

"I don't like him," Pekko said.

"What's wrong with him?" I put my jacket on a chair and took three mugs from the cupboard.

"I don't want coffee. He was on the board of the shelter with me."

"He said so. He seems nice. He has a room full of papers he wants me to sort out."

Pekko walked out of the room, but a minute later, as I was measuring coffee, he returned. "A little too clearheaded," he said. "Sees things *just* as they are."

"What's wrong with that?" I said. "You're the one who's always claiming to be a realist."

"If I were a realist," said Pekko, "I wouldn't rent an apartment to the man I just rented an apartment to."

He was standing in the doorway, filling it, but now he turned away again. Roz called after him, "Speaking of apartments, Pekko, I need a good deed."

"Yes?" he said, sounding friendlier. "How are you anyway, Roz?

What are you up to now?" My mother's conscientious vigor amuses Pekko, and he also admires it. "We're friends," he says, which is also what my mother says, though she's more detailed about it: she claims they made friends because they went through the war together, meaning Vietnam. They didn't meet until years later, but she says they thought the same way about it. She marched, wrote letters to editors, and affixed bumper stickers to her car reading SUPPORT OUR BOYS: BRING THEM HOME. Pekko was drafted and spent a year in Vietnam. "Not as bad as some people's year," he says, "but bad enough." Discharged, he returned to New Haven and, while taking courses at Southern Connecticut, began organizing against the war.

They're a little superior about it. During the war I was busy marrying Bruce Andalusia, who had a good lottery number and wasn't drafted. I tried not to think about Vietnam. Now and then, all my life, I've imagined myself tossing something over my left shoulder with my right hand, walking on and not seeing where it falls. I tossed the war like a button I pulled off my coat and didn't keep to sew on again.

Now my mother said to Pekko, "I promised Daphne I'd ask if you have room for her anywhere."

"She getting evicted?"

"Oh, no," said Roz, "but her place is expensive."

"How old are her kids?" Pekko said.

"I think nine and seven."

"I suppose she'll pay the rent if it's me."

"Of course," Roz said. "Thank you."

"I haven't done anything yet," Pekko said. He climbed the stairs at his steady pace.

I'd offered my mother a cup of coffee not to be hospitable but because I wanted one myself. She was too pleased to have had her leaves raked by the remarkable Daphne, and I wanted her to leave so I could call Gordon back. That impulse made me angry with myself, so I drank the coffee too fast and burned my mouth. As I drank, I formed a policy about not making client calls over the weekend.

My mother drank only a few sips of coffee but lingered, talking about my brothers. The oldest of us, Carl, is gay and lives with a man and two adopted children. Stephen is still married to his first wife, and they have a daughter. Sometimes I am sure Roz is about to blame me for being childless, but the truth is that Roz doesn't want me to be more conventional than I am. She wants to prove that she's as unconventional as I, and she wants me to delight her with stories. That day she probably hoped for confidences and intimate talk. When I was single, I often told her about my men. She didn't disapprove, nor did she grow wistful as I aged out of my fertile years, but prided herself on her appreciation of another way.

Married, though, I'd gone into our bedroom, so to speak, and closed the door. I thought my mother disapproved not of any way of life but of people who don't know how to get what they want. Possibly, these days, my silence made her think I was unhappy, but I didn't want to talk about Pekko. Now she said, "After she finished raking, she came inside and I gave her a glass of water. Then we talked for an hour. I couldn't believe it when I saw the clock. I never do that with anybody but you. She's a lonely person. She hasn't time for boyfriends, just taking care of those kids. All of a sudden she looked at her watch and skedaddled—time for school to let out. She's so skinny she looks twenty, but she's past forty. Would you have guessed that?"

"Yes," I said.

"How well does she know Pekko?" she asked.

"How should I know?" Finally my mother left, and I called Gordon right away. He needed to change our next appointment. And he wanted to know if I minded that he wouldn't be in the office while I worked. He'd just let me in and leave. I said I'd be fine.

☙

Katya was tall and wide, given to exaggerated gestures and mild bullying ("Use your body, Daisy! This isn't radio!") but maddeningly wary of deciding anything definitely. While the rest of us—except for Muriel—sat on the floor, Katya would pace, looming hugely when she came near. She'd expostulate—and then say, "But what do you guys think?"

I found I looked forward to rehearsals, though after each one I promised myself I'd quit. Then I'd decide to stay in but keep silent as much as possible. Yet I always went, and talked a lot, both in character and out of it. As I'd begin to move around the area we called the stage—with exaggerated gestures and speed—I'd feel a familiar, anxious pleasure in my throat and at last I identified it as the sensation I'd get, in my single years, when I was about to sleep with a man I scarcely knew.

Denise always had an opinion about what we were doing, and she was always wrong. She wanted the play to be innocuous, so it wouldn't upset anybody. Invariably I disagreed, and then everyone would offer a view, and we'd be back where we started. We were now a group of six actors, not counting Katya. She'd found another man, a rotund black storefront preacher with a glorious, deep voice. His name was Jonah. "I was swallowed . . . by a *whale*!" he said the first night. He had been a drug addict many years ago, he told us, so he was not shocked by swearing. We mustn't become shy, just because there was a reverend in the room.

We were not shy, and we weren't a coherent group of rational adults. David, the computer kid, had a habit of scooting his mat around the floor while people talked, like an eight-year-old. Chantal was tall and sharp-looking, with her quick glances and glittery glasses. She was bright but illogical. At least she no longer rushed around as much. Denise, the little Puerto Rican lady, used to hug her knees as we sat there, as if she was so anxious not to be in the way that she'd decided not to let herself stand up. When she talked about the play, she urged blandness, but her acting wasn't bland. Something was freed in her, and she often startled me. Muriel retained her dignity and always seemed grown-up, but even Muriel had a fault: she could be boring. Sometimes I had to remind myself that she'd been a prostitute, to make her seem slightly exotic. She looked exotic, and I couldn't keep up with her long stride as we walked to our cars after the rehearsals, but she was as likely to talk about her special red-and-green Christmas plates as anything else.

That night we decided, after some debate, that we needed a couple of kids to play the two-headed little girl if we were indeed presenting a sort of biography. I was opposed, but when I lost the argument I didn't lose my usual desire for control. Somebody said she knew a cute ten-year-old, and I thought of Ellen's not-cute Justine, with her cool, intelligent look. I didn't want Ellen involved in the play, but I often can't help trying to seem more competent than anybody else, so while the others shrugged, I scribbled her phone number on a bit of paper and handed it to Katya.

Then we acted out a scene in which the mother of the two-headed baby tries nursing both heads simultaneously, one on each breast. Denise was the mother this time, and she arranged the doll on her chest. "My kids had only one head, and still I could nurse and keep private," she said serenely. As friends and family members, we circled her, offering imaginary cushions and other props, as well as advice.

"Just nurse one head! Maybe the other will drop off!" I said. Nobody noticed what I considered my funniest lines, but I hoped that Katya's tape recorder was picking them up. We had played back some of what we'd done. Parts sounded more like scuffles and panting than speech, but Katya insisted she had plenty to transcribe. She also took notes. When she wasn't pacing, she sprawled with her back against a wall, a big drawing pad in her lap, a felt-tipped marker in her hand. She said she wrote faster if the writing was big.

"May I ask a question?" Jonah said in measured tones. The current parents had flopped onto their mats after trying a scene we all hated, in which the father (Chantal, that night) tried to persuade the mother (me) to go to bed with him, and she said, "Yeah, and get a three-headed baby?" while as a baby-sitter, Denise tried walking with the two-headed doll. Wiping sweat and patting our hair, we nodded and looked at Jonah, who had not participated so far. "What is the *meaning*?" he said.

Somebody explained the headline. We were working up to a wedding, we said. "We're searching for the story," Katya offered, easing herself to the floor. "There will be a process of decision making later."

"Is it about *prejudice*?" Jonah persisted. "I think it's about prejudice."

"You mean race?" said Muriel. "I'm tired of talking about race."

"Her race, or maybe her handicap?" Jonah said. "I'm just asking."

Chantal said, "No, no, nothing like that. I think it's about not being able to make up your mind. Some days I feel like I have two heads."

To my astonishment, I was suddenly angry; I felt the kind of anger that burns the veins in your arms. I almost said, "But I brought the headline!" as if that made me the boss. I knew the two-headed woman had nothing to do with indecision, and I thought she had nothing to do with prejudice either. I was surprised to be angry, because I didn't know I cared about the play at all. All I could say was "That's too simple, don't you see?" They looked at me. They did not see. "We're talking about having two heads. Don't you see how interesting that is? Having two heads is—having two heads. It's not *like* anything." To myself, I sounded childish and obvious, and everyone looked at me with careful politeness.

"Then why do it?" Jonah said. "Nobody really has two heads. It's about being anyone who's looked down on. We need reminders about that."

"I guess I think it's something like that, too," Katya said.

"No," I said from my mat, pressing my hands into my thighs. "I have no interest in that."

"You don't think it's important that people are prejudiced?" Denise said.

"Of course it's important." I couldn't explain further because I didn't know what I meant. All I could think of was Pekko saying that Gordon saw things as they were. I wanted to *look* at that two-headed person, at the two-headedness of her. "Comparing her to *anything*," I said, struggling to control my voice, "is disrespectful. She's not *like* anything."

ॐ

Gordon had changed our appointment so he wouldn't be late, but he was late. I thought of Ellen as I again stood waiting on steps, but this time I had no key, and the day was colder, though it was later in the spring. At last I saw him coming quickly toward me down the other side of Temple Street, past the gray stones of the back of St. Mary's Church. He was not just hurrying but running, the bottom of his jacket flapping. He crossed with a glance at the traffic and stopped, puffing, at the foot of the stairs I stood on. "It's worth it, because I have more time than I thought. I can stay a little."

I didn't need him to stay. I had learned enough to get started, which probably meant sitting and reading at random. But once we were inside I began to talk about how I usually worked. I was unsure of myself, uncomfortable because I'd expected him to leave, and so I found myself talking about Ellen, the client who made me feel unsure and uncomfortable. "I've got a client now who doesn't *want* to keep anything she has," I said. "She just thinks she ought to. I can't deal with conscience."

"Conscience isn't the usual reason for clutter?" His pointed eyebrows moved up and down, and he stroked the doorjamb.

"No, avarice," I said. I was trying to sound provocative; I had no idea what the usual reason for clutter is, but I wished I hadn't mentioned Ellen.

He said, "You're thinking I'm the greedy kind, or you wouldn't talk about her."

"No, no."

"So what's she like?" Gordon Skeetling said, resting against his raised arm. He was wearing not the tan sweater today but a similar blue one. He smiled and encouraged me to make a funny story out of Ellen, but New Haven is too small. He'd recognize her—he'd turn out to be her next-door neighbor. "Why does she do this?"

"I have no idea," I said. Then, "I took something from her."

"You stole it?"

"It was worthless."

"To you. What did you do with it?"

"I threw it away."

"Hmm."

I could tell he was more curious than troubled, that he didn't care whether Ellen was deprived of her possession or I turned out to be a thief. Have I described his face? Bony planes, lots of forehead. The expressive black eyebrows moved one at a time, and the gray, straight hair flopped when he gestured. A face ready to listen attentively, and then laugh. Now he was getting ready to laugh not at Ellen but at me. At least I'd deflected his attention from her. Usually someone who looks about to laugh doesn't bestow permission here and there, as Gordon Skeetling did, but his wasn't mocking or condescending laughter. What amused him was apparently the oddness of human behavior. He seemed to exist, just then, in order to hear me, and so he satisfied a longing I've always had: to explain, as if something would be accomplished forever if someone would only listen until I was done. . . .

"What did you *take?*" His voice rose zestfully with the question.

"A sugar bowl."

"Sugar bowl? Hmm, a sugar bowl!" Was a sugar bowl a symbol of something? The womb?

But he didn't keep on listening. He looked at his watch and gathered some papers, telling me to leave the key in the mailbox. "Take your time and don't steal anything. No, if you want to, take whatever you like."

"I usually steal cars."

"Then you're stuck, because I'm taking mine with me. But speaking of conscience, remind me to tell you about my dream. Oh, I'll tell you now and be late. I had a German shepherd—a lovely dog—and she grew old and died. This was a dog with a conscience. If she did something she thought she shouldn't have, she'd incarcerate herself in the bathtub, because she hated baths. So one day, after she died, I dreamed about a minister—a pastor, he was called in the dream—in Germany who was so conscientious, he threw himself out of his own church. Excommunicated himself. When I woke up, I remembered that *pastor* means "shepherd." He was a *German shepherd.* Isn't that good? Don't I have great dreams?"

Now he hurried away, and I missed this friendly man, who I thought probably resembled his dog. He'd have a functioning conscience, not one that operated like Ellen's, without meaning, or that failed to operate, like mine. His would keep him from doing harm, and I wanted to stop stealing sugar bowls if only to please him.

In the archive I began by dusting, and then I read. I read or skimmed a stack of articles copied from magazines or torn out: an old account of an election in Albany, a recent story about the New Haven homeless shelter. I could see no unifying principle or subject.

It made no sense to group them by city, except that New Haven came up often. I was interested, because around here it's a little hard not to focus on big, bold New York, which is only seventy-five miles away.

I could already see that some stories could easily be discarded. I grouped the rest by subject: poverty, public transportation, crime. At the corner of the table I gathered those that piqued my interest the most. They were invariably about New Haven, I noticed. Then I noticed that they were almost all about a death, not the predictable death of an old person with a cluttered house but the shocking death of a young man or woman who hadn't had time to accumulate much—the violent death of some young person, a violent death in New Haven.

When I notice a selfish or unselfish act I've committed, I can't seem to help balancing it. Half the time, that is, I fail morally. After being friendly to Ellen about dead pets, I took a sugar bowl. I took a sugar bowl, so I told Gordon. I told Gordon, so I complained about Ellen on the phone to my friend Charlotte. "I guess in your field there's no such thing as confidentiality," Charlotte said. As I add to this narrative, I'm sometimes ashamed of one detail or another, but more often I'm pleased to describe what I did, how I am, as if being an identifiable sort of person matters more than being one sort or another. Accounts like this are supposed to record a change: this is how I became different. But I didn't change. What could I be except myself?

What I don't like is rest. Only when I have a cold do I understand the wish to snuggle and stop striving. "I like to think of finding a place to rest here," Ellen said, fluttering her hand at the confusion in her living room, where extra dining room chairs in many styles were lined up along one wall, one behind another as in a train. On them, as it happened, her children were playing train, but they stopped to listen, tilting their heads: wary Justine, who gave me the same shrewd look that had caught my attention before, and the younger one, with short, blond hair, the one I kept forgetting wasn't a boy, who'd pull his or her shirt up when thinking, baring the belly.

"A nest," said Ellen. I dislike the word *nest* unless a bird is involved, and I loathe *nestle.* Ellen said, "I keep imagining that if I moved things just a little, I could hide properly. Wouldn't you love a curtained bed with red velvet hangings?"

"Dust," I said. "You'd get entangled with the curtains and wouldn't be able to escape if there was a fire."

"Or if your lover refused to perform," said Ellen, now laughing at herself. Justine looked alert. She'd been asked to join our cast. I'd given Ellen's phone number to Katya without permission. Ellen was grateful. She approved of me too heartily. She wanted some connection with the play, because I was in it.

The kitchen, a week after the day we'd emptied the cabinets, was subtly altered. Ellen and the children had not cleaned up but had transformed the mess into an intricate domestic installation, half nostalgic, half critical of the trammels of household, something you might almost see in the Whitney Biennial. They'd washed everything, then arranged the objects in neater groups: platters, teapots (red, blue, patterned), bowls (handmade pottery, old china with pink flowers, Danish stoneware). Silverware, separated by function and pattern, was spread on a blanket under the table. The children fussed importantly, lending Ellen more direction as they explained that after meals they replaced the dishes on the floor. They tried to use different plates and bowls at each meal now. Walking from doorway to sink was tricky, and the smaller child—Celeste, she was a girl called Celeste—hopped, as if to suggest that the aisle wasn't wide enough for two feet, though it was.

Ellen didn't want help putting the kitchen back to rights. "The girls and I will do it," she said. I knew they couldn't. They couldn't keep everything, yet everything seemed to be cherished. Ellen was transforming herself into my other sort of client, making her own the objects that had been thrust upon her. I said, "You're appalling," which Ellen took with one of her accepting shrugs. The children disappeared, and Ellen led me to a spare bedroom. The closet was crammed with clothing.

"I suppose you want to do the same thing here?" I said.

"Let's just see," said Ellen.

She wasn't a real gatherer, not one of my glinty-eyed, irrational but avid accumulators. Her stories were always of imposition, even about her own clothes. "My wedding gown. I never liked it. My mother chose it."

"And now you're planning to force it on your daughters?"

"Celeste might like it. Justine will marry in a black leotard."

We piled clothes halfheartedly on the bed and in a heap on the rug. She'd brought a garbage bag, but it remained empty. Ellen had the profound stubbornness of passivity. As before, when she was out of the room I took something, at greater risk this time. I rolled a green print cotton shirt tightly, then stuffed it into my jacket pocket. And as before, shortly after I left her house, I passed a trash basket on a corner, stopped the car, got out, and threw the shirt away.

I am good half the time. From Ellen's house I went to my

mother's, thinking she'd be alone and maybe lonely. Roz and I visited each other uninvited, but while she justified or explained her visits, I acted as if mine were treats. It was a hot spring day, one of those early summer days before the leaves have come out, which make me dread sweating for the next half year but please some people. Instead of moping at home, my mother might be striding briskly through the park, swinging her arms and smiling under her white curls, being the sort of older woman who heartens younger ones. Roz, however, was neither out walking nor home alone but drinking iced tea with Daphne in her little kitchen. Both were in shorts—a picture of midsummer, though clouds were gathering, and we'd be back to April the next day. Daphne said, "Hi, Daisy," her mouth barely opening.

The iced tea was from a mix, so with the disapproval daughters feel they may express toward their mothers' choices, I filled a glass with tap water and stood leaning on the sink—the interloper— while the two women sat at the table. I could hear a wind starting outside, but in the kitchen it was close.

"Daphne has a nine-year-old daughter," my mother said significantly, after they'd talked for a few minutes about people from the soup kitchen. I'd described the rehearsals to Roz and mentioned the quest for little girls to play the two-headed kid. "I've been telling her about your play. Maybe Daphne's daughter could be in it."

"Katya is pretty much set," I said. "I gave her the name of a child."

"But you need *two* children," my mother persisted. To Daphne she added, "She'd play a girl with two heads."

"Like, two of them inside a big dress?"

"Something like that," I said reluctantly.

"Oh, Cindy would love that. Does the girl die? She'd love playing a corpse."

"No, she doesn't die," I said. "Most of the play is about when she grows up."

"So it's a small part? That's okay, I'll explain it to her."

I pointed out that by now Katya had probably found many little girls. Nonetheless, I was talked into giving her number to Daphne, and before I left I also promised to remind Pekko that Daphne needed an apartment.

And I heard the details of the plan to install kitchen cabinets. Daphne described the carpentry for women course she'd taken. "It was supposed to be job training, but guess what." She had a two-dimensional look—a flat face with a small nose, small breasts, no belly, no backside. Her face, with thin, shoulder-length brown hair around it, was expressionless at rest, then quickly cheerful or combative, then expressionless again. She was well-defended. I doubted that she could laugh easily, and to test her I told a joke Charlotte had told me the night before, about a cocker spaniel who rides a motorcycle and won't wear a helmet—or condoms either, it develops. I like dog jokes, and my mother stared, then laughed. Daphne glanced at her, as if for permission. Then she banged her empty glass on the table, laughing and laughing. She was somebody else, as if she'd stepped through a transforming curtain, and I knew why I had a suspicion about her and Pekko in the past.

"Tell Pekko I still like roller coasters," she called as I left. She and my mother remained at the table, sucking half-melted ice cubes, while I let myself out. As far as I know, Pekko dislikes roller coasters. I didn't reply.

⏧

One afternoon I had an unexpected cancellation, so I went to Gordon Skeetling's office without an appointment. He let me in, surprised but apparently pleased. He led me inside, then crossed to the coffeepot and gestured, one eyebrow raised. He stepped into sunlight near the window, and his thick, gray hair seemed to lift slightly from his head, as individual strands became visible in the spring light. I wanted coffee and nodded. He paused, slightly puzzled, as if he hadn't expected me to understand, then smiled in appreciation of his own peculiarities.

"Last time I was here," I said, "I kept noticing clippings about violent death."

"I don't remember collecting stories of violent death," he said.

"I'll show you."

He followed me into the side room, and I handed him the pile I'd made. He sat down on a tall stool, leaning forward to establish his feet far apart on the floor. I was facing his crotch, and as sometimes happens, I imagined him undressed, how his penis and balls might rest on the edge of the stool, how a hand might hold them. I sat down with my back toward him and reached for a folder, so as to fill my hand with something else.

"This is terrible," he said at last. "This murder on Hillhouse Avenue. I remember it." His voice sounded tense with grief.

"It happened a while ago," I said. A Yale student had been killed in the middle of the night by New Haven kids. The case had made national headlines. According to rumor, Yale's enrollment had suffered afterward. "Do you know why Hillhouse Avenue intersects with Sachem Street?" I said, again changing the subject, this time because Gordon's burst of feeling made me uncomfortable. "It's named for James Hillhouse, a nineteenth-century treasurer at Yale. He was called Chief, and that's what *Sachem* means."

"An Indian word."

"I think so. I can't remember who told me that," I said.

"I remember when that kid died," he said. "Christian Prince. What a name. I read everything about it. I cried. My wife thought I had some kind of weird Freudian identity thing."

"You mean you thought you killed him?"

"What a funny mind you have," said Gordon. "She thought he represented the child I never had."

"Oh," I said, "you're the victim. When I read about a crime, I'm the perpetrator."

"It was terrible," he said again and put down the stack of clippings. Then he returned to his desk in the other room. When I heard him on the phone, I closed the door between us; reading and sorting, I quickly forgot about him. I was interested and curious as I looked through these stacks of paper—not needing to pretend to be interested and curious, as I often did, while concealing mild frustration or amusement toward a client. My pile of clippings about death—local death—grew. I made a few more piles. This archive also had an urban renewal motif. The unknown scissoring hands had often saved pieces about the unexpected effects, good and bad, of change. There were stories of neighborhoods fragmented by a superhighway, sustained by repair of a bridge, or changed by the placement of a bus route. I had a public transportation stack and an arts stack, but that one rapidly began to seem condescending; everything was about the making of art by people who might have been expected not to be capable of it. I remembered our play with a rush of confusion: I'd stolen the headline, in a way; Gordon Skeetling would surely scorn this unsophisticated venture; I would surely scorn it; I ought to be scorning it, and withdrawing from it. I had no business participating in art by the barely capable.

The door opened. "More coffee?"

"No, thanks."

"Then I won't make another pot."

"Not for me."

"Did I show you the headline about the woman with two heads?"

"Don't you remember?"

"You didn't throw it away?" he said.

"You said I could throw away whatever I wanted to."

"But I said I'd yell if you did."

"Well, I didn't."

He seemed to want something, and I wondered if he hoped I'd tell him more about Ellen and my theft of her possessions. I made up my mind not to take anything else. He stood in the doorway, so I edged past him and asked the way to the bathroom. When I returned, he'd gone back to his desk, but when I sat down, he again came and stood in the doorway. "Call me before coming in next time, all right?" he said.

"Oh, sure," I said. "Sorry."

"I like to know whether I'll be alone," he said apologetically. "I do different work."

Gordon Skeetling seemed to bestow permission with every gesture, but now he was refusing it. "What kind of work?" I said.

"I'm writing."

"A paper for a journal?"

"An op-ed piece. The *Times* has run a few I've done, over the years."

"What about?"

"If I wanted company to hear about it, maybe I could write it with company around," he said.

"Okay," I said, but then he told me.

"I'm arguing in favor of decreased funding for foster care."

"But that's a terrible idea!" I said.

"The state is a bad parent," he said. "Do you know how many foster kids end up in the prison system?"

We argued for an hour. Neither of us got anything done. By the end his hair was in his eyes and his shirt was hanging out because he waved his arms so much. I didn't convince him. "You look as if I've been beating you up," I said at last, gathering my things. When I left, the afternoon was yellow. I drove home and took Arthur on a walk to the river, along a trail through woods near the base of East Rock. The trees hadn't leafed out yet, so I could see a distance in all directions. The forest had a roominess I'd miss when the leaves came. The air was light green and anticipatory. I began the walk angry with Gordon, but as I walked my anger was replaced by that awareness, again, of permission. He could cry over a murder by poor children and then argue for decreased help to their younger brothers, and his very refusal to see a connection—though I'd pointed it out—exhilarated me, it was so unapologetically outrageous. I also liked the willingness to take me on in combat, to take me seriously enough to fight, to tell me what I wasn't allowed to do. "Arthur," I said, as if I had something to tell him. "Arthur, Arthur."

꼭

Pekko and I had dinner one night in April at Basement Thai with Charlotte and Philip LoPresti. I arrived alone in my Jetta, straight from a client, and parked a block away. Approaching the restaurant in the cool twilight, I glanced through a window and saw Pekko and my friends already seated together. Pekko leaned forward over the table with his hands extended—as for clapping— but held steady, as if he was saying, "This big." When I sat down, Charlotte was talking earnestly about a misunderstanding with her younger daughter, Olivia, her pale blue eyes holding Pekko hard, then refocusing on me, as they all smiled to be caught talking so intently so soon.

"We're discussing clarity," said Philip, a man who looks ascetic, like a graying priest. He did spend a couple of years in a Catholic seminary in his youth, before he changed his mind, became a teacher, and married Charlotte. "We've ordered appetizers."

Charlotte is a social worker, as I've said somewhere, and Philip was my colleague when I taught at the community college. I knew Philip first, then met Charlotte, years before I knew Pekko. They liked Pekko and became increasingly impatient with me when I kept breaking up with him. Once Charlotte accused me of being a less serious person than she had imagined. "I always knew your *style* was not serious," she said, her eyes filled with tears, "and I love that. But lately I think it's more than style."

I cried too, though I never cry, and we were shocked into new closeness by her honesty. When I married Pekko, she and Philip were happy and went out of their way to spend time with us.

"I rented an apartment to Daphne Jenkins," Pekko said. Clarity, apparently, had something to do with Olivia, the daughter, and something to do with Daphne. I hadn't known Daphne's last name, but of course Pekko did. I felt at a disadvantage, as if knowing her last name was equivalent to knowing an intimate fact about her, and he probably knew some of those as well. I was also bothered because he'd made up his mind without discussing it with me, though he never talked about professional decisions. I'd promised my mother to ask him again about Daphne, but I never had. Eating a Thai dumpling, I said, "I don't trust Daphne."

"She's reliable," he said, "if you let her know the rules." Again he made the gesture I'd seen through the window—hands held stiffly, facing each other—and I recognized it this time as the way people signal that they will keep a difficult person within limits. Of course he'd meant Daphne that time, too, but I couldn't keep from wondering whether he had said earlier that he'd have to set limits for me.

Charlotte drank some wine and said, "I was just saying that I hadn't been clear enough with Olivia." Olivia has always been complicated, and I've always liked her. She went to medical school and had recently begun a residency in surgery, in which, Charlotte said, "The final exam is cutting off your mother's head." Olivia claimed not to mind being insulted by her professors but was quick to leave sharply worded, offended messages on her parents' answering machine.

"What rules did you tell Daphne?" I asked Pekko, interrupting Charlotte.

"Mostly no extensions on the rent—that's the problem with friends. I'm not worried she'll trash the apartment."

If Daphne did fail to pay the rent, I thought, Pekko might let her get away with it. I sensed an unusual distraction in him. The very fact that he'd told Charlotte and Philip what he'd done: he was less protected than usual. I didn't trust Daphne because she penetrated barriers, and that thought reminded me of Gordon Skeetling.

"I'm working on a rubbish heap at the Yale Small Cities Project," I said now to Charlotte. "I had a fight with the director."

"I never heard of that project."

"One guy in a row house on Temple Street."

"Yale has hundreds of tiny kingdoms," Charlotte said. "Some do evil, some good."

"What did you fight about?" said Philip. By now we were eating our main course. I probably had seafood curry.

"He's in favor of reducing funding for foster care."

"A reactionary?" Charlotte said, the lines around her blue eyes deepening.

"He says he's a sensible lefty."

"He's a pile of shit," Pekko said. "I was on a board with him. He's one of those people who's too damned clearheaded. No feelings."

"Oh, he definitely has feelings!" I said, remembering Gordon's reaction to the clipping about the murder. I wanted to see if by chance Charlotte agreed with him about foster care—I wanted to see if I'd been arguing on the wrong side—and she agreed heartily that, as Gordon had said, the state is a bad parent.

"Maybe it *would* be better after all . . . ," I said.

"If kids were left with abusive parents?"

"Or their relatives had to take them in, instead of having foster care as an option." I was arguing Gordon's position, I saw to my dismay. "Terrible things do happen."

"But mostly not," Charlotte said with authority. She works with the elderly, but she knows about all parts of the system. She wanted to talk about Olivia, though. Her older daughter, Amy, is easygoing, but cranky Olivia has always been the one who can get her mother's full attention. That week she'd called late at night, exhausted from long hours at the hospital. At first Charlotte was delighted to hear from her, but she was sleepy, and Olivia got angry when Charlotte insisted on hanging up.

"I recognize her," I said ruefully. "That's what I do to my mother. I need her too much, so I'm mean to her."

"I think Roz doesn't mind, in the last analysis," Charlotte said. "I don't."

"She moved here, near me, not near my brothers." The oldest of us has lived in Chicago for a long time, but the brother I think about—my younger older brother, I call him, Stephen—is still in New York, where we all grew up.

"Correct," said Charlotte.

Philip sat back, looking at me. I've known him now for twenty-five years, and he looks his age. "You're still a handful, Daisy," he said. Maybe he aged worrying about me.

I've probably made mischief all my life so as to hear that loving remonstrance in people's voices. When Philip's or Charlotte's disapproval became real, I was wretched. Now I looked at Philip and felt gratitude—I love his attention—and a resolve not to make further mischief. And then I found myself wanting to check my date book, to see when I'd work at Gordon Skeetling's office again. We had set up a series of appointments, so I wouldn't be tempted to come at other times. Maybe I could have another fight with him, a fight that would make his shirt come partway out of his pants once more.

"He doesn't want me to come when he doesn't expect me," I said to my friends. "Does that make sense?" I told them what he'd said. I liked watching them listen.

༝

I was just wondering," Ellen said on the phone. "Did you notice an ugly green print shirt? I can't find it."

"What do you need it for if it's ugly?"

"I like thinking about the woman who left it here. She forgot it after she stayed overnight, and when I offered to send it, she said, 'Keep it.' It wouldn't fit me—and it's ugly—but I thought of her when I saw it, and I want that to happen again."

"I'll help you look," I said.

"Oh, never mind, the kids will help," she said. "I just thought you might have noticed it."

༝

So how much truth am I going to tell, and how far back need that truth go? And, maybe more important, to whom am I telling this truth? When I began writing this story, if it's a story, I had a half-formed idea that I would write it all down, put it away, and someday read it. I was writing for my future self, assuming I'd forget, or forget how it felt if I remembered the events. I wanted to preserve the good parts of what happened and also preserve the bad parts, and I'm still hoping to demonstrate to that future Daisy, Old Daisy, that what I felt was as good as I will claim it was, and as bad.

So will nobody but me ever read this document? Someone could break in and steal my computer. A floppy disk could fall out of my bag onto the street. Or I could change my mind. I could show what I've written to a friend, or even to a stranger.

More likely, I'm doing something I did before. I wrote and published a magazine article. It began as a hundred-page essay about something that happened to my brother Stephen, but in the telling, because I was telling it, my reactions and feelings were central. I wrote it over and over, for years, and each time it became shorter, and contained less detail about me. There's no need to say here what it was about. The point is that maybe I'm doing that again, maybe I'm writing another publishable five-page article or, more likely, a couple of thirty-page pieces about New Haven, and maybe this is how I do it. In that case I can be as revealing as I like, risk-free. The final version won't have the word *I* in it, or it will, but *I* will just gracefully personalize a serious subject. "When I myself had the opportunity to participate in community theater . . ."

Well, if there's going to be a scrubbing of secrets before anyone reads this, I can write down something I suddenly understood some pages back. I know why I wanted to learn about prostitution. It's because there was a time that I paid for sex, or almost did. I'd begun an affair with a student twenty years younger than I was—I was in my forties. He cleaned houses for a living. He'd been to prison. He was slight and dark, and he resembled Peter Pan—about to slide into the air on an invisible wire. He would come to my house— talking fast and cleverly and oddly—we'd go to bed, I'd pay him for not cleaning. I went on the radio, talking about prostitutes, to find out if the *customers* are ever not pathetic. The young man, Dennis Ring, has been dead for years. He was crazy and difficult, and I still miss him.

Three girls came to the next rehearsal: Justine; Daphne's daughter, Cindy; and a bustling, bossy kid named Morgana and called Mo, a black girl with a head full of barrettes. Of course Katya hadn't been able to say no to anyone who called. She thought they should watch for a week before two of them began playing the two-headed girl. "The third one can be her friend," she said. Ellen also watched, sitting in a corner on a folding chair. I was constantly aware of her. I was angry with her because I'd thrown away her shirt, as if her mildness had forced me into wrongdoing.

But I liked Justine, who laughed quietly, with an adult laugh, at moments I wouldn't have thought were funny, so we became funnier. We were a series of baby-sitters and day-care workers trying to look after the two-headed baby. Then Jonah was a minister who baptized her TheaDora. He did a parody of a preacher, which seemed strange for a real preacher, but maybe he wasn't trying to be funny. When Justine laughed, I noticed, Mo kicked her, and she pushed Mo's shoulder. Then Jonah delivered a sermon. "We must examine our thoughts about this child," he said. "We must destroy any prejudice in our hearts."

Playing the baby's mother, I said, "Reverend, I am not prejudiced against the baby."

"The one who's prejudiced," said Chantal, who was playing the father, "is Uncle Fractious."

Muriel volunteered to be Uncle Fractious, who said, "The baby is an abomination in the sight of God. She is too much trouble. Let's sacrifice the whole child or cut off one of her heads!" Muriel stepped forward briskly as she finished, then resumed her vigorous striding, being both Muriel herself in her men's blue jeans, with her hair sticking out in all directions, and the equally energetic Uncle Fractious.

There followed a debate by the parents, the doctor, and the director of the managed-care plan—David, nodding rapidly, as was his habit in any role though not when he wasn't acting. "The parents' insurance does not cover cutting off extra heads," he said.

"I love both heads!" Chantal screamed.

"How can you leave these parents with this monster?" said Denise, who always seemed to play the doctor, no matter how much we meant to trade roles around.

"No child is a monster," said Jonah, who was not in the scene and was seated cross-legged on his mat at the edge of the open area where we worked, his big knees sticking up. It didn't matter; the managed-care company was adamant.

Later, Jonah played the minister again, and as the mother I found myself giving him a species of confession, explaining how hard it was to love my husband and our peculiar baby, how my husband was afraid of me now, as if I was a witch. Jonah encouraged me to pray.

"He's ashamed to be seen pushing the carriage," I said.

"Because of her deformity?"

"People will think it's his fault."

"TheaDora may be a punishment for all our sins," the minister said.

"She's a sweet baby, Reverend. Both heads laugh. Thea is starting to talk. Dora has three teeth." Getting into the car after the rehearsal that night, I had a momentary feeling of panic: I'd left my baby behind.

The following week, when we moved ten years forward in the life of this family, different combinations of the three girls tried playing TheaDora. Muriel had made a red calico dress with two necklines, and we had two girls at a time try it on, quickly discovering that it hung correctly only when the girls were more or less the same height. Justine and Mo, then, became TheaDora, while Cindy, who was smaller, was their friend. We all laughed the first time our wide little girl, with Mo's confident black face and Justine's sly fair one sticking out of the great big dress, moved toward us, a dark brown left arm and a light-skinned right arm slapping the air as they tried to balance, while four sneakers stepped on one another. The girls stumbled and fell in a tangle but soon were rehearsing out in the corridor, coached by Ellen, while the rest of us reworked baby scenes. Intertwining their hidden arms and counting softly, they were able to walk. By the following week, Muriel had added a flounce to the dress. Their feet concealed, Mo and Justine became a two-headed girl. I watched Muriel watch them, first critically, then with a look of astonishment and pride. Cindy, who commented on everything while twisting or sucking on strands of thin, brown hair, played with TheaDora, teased her, argued with her. "You're not my friend. I don't want a friend with *two heads*."

❦

Pekko thought he might buy a pickup truck from a dealer in Watertown, and on a Saturday late that month I drove him there. Beside me on the front seat of my car, he talked in a slow, steady voice about what he could do with a pickup. At such times we might talk on and on, back and forth, making obvious remarks like a

real married couple. Arthur barked too often in the backseat, and
Pekko told him to be quiet. The stretch of Route 63 that was our des-
tination was ugly, nothing but car dealerships. While Pekko examined the truck he'd seen advertised, I walked Arthur along the edge
of the road. The day was sunny and warm, and we'd seen tulips in
every yard. Arthur yanked on the leash, and I yanked back.

"Did you know that the first act of the first New Haven government was a trial for murder?" I said when we drove off again
together, since Pekko hadn't bought the pickup. I suppose I wanted
to give him details about my work, too: an even exchange. I'd read
this fact in Gordon's office. Then I interrupted myself. "Let's take
Arthur to a park." I remembered a nature preserve in Litchfield I'd
visited with a former boyfriend, and without waiting for an answer,
I made a U-turn and drove north.

"It wasn't well-maintained," Pekko said. "I want a truck that
belonged to someone who appreciates trucks."

"Right," I said. "Did you know that the first act of the New
Haven government, when they set it up in the sixteen hundreds,
was a murder trial?"

"And what does *that* mean?" said Pekko, suddenly paying attention.

"What does it *mean*?"

"What are you implying?"

"I'm not implying anything," I said. Gordon had been away at a
conference that week, and I'd read for hours without a plan, obeying
impulse. The archive included pages photocopied from a history of
New Haven. Its government, I explained to Pekko, had been mod-
eled not on the English common law system but on one derived,
somehow, from the Bible. It was based on a system that had been

established for Massachusetts but never used. New Haven—briefly called Quinnipiack—was established while an Indian named Nepaumuck awaited trial for murder. Once the state was set up, he was tried and decapitated.

"Why are you so interested?" he said.

"It's a good subject," I said. "I've been making a pile of material having to do with murder in New Haven. Obviously somebody who worked in that office was thinking about it, because there's a lot of stuff, and I know I could find more—I mean, when you think about some of the murders that have taken place here, just in the years I've lived here. And their importance. What happened on account of them. Alex Rackley. Penney Serra. Christian Prince. Malik Jones."

"Malik Jones wasn't murdered."

"Technically, no."

"He wasn't murdered."

"I read the police report on Malik Jones the other day," I said.

"What are you up to?" Pekko said tensely, turning in his seat, angrier than I'd seen him in a long time.

I was interested in his anger, not afraid of it, almost amused. I don't know what I should have done, but I pretended I was alone, monologuing in the shower. "Marie Valenti," I said. "Marie Valenti. The one nobody can forget. Oh, God, and Suzanne Jovin."

The truth is that except for Nepaumuck's victim, nobody can forget any of the abovementioned people (and quite a few others), all murdered or at least killed in New Haven. Alex Rackley, a Black Panther, was executed by the Black Panthers in 1969. Bobby Seale and Ericka Huggins were accused of conspiracy leading to the murder, and the trial, in 1970, was the occasion of rallies and riots. Penney Serra, a young New Haven woman, was murdered in a big downtown garage in the summer of 1973. Marie Valenti was eighteen years old, an honor student, when she was found dead on the New Haven Green in 1976. Christian Prince was the Yale student whose death Gordon remembered, killed by New Haven kids who robbed him. Malik Jones was a black New Haven boy who was shot by an East Haven cop after a car chase. Suzanne Jovin was a Yalie killed on a December evening on a residential street—the street where Ellen lived—in 1998. A professor was suspected of the crime, but he's never been charged.

Penney Serra's death, in the garage, increased the public's loss of faith in the safety and bustle of downtown, which grew less bustly and less safe after she was killed. The murder was unsolved for decades. A Waterbury man, identified by DNA, has just been convicted of her murder—in the spring of 2002, as I write this. But the murder of Marie Valenti—unsolved after almost as many years—might make people feel even worse. She was the granddaughter of a New Haven grocer, and hundreds of people had watched her playing with her little brother in the aisles of the Italian market. People who hadn't seen her decided after she died that maybe they had. Marie Valenti had been a student at Wilbur Cross, a reporter on the school paper—and she'd just been accepted at Yale. Her body was found on the green at nine on a Tuesday evening, a couple of weeks before she'd have graduated from high school. I'd lived in town just a few years then. I hadn't seen Marie Valenti playing on the floor of the grocery store—which had closed when the highway cut through its neighborhood—but I remember the headlines.

I said much of the above as I drove, talking more to myself than to Pekko. In my peripheral vision I saw Pekko holding himself tightly next to me, as if gathering his strength to strike—or keep what he gathered. He became more solid, more compact. He didn't speak.

I knew it made no sense to find him funny, yet I coaxed, as if he were four, "*What?*"

He shook his head. When I slowed, driving into the park I remembered—a wooded nature preserve—Arthur whined. In the parking lot, I opened the back door for Arthur, reaching past him to take hold of his leash. But Pekko had detached it when we left Watertown, so now the dog bounded out of the car and took off across a meadow.

Young and disobedient, Arthur ignored my shouts, cantering toward the nearby woods. I couldn't help delighting in his poodle, squared-off directness, his pleasure in motion. I hurried after him, and Pekko followed me at a steady pace, snapping the folded leash against his leg. Pekko is the sort of powerful man who looks more natural on a ladder than walking in a forest.

A family with children and a small white dog came out of the woods, and Arthur and the dog ran off together. I called Arthur once more, but on his way to me, he veered off and put a paw on the shoulder of a little child, who fell down and began to wail. Pekko came puffing up behind me, shouting, "You damned dog, get your ass over here!"

The father of the child had picked him or her up—it was one of those indefinite stubby children, recently a baby—but didn't look concerned. I rushed to apologize, but the people were untroubled. Now Arthur let himself be put on the leash, and we walked into the woods, where the trees were evergreens but the undergrowth on either side was all but ready to leaf out. In the oxygenated quiet, I began to calm down. I'd been afraid the family would be angry, and

I might have become angry myself in response, though the mishap was my fault. As I grew calmer, I remembered that Pekko had been angry with me, and I'd laughed at him. I didn't know why he was angry.

It was new for us to walk like this. Ordinarily one of us walked Arthur alone. "So why don't you want me to be curious about murder?" I said. "Are you afraid I'll become a murderer?" I felt tender toward him, ready to get along with him, to compromise, as if that relaxed family had argued his case.

"You don't know why?" he said.

"I don't know why."

"New Haven," he said, gesturing at the woods that were not New Haven, apparently imagining New Haven superimposed on them. "I've been there longer than you have. I was born there."

"That's why I married you," I said. "I was bored with people who complain about New Haven."

"Then why spread bad news? Penney Serra. Christian Prince. Haven't we been criticized enough?"

"By *we* you mean the citizens of New Haven?"

"What else would I mean?"

"Why would my curiosity make people criticize us?"

"Next thing you'll be on the radio again, talking about New Haven murders."

I hadn't had such a specific idea yet. "It's a thought," I said, "but wouldn't it be possible to present it in a such a way that—"

"No, it wouldn't. You presented prostitution with all sorts of do-gooder, scholarly fuss, and the message was, New Haven is a city of whores."

"*No.*"

"That's how it sounded to me." His stubborn bulk moved beside me.

"You barely heard any of it," I said.

"I heard enough."

Now I was angry. "You're acting as if I arrived three days ago, determined to destroy the place."

"You and your Yale friends."

"Oh, come on! Yale barely tolerates Gordon, because he cares about the stuff *you* care about!"

To my surprise, Pekko bent and released the snap on Arthur's leash. We hadn't seen any people or dogs for a long time. Arthur had been sniffing and peeing, behaving as politely as he ever did on a walk. Of course he bounded away again. Pekko watched with satisfaction, standing still and nodding, so his beard rose and fell. "It's time to turn back," he said.

As we turned, he brushed my shoulder with his arm, a rough, apologetic gesture of amity. I turned toward him and took his white-bearded face in my hands. "Let's not fight," I said. "I won't do anything without telling you all about it."

"Well, there *have* been murders," he said gruffly. Then he took my shoulders in his hands and almost harshly thrust his tongue into my mouth. When he pulled away, he said, "I can't bear it."

"I know," I said, and we set off, while Arthur followed us, running ahead, then turning to look for us, staying away from other people, behaving—after all—like a dog who didn't need to be restrained. The air was cooler, and the light jacket I wore was no longer enough. I zipped it and wound my arm around Pekko's, drawing warmth from his body.

We were silent a long time. Then Pekko said quietly, "Look. I know something about Marie Valenti."

"About her?"

"About how she was killed."

I said, "You mean New Haven killed her. Unidentified poor black kids with unstable home environments killed her. You mean that if I start talking about murder, some of the time I'm inevitably talking about poor blacks killing middle-class whites. You mean I ought to publicize something else about New Haven. Successful black middle class. Integrated neighborhoods. Falling crime rate."

I stopped and sighed and tried to gather my thoughts. New Haven does have a successful black middle class, some integrated neighborhoods, and a falling crime rate. I had no impulse to study those subjects. Death had seized my imagination, which has always gone where it wants to go. Surely there was a way to make a public presentation on murder in New Haven—whether I was talking about radio or something else—that would not just encourage the city's critics. I suddenly remembered a short, obnoxious woman who thrust herself in front of me at a gathering I once attended in Philadelphia. "*How* can you live in New Haven?" she said.

Pekko didn't reply to my account of the causes of Marie Valenti's death, so I kept talking, trying to explain that something about murder intrigued me, and it wasn't the sensationalism. "I wanted to think about prostitution for the same reason," I said. "Honestly, it isn't just sex and violence." We approached the parking lot again, and I crouched to call Arthur, who thrust his hard head into my breasts as he did at home, letting me snap the leash on once more. "I want to know," I said, rising and understanding myself a little better than I had—entranced with what I now understood—"I want to know what it's like to be someone else. And it seems easier to find out if I can think about someone going to bed with a stranger than if I think about someone cooking a chicken." I asked myself what about murder interested me. Not the moment of being murdered but the moment of murdering. I thought if I could fasten on that second—the second of pulling the trigger, pushing in the knife—then I'd know someone. I'd know someone just when everything came apart for him, when he did something terrible, secret, and amazing.

I didn't want it to sound as if murder was good. "I'm not saying," I said, as I put Arthur into the car, then got into the driver's seat and waited for Pekko—who hadn't spoken for a while—to walk around to his side. "I'm not saying prostitution and murder are good. I'm not saying it's fine to have them in New Haven because they're great!" I drove out of the parking lot. Wasn't that what I was saying? Wasn't my defense that prostitution and murder were so inherently interesting that a city was all but enhanced by their existence within its borders? Well, if that was the case, I'd better deny it, I thought, turning the car toward home. Eventually I'd figure out something more plausible and less shocking. "I'm definitely not saying that," I finished and was finally silenced by my inability to make sense of my feelings.

We drove without speaking for most of the hour it took us to get home. Without consulting Pekko, I stopped at a Dunkin' Donuts and brought containers of coffee to the car. He took his and drank it.

As we crossed the New Haven line, making our way through the trafficky western edge of the city, with its shopping centers and strip development, Pekko seemed to come to himself again, studying his fellow New Haveners on Whalley Avenue. He no longer seemed angry or impassive. The people on the street were indeed different from anybody we might have noticed up north in Litchfield County. It was late Saturday afternoon by now, and Orthodox Jews in black hats, leading big families, were walking near a synagogue. Two black teenage girls in shorts, intent on their conversation, waited to cross Whalley, not seeming to mind the evening chill. A small child lingered behind them, one finger in mouth, eyes on the passing cars, looking just about to figure everything out. I stopped for a red light. Pekko said, "I know who killed Marie Valenti. I've been alone with this. I want to tell you. Can you listen? Can I trust you?"

"Trust me?"

"I know if I tell you something in confidence, you'll keep it a secret. I want you also to forget this plan to find out about murder in New Haven. It's not a good plan. You have to trust me, and I'll trust you."

"Sweetie, I don't know what you're talking about, but you can trust me."

"Marie Valenti was not killed by a black teenager or a group of black teenagers. She was killed by a white kid she'd known in middle school. Nobody knew he was here that night. He'd moved away."

"How do *you* know?" For a moment I thought he was just pretending to know something, something he'd somehow deduced. "What paper do you read?"

"I don't live like the rest of you, speculating from headlines. There are people in this town who know what's going on, and I'm one of them."

"But how?"

"I knew them both. I was a sub when they were at Fair Haven Middle School. I made friends with the boy. He'd come to see me now and then when he was in high school. Two, three years after she died, he came and told me. By then he came to New Haven occasionally, to see his grandparents. Nobody thought anything."

"You didn't turn him in?"

"He wasn't going to hurt anyone else," Pekko said, "so there was no reason for me to ruin his life. Turning him in wouldn't bring her back."

"What happened to him?"

"He went to UConn. He lives out of state."

"But if you'd been wrong——"

"I know, if he'd killed again. But I knew him. I was one of those teachers who have a little group of kids who stay after school and wash the blackboards. I had a long-term appointment that year. I was teaching eighth-grade English, figuring it out as I went along. I had kids keeping diaries. I never told you?"

"You told me about the diaries," I said. "You made them read *The Great Gatsby*."

"Right, *The Great Gatsby*."

By now I had reached our street and parked in front of our house, but we sat, not moving, though Arthur began to whine.

"That boy had a cute diary. Always figuring out how to please his dad. An old-fashioned Irish family. Never imagined not going to church. But passion in that kid. Anger. I once saw it come out, when another kid got nasty with him. He was little and skinny, then. Later he got bigger. He still talked about pleasing his dad, pleasing his grandfather. His grandfather was a contractor. I knew him a little."

"But if his temper made him kill once . . . Pekko, it's illegal not to turn in a criminal."

"Not if you're a priest."

"You're not a priest."

"The night he told me, I was a priest. That's how it was. He came to me late at night and talked for six hours. Then I took him out to breakfast, to the diner on Whalley. He said, 'Are you going to call the cops?' and I said I wouldn't. I told him if he wanted to turn himself in, he was free to do that. By then he was almost done with college."

"Why did he kill her?"

"She wouldn't take him back. He'd been her boyfriend for a few weeks. Then he moved away. Family moved to Hartford."

"Wasn't he a suspect?"

"Oh, I guess. They looked at a lot of kids. But the assumption was strangers, because she was robbed."

"So he deliberately made it seem as if New Haven poor people had done it."

"That's right."

"And you forgave that."

"I wouldn't say I forgave it. I didn't forgive it."

We sat in silence for a while, and I said, "Was she in your class, too?"

"No," Pekko said. "I only knew her a little. I'd see her in the halls. I knew her name. She had a lot of dark, curly hair."

"But if he killed a woman just because she wouldn't be his girl-friend—"

"I know. He might do anything."

"You took that chance?"

"He was beside himself over her. I didn't think it would happen again. Remember, he told me three years later. He talked more like the boy's psychiatrist than the boy. I thought he was less likely to murder than I was."

"He stabbed her?"

"He talked about the feel of the knife going in, how he did it again and again."

I thought about it. "Do you think maybe it wasn't true?"

"I think it was true," he said. Then he got out and opened the back door for Arthur, who preceded us up our front steps and wagged when we produced a key, congratulating us for remembering where we lived.

§

The other night I was writing this thing I write, this account of a piece of my life, more than a year later (it's the oddest thing, proceeding in time as time proceeds, but not at the same rate; I began in February, writing about the previous February, and now it's June and I'm only in April), when the doorbell rang, and in, unannounced, came my brother Stephen. Maybe Roz knew he was coming to New Haven and forgot to tell me. He'd had supper with her. Or he'd shown up there unannounced, too. He likes to do that, to prove he's still a boy. He'd taken the train from New York. I hardly ever take the train, I'm too impatient, but Stephen likes it, though he lives an hour from Grand Central, in Queens, and would get home in the middle of the night. He's married, as I've said, and has a daughter, and yet he seems alone all the time, and seems most at ease when he's put himself into a place where there's a slice of emptiness around him, like someone who lived in Montana or Alaska, someone who didn't want his neighbors near enough that he could hear their dog bark. I was alone. He came into the kitchen and sat in a corner of the old green sofa while I opened a bottle of Sam Adams for him.

"Did I interrupt something?" he said.

"I'm writing." I gestured upstairs, where my computer is.

"Writing what?"

"I'm writing about half a year in my life."

"Just any half year?"

"No, February to October of 2001."

"Any special reason?"

"None of your business."

"When can I read it?"

"Maybe never."

"Then what's the point?" said Stephen. I wonder if he dyes his hair. He still seems young, and his hair is dark brown. He carries an expensive ballpoint pen in his pocket, as if he were the writer, and he takes it out and removes the cover, as if he couldn't wait to write, then puts it back on, as if he can't think what to say after all. "Let me see it now," he said. "Is it about that guy?"

"What guy?" I asked, though I knew. I knew he meant Dennis Ring, my young ex-con dead lover, about whom I'd told him one teary night a couple of years ago.

"You said he drank herbal tea with you. He had complicated opinions about herbal tea, which kinds were good."

"He had opinions like that about everything, but that was ten years ago." Denny the occasional thief, drug dealer, drug user, and maker of mischief had opinions about shapes of pasta, opinions about cookies. He knew where to find European cookies made with dark chocolate in the days before you could pick them up at any convenience store. I stopped and calculated. Denny would still be under forty if he were alive. He'd been on and off drugs, and he died—in Pekko's frozen yogurt store—of an overdose. He'd broken into the store. He wasn't my lover then. I hadn't seen him in months. Sometimes he bored me. That was my big secret about Denny, sometimes he bored me. And sometimes he charmed me. He was my lover before he was my student. He signed up for my course as a tease, I think. We weren't planning to sleep together anymore, until he got into the cleaning business. Again I talked to Stephen about Denny. I told him Denny had nothing to do with what I was writing.

"Then do I?"

"No," I said, understanding that Denny and Stephen were linked in my mind, somehow—because Stephen had been the kid with trouble in our household. But that's not true anymore, is it—that neither Denny nor Stephen is in this book? I didn't show it to Stephen. He left late at night. I drove him to the train. Driving home, I thought it had been the first time since September 11— nine months ago—that Stephen and I didn't talk about it, then remembered we had. I'd rinsed his beer bottle and put it into the recycling bin, and Stephen had said, "We don't recycle plastic anymore."

"Why not?"

"Because terrorists knocked down the World Trade Center, and now we can't afford it." I'd thought he meant his family by *we*, but he meant New York. Stephen was wearing a jacket too warm for the weather, though this is a cool June. My brother's lifelong gesture was fixed one summer afternoon when we were teenagers, when he stood up, not quite surprised, and took a step backwards but grasped a chair as if to keep himself from stepping too far back. He is always receding but never goes far.

☙

Gordon called me to change some of the appointments we'd laboriously set up. "Sometimes I want to avoid you, and sometimes I want to be there with you," he said in his frank way.

At least he didn't always want to avoid me. "How do you know now that you'll feel like avoiding me two weeks from Wednesday?" I said.

"I have a schedule. I write on Wednesdays and Fridays in alternate weeks and on Tuesdays and Thursdays during the other weeks, so sooner or later I can make appointments with people who are never free on a particular day." He added, "But sometimes I have to change my schedule." He was odd, but I liked his willingness to answer me, to answer more fully than I expected. The trait compared well with Pekko's silences. "If I'm not writing," he said, "I like it when you're here."

I'd shown him stacks of articles about urban renewal, community gardens, community policing. Sometimes he said he'd already worked on a topic, and I filed what I'd found, but sometimes he said he'd like to think about the subject matter, and I should find a way to keep it from disappearing. I imagined my stacks going slowly by on a circular moving sidewalk, so he could glance at them now and then.

Before we hung up he said, "Let's schedule a lunch, too. I need to fight you some more about foster care. It clarifies my thoughts to argue."

"Did you tuck your shirt in?" I said.

He didn't know what I meant. "There wasn't any hanky-panky, was there?"

"You mean you don't recall whether there was or not?"

"I recall there wasn't."

"So do I. You waved your arms around so much, arguing with me, that your shirt came out."

"Oh, it's always out. Doesn't that happen to everybody?"

Was I flirting? Yes, but I always flirt. In my single days, I didn't bother to flirt, I'd just proposition a guy. I might say, "If you're interested, by the way, so am I," and often he became interested whether he had been or not. I think my flirting with Gordon was a sign, given my nature, that we were going to keep the relationship businesslike, with an admixture of casual comradeship. Flirting can be a substitute for sex. I have flirted with Philip LoPresti for years but never considered sleeping with him.

And the next two times Gordon Skeetling and I were together, nothing much happened personally. We had lunch without arguing, talking about dogs. Nobody flirted. I interrupted him a few times to show him material I'd gathered. I continued to amass a pile about murder in New Haven, though I told myself I was simply doing it out of curiosity and, in deference to Pekko, would not use it for any public purpose. I worked at Gordon's office alone a few times, too, when he was away. By now he'd given me a key. Then I saw him again on a cold day, a return to March-like weather after the warmth earlier in April. It was chilly in his office. I was sorting dusty papers from the bottom of an old pile in a corner of the floor, and I frequently went to the bathroom to wash my hands.

Gordon was restless, leaving his desk every few minutes to pace, look out the window, or take his own trip to the bathroom. He seemed to forget I was there. I had given up trying to stay out of his line of sight and mostly didn't close the French doors, since I could hear him on the phone whether they were closed or not. I'd look up and see him ambling back, automatically checking his fly, his eyes unfocused. I looked as I always did at his clothes. By now I associated him with tan and brown, colors I hadn't much liked before. They looked woodsy and comfortable on him.

"Did I tell you about the conference?" he asked, on one of these walks, and I'd been so sure he'd forgotten me that I glanced to see if he was speaking on the telephone.

"Me?"

"Who else? I didn't, did I? The project hosts a conference in October every two years. This arises out of a byzantine arrangement with two other Yale projects, but lately they've essentially dropped out. Do you want to do it? Obviously I'd pay you."

"Do you have a topic?" I said.

"No, that's the carrot. You can host a conference on anything you like that's remotely connected to urban life in small cities."

"How about murder in New Haven?" I said immediately.

"Whoa. I guess so. It's not our usual pedantic crap, but I suppose you could turn it into something academic enough."

"Sure," I said. As I talked with Gordon about it, I scurried around in my mind to discover why I was completely willing to oppose my husband. I decided, with the kitchen of my mind—while its parlor and dining room decorously considered what Gordon was saying—that I was angry with Pekko after all, because I'd felt morally bullied on the walk, shamed out of thinking about what I wanted to think about. Moral bullying seemed like a crime bad enough that I could now do whatever I liked.

"I mean," Gordon said now, "could you plan this conference in additional time? I don't want you to stop the sorting-out project."

"I guess I'll be spending most of my life here," I said.

"Fine with me," said Gordon, "except for those afternoons I write. Well, maybe we'll have to rethink that, if you're going to have time for this." Then he said, in the tone in which he might have proposed still another schedule change, "You could also become my mistress, if you choose to."

"Your *what?*"

"Obviously we'll continue with both projects whether you say yes or no."

"I didn't think you were asking for sexual favors," I said, "in exchange for the right to organize your trash."

"Or even put on my grubby little conference, eh? Oh, I know. The word *mistress.*"

"It's a rather startling term. But I suppose you required a word that could have the possessive adjective *my* in front of it." What I primarily felt, that is, in response to his suggestion, was even greater permission—the right, now, to say anything whatsoever.

"Oh, I'm a possessive bastard, indeed I am. Will you go to bed with me, Daisy?"

"Where?" I said.

"Good question. Not here. Not in my house in Madison, which is too far."

"Not in my house."

"You don't seem like a motel girl."

"I know where to go," I said. We seemed to have skipped over the question of whether. Ellen's children were on vacation, and she'd taken them to Florida to see her mother. Or her father, whichever it was. I had a key. It was a nice house. I was going to accept *mistress,* apparently, and even *girl.* My body had just turned into an object that required touching by Gordon Skeetling. My arms and legs seemed to be located where they were only to serve as lines pointing directly or indirectly to my crotch.

I'd never touched him. I wasn't in love with him. I believe in work relationships. That is, I believe passionately that people can express what is inside them by working together as authentically as by sleeping together. I don't imagine that work is a substitute for love or sex in any way. I wanted to work with Gordon Skeetling, and the fact that I'd considered him attractive from the beginning, with his dangly, mobile, bony arms and his up-and-down eyebrows, just made the work pleasanter, maybe more likely to be good work. What I'd just agreed to do—though I was eager—seemed as unlikely as if I'd moved comfortably through his rooms and he'd offered to lead me to the bank on the corner and arrange a mortgage so I could buy them. (Not that I was buying Gordon Skeetling. I knew from the first he was a rental.) We didn't leave immediately for Ellen's house, once I told him where I thought we could go and he'd nodded quickly.

"An hour?" he said and went back to work. I had another appointment. I phoned and canceled. Then I went back to work, too. Sorting through piles of documents that seemed to be connected with the building of the New Haven Coliseum, throwing most of them out, was more fun with a tingling crotch. I'd made several decisions in a row, and as I write this I remember writing not many pages ago that my habit is to be good half the time. Deciding to do the conference over Pekko's objections felt good, as I made the decision, not bad. Deciding to be Gordon's lover felt good, not bad, although I was surprised to notice that. Deciding to use Ellen's house was decidedly bad and felt that way, and I also felt guilty about canceling that appointment. You could say my conscience works well about the minor issues and less well about the major ones. Or you could say I have an original notion of right and wrong. Writing this now, I am not sure I disagree with the assessment my overburdened conscience, working in a hurry, made then. During that hour I did not think for long about the right and wrong of it, although I believe I did total the thing up in a rough way, something like the way I've just described. Mostly I spent the hour doing good work, and waiting.

I'm writing because I want to, but when I sit down to it, I don't always want to tell the story of Pekko, Gordon, and the play about the two-headed woman. Sometimes I feel like writing about the moment that changed my brother Stephen, more than thirty years ago. Stephen called me, a few nights ago. (Now it's July 2002.) "When are you going to show me what you're writing?"

I liked his curiosity. I said, "You didn't tell anyone, did you?"

"No. But I want to see it."

"Why?"

"Because you're my sister. Because you didn't tell me what was going on, and now I'll find out."

"What was going on when?"

"Last summer. I knew something was going on last summer. I wondered if that guy was really dead. The guy from ten years ago."

"How did you know something was going on?"

"It was clear, the time you were in New York."

That's still to come, the time in New York. Talking to Stephen the other night, I changed the subject.

I didn't invent Denny's death. He died ten years ago, two years after I met him. I met him at his grandmother's house. That wraith had a grandmother—a canny woman who loved him, a school-teacher who'd taken her small grandson for pancakes each year on the morning of his birthday, and when he was grown (and not in prison) bought him Thai dinners whenever she could invent an excuse. The grandmother had a Fourth of July party, at which I was somebody's date. Denny and I met over salad: he was tossing his grandmother's salad.

"Did you ever go to bed for money?" he asked me, when I hardly knew him. Not that first night, and not after we slept together—yet I think I remember that we slept together the second time we met. I suppose there was a time in between. When he asked the question, we were in my car. I was driving.

"Did *you*?" I said.

"Sure. It's not so bad. I've done everything."

"Was it a woman?" I asked.

"I wouldn't go to bed with a man for money. With a woman, I figured I was cheating her." Of course this was before I gave him money when we went to bed. Which I did because he needed money. I think. He persisted. "Did you? Did you ever?"

"Not exactly." I told him a story nobody else has ever heard. I was in my thirties. A blond, pudgy man in a bar took me to his sister's apartment, to which he had a key. I suppose he was married. When I walked in, I noticed the smell of gas, and I checked the stove. One of the burners was slightly on. I turned it off on my way to his sister's couch, taking my clothes off. After we were done, he handed me two fifty-dollar bills.

"What's that for?"

"You saved my life. My sister deliberately left the stove on. She did this to asphyxiate me."

"That's ridiculous," I said. "I'm not taking your money."

"You said you like to read. Buy books."

I shrugged and took the bills. In New Haven, there are people you know whom you never run into, and others with whom you have a high coincidence rate. For years I kept noticing that man. Sometimes he smiled. After a while I knew I'd been a whore—he'd wanted me to be a whore and I'd complied—but when I talked to Pekko and Gordon about my interest in prostitution, I left that incident out.

Right now I'm recounting, however, not Stephen's early life or what I told Denny, but the day I agreed to go to bed with Gordon Skeetling for the first time. I enjoyed the postponement and the anticipation. I felt clever, having acquired something I wanted that wouldn't become a nuisance, like a travel bag of just the right size, one that would fold up later, using little space in the corner of the closet.

We worked for an hour, then Gordon walked in and put his hand on my shoulder. I murmured, "One second," and made a brief note on my pad. The room was becoming more orderly, something like Ellen's kitchen, an artistic arrangement of chaos reduced to categories, and Ellen's kitchen was where I led him first—so he could see it—after we'd clumsily walked out of his office (suddenly I was nervous), bumping into each other and apologizing, and had gotten into my car, almost without discussion. I drove to Ellen's house, parked boldly in front, unlocked the door, and led Gordon in.

It was several weeks since we'd dismantled the kitchen. Ellen and her daughters still ate meals in that complicated array, that statement of the value of detail for its own sake. Everything she owned could be connected to someone in her life, some painful or joyful event. When Ellen was home, memory ruled that room, but now she was not home, and the objects themselves sat there like "the plain sense of things" as Wallace Stevens put it. "Look at that!" Gordon said, bracing his long arm in the kitchen doorway and taking in the view with some amusement. "What a conglomeration!"

He was delighted, which delighted me. He blocked the doorway, but moving up behind him, under his arm, putting my hand on his waist as if I'd done that before, and looking into the room as if he was showing it to me instead of the other way around, I saw it his way. When Ellen was home, everything was fogged with meaning—often with loss, disappointment, or betrayal. "This was the teapot my college roommate left behind when she moved out. She liked the man I was dating, and she moved out when she couldn't bear it any longer. I hadn't even guessed." Ellen's memory dulled the blue glaze even for me, but when Gordon stared at the teapot, and everything else, that glaze shone bright. Each object was simply itself, and even I could see the difference, with my partial view under his elbow. "It is as if we had come to an end of the imagination," Stevens wrote.

I led Gordon to the spare bedroom in which Ellen and I had piled clothes. Heaps of coats, men's suits (her father's?), dresses, and blouses were still on the bed. I removed the piles carefully, lining them up on the floor so I could replace them. I felt a pang about the lost green print shirt, and even looked around for it, as if I might have incorrectly remembered my theft and disposal of it. Then, in that roomful of piled clothing—which Ellen was reducing to cleaner, neater, but never smaller piles—I began unbuttoning my shirt, and Gordon stepped forward and put his hands over mine. I didn't become completely passive, though I let him do it. I knew we had to keep track of our own clothes in this array of clothes, not mislaying Gordon's tan sweater or the silk scarf I wore. We made two neat piles, both moving unself-consciously, usefully, though we were becoming naked. I liked Gordon's substantial but bony torso, his rounded, surprisingly fleshy ass. Standing next to our folded clothing, Gordon put his hands on my breasts. He laughed, then kissed me, a long, good kiss that made me forget everything but the tongue in my mouth.

When I drew back the old pink chenille bedspread, I found that the bed was made. We'd have to do something about the clean but slightly musty sheet we were about to muss and stain. I left the room, found Ellen's linen closet in the hall, and returned—while Gordon looked at me with open curiosity—with a towel, which I spread between the sheets, postponing the question of what I'd do with it later. If the plan I'd made was awkward, that made the enterprise better—touchingly amateurish, like a homemade greeting card. We were laughing when we lay down, and I drew this new, differently shaped man to my body with nothing but pleasure in chance, pleasure in possibility, and my old, too-long-forgotten delight in the variety of captivating male bodies available to someone who kept an eye open.

"I didn't know we'd do this," I said, marveling, after he'd entered me and we'd both come quickly, too excited to take it slow. What if we'd missed it, as people do?

"You're married."

"You're not, or so you said."

"I'm not."

"Well, that's good." He had multitudes of girlfriends, of course. All right. We hadn't used a condom. All right.

We lay companionably on the scratchy towel, and he began to talk about work, telling me with some excitement about the next article he intended to write. He was now thinking about a new way of organizing the categories in municipal budgets, and he talked fast, rising on an elbow to explain better. Like a cup of coffee, sex had awakened him.

When I laughed, he said, "Work is sex." He kissed me again, longer this time.

"I know," I said when we stopped. "That's what people don't understand. Work is sex. *Good* work. Putting on a conference."

"Can you do that? Can you put on a conference?" Another kiss.

"Oh, sure, I'm terrific," I said.

I did not steal the towel but put it in the clothes hamper, assuming Ellen wouldn't notice an extra dirty towel. That morning, I had told Pekko I wouldn't be home for supper, because of an appointment so late it left little time before a rehearsal. I dropped Gordon off near his car, an old black Saab (he got out without kissing me, but that was only sensible) and arrived late for that last appointment. It was disconcerting to be with a different man, someone who didn't count, a man who chose not to clean up his clutter when he heard what I charge. Then I ate Chinese takeout in the car, irrationally elated by good food, and elated that my old capacity for mischief wasn't gone. I walked into the rehearsal room feeling at peace in my body, as if I'd swum a long, slow distance.

With Justine away, Cindy could have joined with Mo to play the two-headed girl, but she didn't want to. "I don't like being squashed together with somebody," she said.

"You think I like it?" Mo said.

"Could we record that?" said Katya. "Could you kids say that again?"

They couldn't remember what they'd said. "That you don't like being too close . . ."

"I don't want you breathing on my face," Cindy said. "I don't want to be in that dress with anybody."

"There's nothing wrong with my breath," Mo said and blew into Cindy's eyes, so Cindy's lank, brown hair flew up. She had a tense little face like her mother's, and she looked as if she might cry, but then I saw she was trying not to laugh.

We were different people when involved with a two-headed person. Maybe I had become different in the rest of my life as well. Gordon didn't know about the play but had been the source of the idea. Maybe I wouldn't tell him. Right then, being in the play felt like a magnificent urban act. It was art being made by the untaught but well-intentioned wit and instinct of plain people. I liked considering myself one of the plain people, though sometimes I caught myself faking it, adopting an attitude and even a vocabulary that weren't mine. That night, with Justine away, we worked on scenes in which the child TheaDora was not present: first a conversation about her between her mother (me) and a social worker who believed in mainstreaming, played by David, and then a conference with her teacher. The scene with the teacher, played by Muriel, was hard, and we did it over and over, changing it.

"Madam," Muriel said, "your daughter is so busy arguing with herself she can't color. If one head says red, the other says blue. I don't know what to do with her."

"Don't *your* heads ever argue?"

"My dear lady, I have only one head." The teacher turned it slowly in my direction—her good, big head.

"I'm sorry to hear it, but I shouldn't hold it against you, because I too am not all there in just that department."

"The other day they had a fight about whether she needed to go to the bathroom, and then she wet her pants." The teacher had been sitting in a chair, but now she stood and paced, while I folded my arms stubbornly and twisted in my chair each time she passed me.

Then she said, stopping, "Oh, that's not the problem. I'm afraid of your daughter."

"What are you afraid of?" I said, turning as she strode past.

"What am I afraid of?" the teacher said. She stopped walking. "I'm afraid of anger. I'm afraid of love. I'm afraid of sex. I'm afraid of white people. I'm afraid of black people."

"I understand why your fear of black people and white people makes you afraid of my daughter," I said, "because she is both black and white, but why does your fear of sex, love, and anger make you afraid of poor TheaDora?"

"I don't know," Muriel said, no longer sounding like the teacher.

"I know," I said. "Anger comes out of the head. Love is all in the head. Maybe even sex is all in the head, I don't know."

"So if you have two heads . . ."

"More anger. More love. More sex."

"Does she eat twice as much as other people?" asked the teacher, resuming her role. Now she stood still in front of me.

"Maybe not twice," I said, "but a lot. Both mouths are always busy. You can see she's fat."

"Do you like having a two-headed child?"

The mother answered, "I like having a child of any sort. I never thought I'd have a child." The mother teared up at that point. "It's good to have somebody to love!"

"Don't you love your husband?" asked this nosy teacher.

"Oh, him," I said. The rehearsal was over, and Muriel and I grabbed each other. Hugging was big in this group.

ॐ

I decided I'd go to bed with Gordon five times. Once was not enough, twice would give the second occasion a dolorous weight, and three times, I thought, would have the same effect, except that both the second and the third would acquire that sentimental portentousness. I don't like the number four; I prefer odd numbers. Five beddings would constitute a short affair, not just an indiscretion, but more might cause difficulty: I'd need to tell others, or he would, or I'd get bored, or we'd become careless and someone—Pekko— would find out. I was more comfortable embarking on a limited series of sexual meetings, rather like my limited run on the radio, also a series of five. I considered discussing the number five with Gordon but decided not to. I did say, the next time I was in his office, "That was lovely, the other day. I don't want to make a habit of it, but that doesn't mean I'm through already."

"Fair enough," he said. That was our only reference to what now felt, as we conferred on work issues, like a different existence that didn't overlap, as if we knew each other two ways. I was glad we didn't rush off to Ellen's house or some other place that day, but also glad when, the next time we met, he said, "I have a towel in my car."

"Well, that's remarkable!" I said.

"Is today a good day?"

Ellen was back, but surely she was at work. It was eleven in the morning, and the kids would be at school. I'd ring the doorbell, and if somebody was home, I'd make up an excuse for being there. Of course, somebody could come in while we were there. That felt so scary, so exciting, that I was glad we were doing it, and glad we'd do it only five times altogether: limited suspense, like suspense near the end of a movie. Maybe we'd think of another place pretty soon. We went, we were brief—Gordon understood the danger, and like me was stimulated by it, not repelled—and we were back at Clark's Pizza, eating souvlaki, talking about work, before the lunch rush was over. This time, in bed, Gordon did something I particularly liked with his tongue, which was long and flexible, comparable in its way to his arms.

𝄢

As April turned into May, as I bought a few flowers and tomato plants and forgot to plant them, I contentedly made lists to myself of Pekko's good qualities and Gordon's, and how the two men were different, what each would never do or never say. Pekko would never say "Good haircut"; Gordon would never keep silent, as Pekko did habitually. They were different about dogs. Pekko regarded Arthur as his responsibility; Gordon spoke of that German shepherd as if she'd been his drinking buddy, a coconspirator. I was fascinated by his curiosity. One afternoon in the office, he came uninvited to sit on a table in the archive. "Tell me about your brothers," he said.

I'd mentioned them. He even remembered their names. "Which are you closer to, Carl or Stephen?"

"Stephen."

"I don't just mean in age."

"Neither do I."

"What does he do?"

I told him Stephen worked in the shop at the Metropolitan Museum of Art in New York.

"Running away from something."

"What makes you say that?"

"It's so indoors."

"Like a store in a mall?"

"Further in."

"I need to concentrate," I said, "I don't have much more time today." And he apologized genially and returned to his own desk.

Knowing we'd have only five times together, I was glad they were spaced. "This is the solution," I said to Arthur, as we walked by the river one morning, sidestepping birders with binoculars. Now the leaves were out: light green. "I'm too old and independent to be married, unless I have a lover from time to time. Maybe every spring." I wondered if they'd always be so easy to come by, or so nice.

I noticed that my habits changed slightly during this time. I was

messier, and might leave a pile of laundry half folded to cut up vegetables, then leave them for some third task. I didn't take up a craft,
though I believe crafts often arise out of sexual complexity. Two
women I've known started making stained-glass hangings when
their marriages were in trouble, and I think pottery has to do with
sadness, if the shapes have enough space inside to contain darkness.
Women knit when their lives are changing, and make patchwork
when they are trying to reconcile contradictory urges.

I don't know what makes people weave baskets, and I kept forgetting to ask Ellen if she'd woven some of the baskets in her house;
the rough, chunky ones looked homemade. Ellen came home from
vacation full of resolve to change her life (though she didn't seem to
be knitting). She'd dyed her hair blond like mine, and she wanted to
spend more time with me, even though she had to pay for it. I'm
firm about hours, and the customers pay for talks that take place
while I stand on the porch, ready to depart, as they think of one
more question. I try not to prolong the conversation, and I look at
my watch and write down a number when the door closes.

The first time I went to Ellen's house after being there with Gordon, I was scared. She might have known I took the sugar bowl, she
probably suspected I took her green shirt, and how could I be certain Gordon and I hadn't dropped something revealing? What if
she'd sniffed the towel? I scolded myself for repeatedly risking the
disapproval of someone who wasn't important.

Ellen was glad to see me and had no accusations. I'd pictured her
more determined and angry than she was likely to get. She fluttered
and shrugged and led me to still another room, the dining room,
which contained more baskets and several big bookcases. The baskets were filled with magazines, and additional piles lay on the floor.

Beyond an elaborate mahogany table, windows overlooked Ellen's big backyard—full, I was sure, of shrubs and budding stalks that had also made their way into her life unbidden. An old oval mirror hung to the left of the windows, and when I glanced into it, for a moment I thought Ellen, with her new light hair, was I.

"I met someone," Ellen said, and I almost said, "So did I."

"It's the first time in years," she said. "I met him just before I went away, but we talked twice while I was gone."

I suddenly felt uneasy lest Ellen's new boyfriend, somehow, was Gordon, so I murmured, "Tell me," but she didn't.

"I apologize for bringing this up," she said. "I'm letting you know because it explains my distraction." I wanted to say that, though I too had met someone, I was not distracted, but I said nothing. Then she said, "No, you're just a good person to talk to."

Then she wanted to tell me her thoughts about the play, which were numerous. "I shouldn't always stay," she said. "Justine should have time there to herself, so it's not as if I'm a friend of the adults. She's the friend. Of course I know she's not your *friend*, but—"

"She's part of the troupe," I said impatiently.

"And I'm not," she said. "I ought to find something comparable to do, but I keep wanting to help. Katya needs help."

"Help how?"

"I'd direct. I'd be the assistant director."

"Well, ask Katya," I said. Katya couldn't say no to anyone.

"But then Justine wouldn't have her experience—"

"I see," said I. "Maybe talk to Justine first."

"Maybe *you* would? She'd be honest with you."

"I guess I could do that." I decided I'd encourage Justine to say no.

In the meantime, we turned to the magazines. Presumably because she'd acquired most of them herself, Ellen was willing to consider disposing of them, although not without looking them over pretty carefully. For once our morning felt useful, and we produced a good bit of material to be recycled. I stayed longer than I'd meant to, and as we worked, the phone rang, and Ellen went to answer it. Alone in the dining room, I stood and stretched, staring into her yard. I could hear Ellen's voice, though not individual words, but then she must have turned as she spoke, because I did hear. "Louie," she said, "get your ass over here and fuck me."

෨

Two days later, I called to Gordon from my desk to his, "You want to do that again?" It would be our third time, and the little affair would be more than half over. I'd be better off, I thought, moving things along.

"Mmm."

"When?"

"As soon as possible."

He lay on top of me, an hour later (of course he liked being on top), again in Ellen's house. She had told me, when she got off the phone, that she and her lover were going to New York for the day, two days later. Gordon lay over me, and I delayed letting him go when we were done, holding his buttocks, though his weight made me breathless. Then I pushed him off and kissed him lightly, swinging my legs out of bed, reaching for my bra. I felt free as I never had with a man before, despite all my experience. I liked getting my clothes on and getting back to work, while he told me with excitement what engaged his mind that day. I liked knowing we had only two more times together, while he didn't know. Nervousness about Ellen——she might have changed her plans——added to my haste, but also to my pleasure.

"Help me pick out new glasses?" he said as we got dressed.

"But you don't wear glasses."

"I wear contacts. Sometimes my eyes get tired, and then I wear glasses."

It felt disconcerting not to have known I'd been kissing eyes with little disks in them. I didn't want to do anything more with him, just get back to the office, have a cup of coffee from his pot, and resume work. I'd started planning the conference, and sex stimulated my brain, too. But I thought tenderly of Gordon with tired eyes, long, knobby, gray-haired Gordon wanting me to look at him in glasses, some of which wouldn't look good. It was a nice lovers' errand: nobody would suspect, if we met anybody at the optician's, a block from Gordon's office. We'd be a man taking advice from a woman he knew and worked with. So I accompanied him. In the car, I asked him, "Do you imagine going to bed with me before we do it?" For me, the imagining was particularly delectable.

"I don't imagine," Gordon said.

Coming from bed, it was hard not to walk too close, rubbing limbs. I loved helping pick out glasses, teaming up with a stylish saleswoman whose good ideas resembled mine. Together we talked Gordon into the best frames, though they cost more, and he said he hardly ever wore them except alone at home in the evening. I was pleased to hear that he spent his evenings at home, alone.

❦

What were you doing buying eyeglasses?" my mother asked me on the phone. "Do you need glasses all of a sudden?"

I've used reading glasses for a while—not as long as most people my age—but a pair from the drugstore seems to work. Sex with many partners kept my eyes young, I used to tell my friends. Sex lubricates the entire body.

"I saw you in Kennedy and Perkins," Roz continued. "I was on my way to the ATM machine. You were with someone, or I'd have stopped to say hello."

I told her who Gordon was, how I had met him, and how I'd helped him pick out frames. My mother, who also wears glasses only for reading, turned out to be an expert. She said, "You have to try on glasses different ways— wearing a hat, or pretending you're angry. You have to frown at the mirror."

"He mostly wears contact lenses."

"Oh, Daphne has contact lenses," my mother said. "You don't know somebody is wearing them."

"That's right."

"She took them out when she clipped the hedges. Something got in her eye. How's her daughter doing?"

"Fine."

"She has those kids trained. The minute they get home from school, the phone rings. She doesn't let them play outside until she gets there."

"Did she move?" I asked, remembering that Pekko had offered her an apartment.

"Oh, sure. She says she's glad to have it, even if it's not perfect."

"What does that mean?" I said.

"Pekko has so many places, he can't keep them all just so," said Roz. "When she has more money, she'll move again. She's installing those kitchen cabinets for me."

"Mm." I was in my kitchen, watching Arthur in the backyard as he sniffed and paced, stopped to pee, trotted to a corner of the yard, then trotted back.

"She's good at things. I don't know why you're suspicious of her," my mother said.

"I'm not," I said.

"Maybe you're jealous because I have a friend younger than you."

"I'm not," I said again. Then something made me remember and speak. "Mom, was your cousin a call girl?"

"Actually, she did it only once," said Roz, after a long pause. "As far as I know."

"You weren't shocked," I said. "You liked it, didn't you?"

"I used to imagine it," she said. "Stupid of me. As if it carried no risks."

❦

The next time I saw Justine—on her way into the building where we held rehearsals, while Ellen's car paused at the curb and took off—I remembered that I'd agreed to ask if she'd mind having her mother participate. She'd missed one rehearsal because of a school project, and in the intervening time warm weather had come, or children thought it had: she was in shorts. I envied Justine's perfect skin, and said so.

She shrugged.

We were the first ones there. I had no idea what to say next, then began with "Are you at all worried about your mother?" As if we were both older than Ellen, or as if Ellen might be senile.

"A little. But I think she's all right. She's got a boyfriend."

"I think she might like to be in the play—maybe to help direct," I said. "But I thought I should check with you first."

"Fine with me," Justine said. I was sure it wasn't true, but I didn't know how to encourage her to say something different, and to my surprise, I didn't want to. I'd been pretending to myself that I liked Justine better than her mother, but Justine was a child, and though I wished Ellen had her daughter's restraint, I would always be more comfortable with an adult.

At that rehearsal, Jonah said, "I don't think we should make up one more scene without deciding what the two-headed woman *means*. What's the point of her?"

Nobody answered. Then I said, "We won't know until she's grown up, Jonah. She'll tell us, when she's grown."

"But she's a made-up person."

"Jonah, you're playing characters too much like yourself," Muriel said. "Tonight you have to be the two-headed little girl. You and Cindy. You won't know what it's like until you try it."

"I still don't want to be part of somebody," Cindy said. "And I certainly don't want to be part of somebody with *him*."

Jonah was four times Cindy's size. Finally we did a scene in which she stood on a chair and Jonah sat beside her, with the dress draped like a barber's bib over their chests and shoulders.

"I hate you," said Cindy, as soon as they were joined.

"I hate me too," said Jonah. "I hate having two heads. I don't want to be the same person as this little white girl! Nobody understands what it's like to have two heads! All of you talking about tolerance. I do not tolerate it! I will not tolerate it!"

Then he started to laugh. We all laughed. He rolled up the dress and tossed it to Katya. Then he picked up Cindy and gave her a kiss. "Nothing personal," he said.

❧

Calling through the open French doors of Gordon's office one afternoon, I said, "Did you know that the first act of the New Haven government, in 1638, was trying an Indian for murder?"

"Who did he murder?"

"Another Indian."

"White men trying nonwhites for murder. Started early."

"Wanna fuck?" I called now.

"Not today, monkey face," he said. "I've got my period."

"What's that supposed to mean?"

"Monkey face?"

"Period," I said.

"I don't know. I love going to bed with you. But today I have to get some work done."

"Well, so do I," I said, wishing I hadn't spoken. Events at the conference might be: Prosecutor speaking about murder trials in New Haven. Historian talking about history of crime in New Haven. Panel discussion: cop, social worker, head of organization of former prisoners, talking about murder and race: Are murders of white people paid more attention (surely)? Are murders by white people pros-ecuted as vigorously as murders by black people? Or Hispanic or other? Indian? City planner or urban anthropologist or whatever, comparing New Haven with other cities. Who will come to this con-ference? Academics. Public defenders? A public defender should speak. Can a poor person get a fair trial for murder in New Haven? Causes of murder, psychological and sociological. Could a psychia-trist talk about death wishes and destructive impulses?

I'd been writing rapidly, getting over my chagrin at Gordon's rejection. I wanted substance, not just the mouthing of clichés about a violent society.

"Changed my mind," he said.

"Work," I said.

"An hour?" he said.

I had an appointment in an hour and a half. I'd cancel it. "Too late in the day for Ellen's house."

"Let's go to my place," said Gordon.

"How far is it?"

"Not too far, and we'll have a new activity. Riding in my car. Since you don't know the way, and I won't tell you." I'd never been in his car.

Gordon was curious and clever, but he didn't imagine. He seemed to feel close to dogs, and dogs wonder, but like Gordon they perhaps don't picture scenes at which they are not present. Gordon often watched me lie to a client when I canceled an appointment, but if someone canceled an appointment with him, he didn't won-der what the real reason might be. I suppose his lack of a fantasy life made it possible to go to bed with a married woman. He neither imagined me in bed with my husband, making himself jealous, nor imagined my husband finding out, making himself nervous. Each event was what it was until it was over, and trying to put myself in his mental position, I felt as if the world had been freshly washed.

So I felt free, with Gordon, as if I stood on a windy dock, looking over water, letting my hair blow. I knew he didn't have a notion of me that I would have to work to fulfill or contradict. He wanted to know about me—he asked a million questions—but he hadn't speculated in advance. I wonder as I write this whether that's so unusual, and how I knew right away that Gordon looked at "the plain sense of things," though I didn't understand my knowledge until he said, "I don't imagine." I recall that Pekko said something about it when I first mentioned Gordon Skeetling. He'd noticed it too—noticed it and disliked it. To me—as we drove east on I-95, for Gordon lived on the shoreline, in Madison—to me, Gordon's refusal to imagine felt roomy, like the place he took me to on that splendid May day, a middle-sized house not far from the water, with a wide screened porch. I looked in all directions, then turned and looked at Gordon watching me—waiting—one hand on his screen door, waiting without impatience until I followed him inside.

The porch was deep, made of new-smelling pine planks, profoundly shadowed. "Did you build this house? Are you the first person to live here?"

"My wife had it built, before I knew her—my second wife," he said. "She's an architect, and she did some of the work herself. I moved in with her, and when we divorced, she moved to Arizona and I bought the house from her."

"Thank you for telling me more than I asked."

"I have no secrets," Gordon said. "That's how I got my car, too. It

was hers." I liked his black Saab. He unlocked the front door as he
spoke and turned again to watch me admire his porch. As he so
often did in the office, he raised his arm and leaned against the
doorjamb, his palm braced, and as in the office, he took up all the
room. I stepped forward and placed my hands on the sides of his
hips, below his belt on his trousers. Then I moved my right hand
until it covered his fly. I felt him stir beneath my hand, but instead
of unzipping him where we stood, which would have required undo-
ing his belt buckle, I put my arms around him. I felt luckier than
ever in my life, having found a man who had no secrets. But we
were about to go to bed for the fourth of five occasions. We went into
the house, while I marveled at myself. I thought I *liked* secrets.

The house was light despite the deep porch because the first floor
was one big room, with windows all around. It was floored with
polyurethaned wooden planks, and furnished with not much. It was
cooler indoors than out, the way houses are in May in Connecticut.
We moved quickly upstairs to the bedroom, where without hurry,
and without having to be neat, we took off each other's clothes.
Some men find this funny—bra hooks and so forth—and some do it
sentimentally, as if undressing a bride. Others are matter-of-fact,
completing a task. But the best men are aroused by it, and do it
aggressively, and that's what I like, and that's what Gordon did.

"Come," he said and pulled me by the hand toward the bed,
while with his other hand he shoved the comforter, which was
white, onto the floor. I was cold and warmed myself with his body
on the bare bed. He seemed like a young man—like Denny—as he
seized me, his hands everywhere: someone who didn't plan his every
move, didn't remember what he'd done last time. For the first time,
I felt an exuberance in the man that had to do, it seemed, not with

the fun of taking a business connection to bed but with me. And as always I felt his clarity. Making love to me, he was doing nothing but making love to me. I tried to keep myself from coming, because when I did, we'd have only one more time together. As Gordon thrust and thrust again, I thought that if I didn't come, it wouldn't count. There would still be two times to go. But he'd raised me to such a pitch that I had to let the release happen, and then we lay silently, getting colder until I snagged the comforter on my foot and sat up to pull it over the two of us. I lay down luxuriously in its warmth and Gordon's, pressing myself into his body. He put his arms around me. "We're getting to be friends," he said.

There were no rugs in this house. After a while I got up to pee, finding the bathroom without directions because Gordon had fallen asleep. I tiptoed on the cold floor. Alone, I had a sudden sense of completeness, something exquisite. I'd found a man who could finish me, put his semen into me in a way that made me feel I needed nobody's semen for the rest of my life, not even his. From now on I'd make friends with women. I'd call Charlotte, whom I hadn't talked to in weeks. Maybe I wouldn't go to bed with Gordon again. Maybe I'd keep that fifth time unused, like a framed dollar bill on the wall of a restaurant. I flushed the toilet and walked out of that bathroom as if into the rest of my life, almost expecting Gordon to have vanished, his role completed, like an insect who achieves his destiny by copulating, then flies off in an iridescent flicker.

But Gordon was present, and now awake. "I thought you had a dog," I said. Suddenly I remembered the way I'd imagined his house: old, old-fashioned, crammed with books, cracked leather furniture, and dusty end tables, and festooned with dog hair; I'd pictured a big, shaggy dog greeting me solemnly, swinging his tail. This place was clean.

"She died. I told you."

"You didn't want another dog?"

"I wanted that dog."

I reached for my underwear; then, chilled again from getting up, I relaxed into the empty space next to Gordon and pulled the comforter, once more, around my shoulders. "That's how my brother lives," I said.

"Carl or Stephen?"

The man's memory was uncanny. "Stephen. He lives with empty spaces that stand for what used to be."

"I don't. I simply had a dog who died. When my mother died, I didn't replace her either."

"All right," I said, wondering if what I'd said was untrue of Stephen as well. He lives in a small brick house in Queens, with the usual quantity of furniture. Only one child, away at SUNY New Paltz now, but he didn't, as far as I knew, leave her place at the dinner table sentimentally clear in her absence. He and his wife had taken to letting their mail accumulate there, Stephen had said, and had to sort it when my niece came home on vacation. But what I'd said about Stephen was true, I continued to feel. I pulled the comforter more closely around me, and then Gordon stood and began to dress, and I felt a twinge of desolation, though I knew he wouldn't depart, leaving me alone in his house. "Get up," he said. "Let's go back to the office."

I sat up, still swathed in the big, puffy comforter. "Well, in Stephen's case, it's not a dog or a person who's gone, it's a way of thinking about himself. His life is like an exhibit in a museum—it preserves an idea about himself he doesn't have any longer."

"When did he lose it? You said he *works* in a museum."

"Yes. He lost it at seventeen."

And now I come to a difficult point, because I said early on there was no need to describe Stephen's trouble—or talk about Denny—in this narrative. I don't want to write about Stephen, and I don't want to write any more about Denny, and I've been avoiding this manuscript for days—I stopped at "seventeen," doing anything else I could think of, because I didn't want to write about either of them. I didn't talk to Gordon about Denny then, but I did later. Now, it's either write about Denny and Stephen or play computer solitaire, and I'm exhausted with playing solitaire.

For some reason, I seem to need to begin—now that I'm doing it—with a time Denny and I threw sticks in the river. Denny would get excited about something he did as a child. He was a juvenile delinquent and a druggie, but he'd had a normal, middle-class childhood, his respectable mother (or, more likely, that grandmother I mentioned) had read him *Winnie-the-Pooh*, and he liked to go to one of the bridges in East Rock Park, even when I knew him, and play pooh sticks, which if you recall is the game in which you throw sticks from a bridge into the river, upstream, rush to the downstream side, and see which stick emerges first from under the bridge. We'd do this late at night: I'd say, "I'm starving, let's get something to eat," and he'd say, "No, let's go to the river." You couldn't always see the sticks at all, but the river—the Mill River, the same one where I walk Arthur these days—was mysterious and enticing (and I'd have visions of my young lover found drowned at the edge of it). One night we'd thrown sticks, and gone and leaned over the parapet, but we began to talk and forgot to watch for the sticks. Denny told me how his younger brother had come to him recently, crying, saying, "Man, you have to stop making Mom cry."

"What did you say?" I said.

"What does anybody say to a younger brother? Or a younger sister? What did your brother say to you when you asked that?"

"How do you know I asked that? I don't think I did," I said.

"Sure you did. Your brother got in trouble, didn't he?"

"Well, yes, but I don't recall telling you about that."

"You once said I reminded you of him. That's the only reason I remind people of anybody."

"It wasn't that, it was your sense of humor."

"I don't have a sense of humor," said Denny, "I have a sense of sadness."

"You make me laugh, though."

"That's what I said to my brother. I make people laugh, not cry. But he said, 'No, no, you make Mom cry.' See, maybe I won't do that forever, but then I wouldn't be around anymore."

"You mean you'd go away?"

"Go away, die. Same difference, from your point of view."

"You don't seem like a potential suicide, Denny. Is that a signal for me to worry?"

"I don't mean suicide. I'd never commit suicide. It's not my style."

It was winter, and I got cold, or impatient, or came back to my senses and remembered I had to work in the morning, so the evening ended. Something like that. But I did not think about this meeting with Denny on the day of the white comforter, and I don't know why I wanted to write it down now, except for the obvious connection anybody could make, when I say what I told Gordon next, which is "When my brother was seventeen, he was questioned by the police after his girlfriend died."

"Did they think he killed her?"

"In fact, apparently not," I said, surprised that I was about to tell Gordon a story I hardly ever told anyone, and hadn't told Denny, who found out most of what he wanted to know. I was fourteen and Stephen was seventeen. Carl wasn't home, but Stephen and I were being shown off to some cousins from the Netherlands, people my parents scarcely knew, who'd settled there after the war and had come to America on a visit. I was lusting after the son of this family—a boy with a bright, friendly laugh, a look unlike the guarded looks of boys I knew—when the police arrived. We three had gradually moved away from the adults, who were lingering over coffee, and we were listening to records in Stephen's room. The boy didn't have enough English to follow Tom Lehrer's satirical songs, but he liked Judy Collins. We heard the doorbell, and when the record ended, we listened—some romantic, violent ballad still in our heads—as my father talked with the policeman, then led him past the visitors to the room where we were.

Stephen's girlfriend had died a month earlier. It was a shock, but not as shocking as it might have been, because she'd been a troubled girl. My parents had been terrified of her, and that Sunday I was still angry because they refused to regard her death as a full-scale tragedy: according to them her life was doomed, one way or another. I screamed at them about that. She wasn't doomed, I insisted, though her death seemed to contradict that notion. She'd slit her wrists, yes, but that didn't have to be—if she'd had a good psychiatrist she might have led a long, reasonably happy life. Now I know I was right, but at the time, as children do, I secretly thought my parents probably knew better. I thought I was making these arguments, night after night (while Stephen stayed quietly in his room) out of stubbornness. I felt guilty for shouting at my parents.

That afternoon, as a policeman entered Stephen's bedroom, my brother stood up. The visiting boy was sitting on the bed, and I was on the floor, working up my courage to rise casually and sit next to the boy. Now I went through a swift progression of thought: My brother had killed his girlfriend! I was angry at my brother for killing his girlfriend and therefore impeding my lust toward the Dutch cousin. Then I was afraid.

Stephen was questioned in the policeman's car and returned to the house. "It was nothing," he said. The next day the policeman returned, questioned Stephen some more, and left again. My fear didn't dissipate for weeks. Months later, Stephen told me he'd been asked if he knew in advance what the girl planned to do. He'd said no. The policeman had been gentle but persistent. By then it seemed absurd to have thought my brother was a murderer.

For years, I blamed myself for my disloyalty and suspicion. The long piece I wrote was originally about Stephen and also about me: about my slow discovery that it's possible to think mixed-up thoughts and go on, essentially—and therefore about how I finally came to feel that my lusting after the cousin was not proof that my brother was a murderer, that I hadn't retroactively turned Stephen into a murderer by lusting after the cousin. The early drafts contained much information about my youthful sexual life that I gradually omitted. Eventually the article, or a fragment of it, was published. It concentrated on the ordeal that began for Stephen when he made friends with this troubled girl, and went on to make an argument I'd come to understand in the course of revising it. I argued for the importance of wrong guesses. I argued that my mistake was permissible, even though it was to think my brother was a terrible criminal: I argued, that is, for the innocence of imagination. When the piece was published, Stephen told me it was good, told me he was glad I'd written it—he'd read twenty drafts along the way—and quietly said he hoped I never wrote about him again. I said of course I wouldn't.

Half a lifetime later, I think I'm doing something similar. Maybe eventually I will omit, again, the secrets I'd rather keep from this record—and omit Stephen—and publish what is left as an essay in which, once more, my life is merely illustrative. The point might be how, in a city these days, what we consider outside the line we draw around ourselves—the boundary beyond which we do not go—may turn out to be inside, how the boundary may need to be redrawn, and again redrawn.

We got dressed and drove back to town. Even telling Gordon about Stephen, the Dutch cousin, the dead girl, and the resulting piece of writing did not take all afternoon, yet I worked late that evening, completing what I'd hoped to complete, and didn't cook the meal I'd promised Pekko when I left that morning. I hadn't cooked for a while. It occurred to me, as I finally drove home, that if he were a roommate instead of a husband, my account of my afternoon could be my apology. Don't scold, I'll tell you a story.

☙

Call your mother," Pekko said when I arrived. He was cutting up onions, celery, and mushrooms for spaghetti sauce.

"Oh, did she call?"

"I called her."

"Did you think I might be there?"

"It had nothing to do with you," Pekko said. "I wanted to find out if Daphne actually knows anything about carpentry."

"Roz claims she's installing those kitchen cabinets," I said. I began setting the table.

"Daphne said so. Roz says they've looked at everything in Home Depot and now Daphne is emptying the old cabinets and carrying the canned goods to the basement. I can't tell from that if she knows what's she's doing."

"Why did you call?"

"She wants to work off the rent, and I need someone. The guys I used in the other building are impossible."

"Daphne hasn't got the rent money?"

"Or she wants it for something else."

"For what?"

"Not my business," said Pekko. He opened a can of tomatoes. Pekko chops vegetables well, with a cleaver, cooking deliberately, as if listening to instructions in his mind, choosing the correct tool. His back was to me as he stood at the counter, and I appreciated his vulnerable firmness even while I was still appreciating another, different man. No matter; it felt tiresome to limit myself to one man, an odd requirement, no more sensible than a rule that would have me manage with a single woman friend. With his face hidden and mine not visible to him, I asked experimentally, with a mischief maker's need to shift a pile of objects, just to see which one broke, "When was Daphne your lover?"

Pekko hardly ever answers questions directly, but this time he said, "When she was pregnant."

"With Cindy?"

"Is that the ten-year-old?"

"Nine, I think."

"Nine."

Somebody had to be careful, so I asked nothing more, but he continued to talk, without turning. "The last time I saw her she was too pregnant for sex. She pulled up her shirt, and from across the room, I could see bulges move up and down her belly."

I'd known Pekko for ten years—with gaps. I didn't know exactly how old Cindy was. It didn't matter, yet I wondered where I was while Pekko looked at Daphne's belly, whether we were dating then.

"The baby was kicking," I said.

"No, I think it was a knee moving. The baby pulled her knees to her chest and then straightened them."

"The fetal position."

"I suppose. I remember the bulges moving. I never felt so sad."

"Was she your baby?" I thought of putting my arm around him as he stirred the sauce, but it seemed like a sentimental idea.

"No. Daphne was married, and we started when she was pregnant. I was glad it wasn't my baby. I didn't want to marry her. I didn't want to know her after she had the baby, because I knew she'd leave her husband sooner or later, and I didn't want all that. I'd probably fall in love with the kid."

"She's a cute kid."

"I guess she's all right, even without a father." He swept mushroom slices off the cutting board into the pot. "Set the table," he said.

"I already did."

He glanced over his shoulder. "Right. Sorry."

"So did you tell Daphne she can do the carpentry?" I said.

"I did. Against my better judgment. Before I called your mother. I called her to reassure myself, but of course I didn't learn anything." Daphne had appeared in his office to negotiate, taking notes so as to write up a contract. Her main concern was apparently that Pekko would exploit her, and she had negotiated an hourly rate, insisting on weekly paychecks once she'd earned the rent.

"She's not donating one flick of a paintbrush," Pekko said as we ate.

"No nostalgia for lost love?" I said lightly.

"I'm not sure it was ever lost love." It was all right, I explained to myself. My afternoon was less bad if Pekko had leftover feelings for Daphne, and the feelings made him more interesting to me. We were almost done eating before I heard all of what he was thinking—or another part of what he was thinking. "If I asked you to cut her daughter out of the play, would that be possible?"

"Of course not. Is that what you want me to do?"

"Not so far."

"But ever? Pekko, you're not like that. Even if you did feel terrible when you saw Cindy's knee move before she was born."

"It might have been her butt. Maybe she had her back to Daphne's front, and when she flexed her legs, her butt moved."

"Or her butt." He got up and gave Arthur, who'd been attentive, his plate to lick.

"Even if her mother cheats you," I persisted. "What difference does it make if Cindy's in the play?"

"I might need a threat."

"If Daphne doesn't work hard enough?"

"No. If she doesn't work hard enough, I'll be out the rent. That's happened before. But she's complaining about the building. I don't need stuff in the paper."

"Throw her out."

"Civil liberties. That's the one thing you can't do."

"You can blackmail her by breaking her kid's heart but you can't refuse to renew her lease?" I said, wondering if Cindy cared about the play.

"Violates her civil liberties."

But now Pekko had done talking, and as I gathered the plates to wash them—the cook shouldn't have to clean up—he wandered out of the room. When I was done, I took Arthur for a late walk so as to think about my lover—the light on the planks, which were the color of corn oil, the off-white walls and white comforter and nothing much in the room to distract me from the sensation of my vagina pulsing and rippling around him.

❦

I planted my garden toward the end of May, feeling a sudden wish for flashy annuals and something I could eat. I don't like impatiens or pansies, but I put in a lot of zinnias and tomatoes, and then watered only now and then and weeded hardly at all. June was warm but not too hot, cooler than those hot days in April, and when I was home I was often in the backyard, in sandals, throwing Arthur's ball. Sometimes I tried teaching him something, but I soon gave up and spent time reading and thinking about Gordon. Charlotte came over late one afternoon, and being together in the sunshine felt so good, for me at least, that we didn't talk for long minutes, leaning back on canvas chairs in my backyard, looking up at layered maple leaves, and drinking white wine. Then we began, sleepily, listing the epochs of our long friendship, just referring to times we were at ease and times we were not, mentioning them and not needing detail. "The time I didn't tell you about——" she said.

"Yes. And the time you told Philip——"

"About your mother?"

"Oh, that too. I was thinking about something else," I said.

"Oh. Yes. The time at the beach."

"Yes, the time at the beach." Which was the time I found out that Denny was dead. I was staying at the old beach house where Pekko was living, and Charlotte and Philip and maybe her girls—yes, her girls—had come over for supper, but Pekko was late, and it got later and later: a summer evening that began hot and became cool. Olivia ran around in her wet bathing suit to keep warm while we waited for Pekko before eating, then ate without him. When he arrived, it was with the news that Denny was dead. He'd broken into Pekko's frozen yogurt store and died of an overdose. Now Charlotte and I stopped hinting and told each other that story, over and over, it seemed: how I'd slept with Denny, though I was in my forties and supposedly sane, while he was twenty-three and apparently crazy, how I'd stopped, how he'd died.

"You know, he had been *living* in Pekko's store," she then said, after a long pause. "He didn't break in just that one time."

"He was living there?"

"He was homeless. He broke in every night. Lots of street people do that someplace."

"How do you know?"

"Somebody reliable told me the story, not long after."

"Another street person?"

"A case manager."

"Did Pekko know?"

"How could he not? Daisy, how could he not?"

"You've been quiet about this for ten years?" I said.

"Eight, nine maybe. I didn't hear it right away."

"Why didn't you tell me? Why didn't you get angry with Pekko for keeping quiet?"

"Oh, Daisy, Pekko's just like that. He does what he does."

That's why I keep thinking about Denny, as well as about the events of last spring and summer. He was part of them, too. He gets younger in my mind, a sort of imp, laughing at us all. He did laugh at us all. He was thin, with a tough look about him that didn't seem real to me, as if he was playing bad guy, and nothing really bad could happen.

That afternoon in the backyard, I didn't tell Charlotte about Gordon, but I told her all about the play. She was enthralled. It was just her sort of thing—talky, good-natured, naïve.

❦

Rehearsals, speaking of the play, had become three quarters discussion. Katya said that didn't matter, it was our process at that time. She was a great one for following us as we sniffed each bush, and sometimes I tried to follow Arthur on a walk the way Katya followed us. I always lost patience, but Katya, like a big, soft shadow, never did. She'd signed us up for a performance: we were to perform our play in October as part of a community arts festival at the Little Theater, a small theater that used to be an art-movie house and got rescued, renovated, and set up for plays when the movies stopped. In the old days, before the renovation, I remember watching bats flying in the light from the screen. I remember Denny and me together there, but that might be wrong.

Cindy had a sharp directness that made everyone wish she had a bigger part, and someone suggested that, once the two-headed girl grew up, she could have a little sister. That idea led us into a somewhat idiotic discussion about whether these parents would take a chance on another baby. I was against it and found myself ridiculously involved, arguing against Jonah, who thought they should accept the will of the Lord. Maybe I wanted Cindy's part to stay small.

"You're not thinking about whether these *particular people* would accept the will of the Lord," I said.

Ellen had come into the room and was watching at one side, and then Daphne came in as well, to pick up Cindy. Daphne emitted an atmosphere of disdain. Of course she wanted there to be another child, so her daughter could have a bigger part. Finally she called, "Oh, give them a break. Give that couple something good."

We agreed that the play had enough sorrow in it, and Cindy was confirmed as the future sister of the two-headed girl.

❦

Reading about murder, I was more interested in the killer than in the killed. When I wasn't thinking about bedding with Gordon, I'd think about the sensation of killing, the sensation of getting away with it. Many murders I read about were unsolved, or solved only provisionally. It felt strange to begin my research about murder in New Haven—or small cities, we'd broadened the topic that much—already knowing that Pekko had told me about the murder of Marie Valenti, knowing that, if Pekko had told the truth, someone was living his life as if it hadn't happened.

Not all the murders I read about were unsolved. Sometimes crowds saw a killing. I found an amateur book in the local history room of the Main Library about the killing of cops—a typed tribute, all in capital letters, to policemen who died on duty between 1855 and 1970. When cop is killed, another cop is usually around to tell about it, and sometimes there's a crowd of bystanders interested in whatever the cop was investigating. Sometimes it seemed that everybody had lied.

New Haven is composed of Yale and Not Yale, and Not Yale is composed of African Americans, Puerto Ricans, Italians, Jews, WASPs, Poles, Irish, and so on. (I suppose Yale is too, these days.) Reading about dead policemen was like watching outsiders arrive, one group followed by the next. The first cop murdered on duty, in 1855, had been born in England. Before a raffle intended to raise money for a poor widower, neighbors held an impromptu dance. According to the *New Haven Register*, a young girl who went to the dance was tracked down by her mother, who began beating her with a stick. The neighbors grew agitated, and when an officer tried to arrest a drunken man, they beat the policeman to death. The paper reported that everyone in the crowd was Irish.

The next police officer to be murdered, some years later, was Irish. Again the book quoted the *Register*: "In consequence of the inequities practiced in the Fair Street, Italian quarter of the city, Policeman Hugh McKeon, a stalwart member of the New Haven Police . . . [was] the victim of the bullets of a dwarfed specimen of the Italian race." Andrea Laudano, who'd been running "a house of ill repute," shot the policeman three times when the cop broke the door down to stage a raid.

By 1915 the witnesses to the murder of another police officer had Jewish names, and an officer was killed in 1935 by a burglar with a Polish name. Poles seemed to figure in the next murder as well; one of them, known as the Eel, escaped from prison. Near the end of the book, though it doesn't say so, the perpetrators are probably black—to judge from the names and addresses—while the police officers are Italian. And the last murder described, of an undercover agent who posed as a bookmaker, seemed pretty clearly to be the killing of a black police officer.

I was asking around for the names of urban sociologists, looking for someone who'd talk about New Haven's ethnic history and how it connected to murder. I was also looking for a psychiatrist. I wanted to know about New Haven's murders, but I also wanted to know about murder: how it feels to do it, why people do it, and how they sometimes get away with it. I didn't like thinking about Marie Valenti because I didn't know what to do with my knowledge, and couldn't talk to Gordon about it, and I didn't like thinking about Pekko's disapproval. I hadn't told him about the conference. I wasn't afraid to have an argument with him, but I was afraid to think he might be right, that if anybody ever heard of my conference, it would be one more reason people I met outside New Haven might ask why on earth I lived there.

Uncomfortable learning about Marie Valenti, I went searching for information about the murder of Penney Serra, another young woman killed in the seventies. One day I went to the public library to read about the murder itself. I thought the newspaper article at the time of her death would have huge headlines, but sitting in the library basement, trying to work a balky microfilm viewer, I took a while to find the story. I struggled with flapping plastic tape and reels that spun too slowly or too fast, then first came upon not the news story but the death notice. "Suddenly in this city July 16, 1973 . . ." Shaken, I continued looking. Another rattle of the machinery and I found the story, not a big headline—all the big headlines that month were about Nixon—but a story in the lower left-hand corner of the first page, POLICE SEEK MOTIVE IN GARAGE SLAYING. Penney Serra, age twenty-one, had gone downtown looking for a job. She was found dead in a stairwell on the top level of the garage, which was fairly new then—one of those gray concrete, cavernous things; I remember wondering, when I first drove into it, if it could hold up so many cars. She had no reason to be at the top level. Her shoes were in the front seat of her car, and her purse was in the backseat. She'd been stabbed once in the chest, and also in the right hand: that brave child had been fighting back, and reading about that wound, I saw the girl—her useless, reflexive grab at the hand with the knife.

❧

Ellen, in a white T-shirt with a low neckline, walked with her usual hesitation into the bedroom, where I was sitting on the floor amid piles of clothing. She'd left me to talk on the phone; lately, that happened. For the first time, as she paused, watching me, her tentativeness pleased me. Ellen and I now worked together more easily. She still believed that objects own their present locations, or that people who had long forgotten them have a claim that they be well-treated. She argued, but now she was occasionally willing to lose. I guess she'd decided that I too had some respect for the ancient lease-holds of things. We stacked stuff in piles, room after room. Her house was turning into the worst sort of clutter museum, the organized sort.

She lowered herself to a squat beside me, lightly touching my shoulder—a support—on the way down. In her absence I'd contin-ued folding and piling. We were in a back bedroom used for storage of the children's old clothes and of papers and notebooks Ellen had been accumulating all her life. She had so many bedrooms, she could do this sort of thing.

Then she said, "Daisy, are you by any chance having an affair?"

"No," I said, too quickly. "Why?"

"Nothing. Well, the man I'm seeing—you know, he's another castaway. My brother made me see him. He knows my brother."

"Your brother left him here, and you're too nice to throw him away?" I said, hoping to confirm this change of subject.

"He's married."

"Your brother made you go out with a married man?"

We were making no pretense at working. "He's here for a few months, installing computer software for a bank. I was supposed to help him figure out New Haven. We met for lunch, and I brought him here and fucked him."

"That doesn't seem like the sort of thing you'd do," I said.

"I never did before. I'm working on not falling in love with him. It's such a reversal for me—I get handed things nobody wants, and I keep them. Now I'm trying not to want this guy, and of course his wife does want him. She'll take him back."

"Maybe not." I stood up and stretched, then flexed my feet to get the kinks out. "These patterns hold," I said. "You're the drop-off center. I don't think there's anything you can do about it."

"What I want to know," Ellen said from the floor, "is—my God, Daisy, you're using my house for something. If it's an affair, you could help me. I'll continue to pay you for your time, if that's what you want."

There was a chair in the room, and I stopped doing half-remembered ballet steps and sat down. "Paid friendship?" I said, taking things one at a time, carefully.

"Whatever you want."

"Do you think I'm like that?"

"Someone who'd have an affair?"

"No," I said, thinking of my radio series, "someone who takes money to listen."

"A therapist?" said Ellen.

"Never mind. I'm not a therapist, and I'm not having an affair."

"One of my neighbors saw you bring a man here."

"Oh," I said. "Gordon Skeetling. I'm organizing his papers." I told her quickly who he was and how I'd come to work with him. "It's where I saw the headline about the two-headed woman," I finished. Then I added, "Gordon and I were on our way to the library. I wanted to—" I hesitated, trying to think of something I'd legitimately want to do in her house, in her absence, that would justify bringing Gordon in. "He loves old houses. I shouldn't have done it. I just gave him a bit of a tour. I'm sorry."

"Oh, that's all right," Ellen said. "Did he like it? What did he think of the mess?"

"He liked the way the dining room windows look out at the backyard," I said.

"So you're not in love with him?"

"I'm not in love with him." It wasn't a lie. I felt wonderful as I said the words, not because I was misleading Ellen, which did make me uncomfortable, but because as I spoke I felt totally at ease about Gordon. I loved being with him, I loved going to bed with him—and we were going to do that only once more—but I didn't love him, I wasn't going to love him, and therefore I was free and in charge. What I like is power. Who doesn't? But if it was that good—if I was that free—I didn't need to stop at five sexual encounters, did I? I was too wary of myself to abandon discretion entirely, but as Ellen chattered I decided I could add another five, which meant I had six more altogether. What good news.

Then my discomfort about what Ellen had said made me want to appease her, so I told her about the murder conference, and how Pekko would object if he knew. At some point we calculated how much time had elapsed since we'd stopped working, and I said I'd stop charging her then. When I was finished talking, Ellen said she had something to show me, and it was several shoe boxes of clippings and flyers from 1970, from the time of the New Haven trial of Bobby Seale and Ericka Huggins. New Haven's most famous murder, the execution of Black Panther Alex Rackley, took place in 1969, before I came to town. Two local men did time for that murder, but Bobby Seale and Ericka Huggins—nationally known revolutionaries—were acquitted of masterminding it. One of those convicted, imprisonment decades behind him, was now a respected counselor to former prisoners, running a New Haven program. He was on the list of speakers I planned to invite to the conference. ("Your murderer," Gordon said. "Of course you need one actual murderer.")

"I can't tell Pekko," I said, as Ellen and I looked through the boxes. "Where did you get this?"

"I was very interested, at the time. You can borrow it. But I'd tell him, if I were you, Daisy. I couldn't think clearly about something as big as a conference unless I talked about it at home. And eventually he'll know all about it. It's open to the public, right?"

At the time of the Bobby Seale trial, Ellen had demonstrated on the green, a young girl taking days off from college (Smith, an hour and a half away) to come home and participate in riots. She'd stayed at this house—her parents' house—while they argued with her. Ellen couldn't stop telling me the story, which was more about her parents than about the Black Panthers. But that was all right.

I left her house, eventually, feeling that restless emotion that makes you know there's undone business. It's like sitting opposite a drawer that's slightly open, with a bra strap hanging out of it. You have to get up, stuff it in, and close the drawer—but for me, the appeal is in *not* getting up. I don't get up for a long, long time. I like the slightly sick feeling of uneasy anticipation. I like to keep bad things from happening, while preserving the feeling. Now Pekko mustn't know about the conference or Gordon, and Ellen mustn't know what I did in her house. Yet I knew I'd keep on risking conversations with both of them, nearly telling, wondering if they'd guessed.

I took Ellen's boxes, with thanks, and drove straight to Gordon's office, so I could leave them there. Gordon was on the phone. "What was the name of that kid—the girl who got killed? The famous murder?" he called as I passed, apparently not surprised to see me, his hand over the mouthpiece of the phone.

"Suzanne Jovin."

"No, a long time ago."

"Penney Serra," I said.

"No, the other one. The high school kid. On the green."

"Marie Valenti."

"What year?"

"1976."

"Unsolved, right?"

"Right." I went into the archive and waited until he got off the phone, though I could have put my boxes on a table and walked right past and out again. "Marie Valenti," I heard him say. There followed half sentences and mumbles, while I looked out the window at nothing, irritated that he was taking so long but not knowing why it mattered.

When he hung up he said, "I did something good. That was the state forensics expert. I told him we'd do a whole morning on Marie Valenti, and he agreed to come. Maybe we'll solve it. We can put together everything anybody ever knew or said."

"Did he work on it?"

"No, the original guy is dead. But he's aware of it, and he's willing to spend some time on it."

"Let's not," I said. "I thought this was *my* conference."

"Of course we will!" Gordon said. "Why not? It's a great idea. Tell me if I'm wrong. He'd be a terrific speaker. I worked hard to get him interested."

"I think not," I said.

"Of course we will," said Gordon.

I have a red, two-piece bathing suit, and I began carrying it in my purse, stuffed into a plastic bag, after Gordon and I swam off the shore near his house one day in late June. The water was cold. On some days, though I spent time in Gordon's office, I didn't have a use for the suit. Other afternoons, we might look at each other and start figuring out how long to work before leaving. Under the water, he'd work my bathing suit bottom down and, his trunks lowered, stroke me with his penis. Or I'd straddle and squeeze his bent knee. The cold water kept him from having enough of an erection to enter me then, but later we'd fuck vigorously in the still sunniness of his bedroom. I stopped counting our meetings, stopped planning to end the affair on schedule. It would be humiliating to form a resolve and abandon it; letting the future take care of itself seemed alert and mature. I was no longer some fool who thought occasions in bed should be numbered.

Swimming isn't easy to keep secret. At night my bathing suit would be a sodden lump in its plastic bag. I didn't consider leaving it at Gordon's. Why not, I ask myself now, as I write. Did I fear that another woman would see it drying helplessly over the towel rod? Did I think that he'd blackmail me with it, or that I'd end the affair between visits and lose my swimsuit? If you'd asked me, I'd have said I wanted it in case I chose to swim when I wasn't with Gordon, although a woman can buy a second bathing suit. I didn't want to leave it in his power.

I'd be too cheerful after swimming, cooled and refreshed within, with the tang of salt on my tongue or in my nose despite a shower. Pekko isn't a curious man, but he's sensitive, and something in my freshness would appeal to him. He'd often approach me himself the night after I'd been with Gordon. So I'd learn again why I needed both: my husband with his reliable, almost workmanlike attitude toward sex, and my lover, who fucked exuberantly and originally, talking all the time (often not about me or what we were doing), and who seemed eager not so much to please as to interest me.

"Here's this breast," Gordon might say. "What shall I do with this breast? Hmm?" He'd listen to know if I was in suspense.

We didn't go to Ellen's house now, though I sensed that she was encouraging me to use it, to leave my affair there as others left their detritus, and I understood that her role in collecting other people's leavings was not entirely passive. We didn't go to Ellen's, and of course it was better at Gordon's. We'd drive in separate cars because Gordon was generally done with work for the day. Even if he planned to return, I still took my Jetta. I'd learned the route quickly. Driving there was delicious: taking myself to my lover. And driving home was delicious, too. I liked to depart just a moment or two before he might think I would, sometimes while he was in the shower, or dressing. I'd make him kiss me good-bye shoeless, one sock on a foot, the other in his hand.

⟡

One night Pekko and I had a late supper of take-out Buffalo chicken wings and celery spears from Archie Moore's, a few blocks from our house. As we ate, a long-awaited thunderstorm began. Leaving our food on the table, we sat watching the rain and lightning from the top step of our tiny front porch, while Arthur stood behind us, nuzzling our backs and licking our ears. When the rain touched us, we moved inside, and I cleared the table in a desultory way.

"So are you still working with Skeetling?" Pekko said, emptying bones into the garbage. "I saw him at Clark's Pizza."

"Did you talk?"

"Just waved."

"I'm still working with him."

"Just clearing his trash out? You're not doing a presentation about murder, are you?"

"Well, I am," I said. I put our plates into the dishwasher, then sat down, pressing my feet into the floor. The thunder had diminished, and I could hear that the rain had increased. Nothing tentative about that rain.

Pekko stood in the doorway. "You said you'd keep me informed."

"I couldn't think if I kept you informed," I said. "Once you start giving your opinion, it's like a casual chat about sex with the Pope." But it was a mistake to mention sex when Gordon's name had just been spoken. "Or a conversation with a vegetarian about how to cook steak," I said.

"Is it radio?"

"A conference. At Yale. Not until October. Nobody will know about it except a bunch of desiccated academics."

"Not likely. What's the topic, New Haven: Murder Capital of America?"

"No. It's about murder in small cities. New Haven is only one example."

"Which makes a difference?"

"Pekko," I said, "*what do you want?* Even the chamber of commerce doesn't advocate censorship."

"I'm not in favor of censorship, I'm against sensationalism," he said. "This is scholarly sensationalism."

I was angry. "You give me no credit for sense, no credit for decency, no credit for intelligence" was one of my comments. He sat down on the old, faded sofa and fell silent. I washed angry words over him with the speed and intensity of the rain, describing, for example, a panel discussion we planned on perceptions of murder in New Haven—the difference between what happened and what people assumed happened. We'd be counteracting sensationalism, I said.

After a while, feeling safer if I mentioned Gordon impersonally, I began to complain about him. I had plenty of disagreements with him by now. I wanted to include in the conference a discussion of killings by police, including the shooting of Malik Jones, the young black man who'd been killed by an East Haven cop after a chase into New Haven. Gordon said I was losing my focus. Many people considered that killing unjustified, but it was not usually described as murder.

"It's a different topic," Gordon had said that morning with barely suppressed sarcasm, so his words came out as condescending baby talk. "It's a *different... topic.*" As I summarized the incident to Pekko, I realized I'd been accused of stupidity by each man. Pekko had become silent, sitting with his arms crossed, looking thicker in the midsection than he ordinarily does, leaning back. Sometimes when he does that it's kindness at work, an offer to take on your troubles, but at other times he's a police detective, unobtrusively running the tape recorder while you convict yourself. At last I stopped. The rain had lessened, but new weather hadn't come in. The air felt lighter but moist and warm.

Pekko didn't speak and didn't move, and then he did move, and made a sound—the sound a child makes, breathing in so as to get enough breath to sob, the undercry before the crying. But Pekko didn't cry. He walked into the other room, and I stood and followed him. Now I stood while he sat down heavily in a lounge chair I'd bought him for his birthday the first year we lived together. He said, "Daphne's claiming there's trash in the backyard of her building."

I was glad to change the subject. "Is there?"

"Sure. I'm paying someone to take care of the place, but you only get so much."

"I guess she wants her kids to play outside."

"She says she wants to put in a garden."

"She has a lot of energy."

"Energy to leave phone messages."

But he wasn't changing the subject. "When you start looking at things the way Skeetling does," he said, "and I don't mean just because he's a professor—when you start doing that but you can't see the whole picture, you get it wrong."

"Daphne gets things wrong?"

"I have to allocate the resources I have. How does she think I charge cheap rents?"

"Daphne's not like Gordon Skeetling."

"A partial view," he said, sitting up and clamping his hands on his knees. "She's not like him. She just doesn't know, and she's not too bright. He's very bright."

"He's very intelligent. Why are you assuming this conference is Gordon's idea? Really, Pekko, it's mine. Fight with me if you want."

"It sounds like him. It's a way of looking at things as if they weren't attached to one another. If it's your idea, you had it in his office."

I said, "So he's a manipulator and you're not? You think you're aboveboard and he's sneaky? What about Denny Ring?"

"Denny Ring?" said Pekko. Denny had introduced me to Pekko in the first place, one summer night when Denny and I were walking and we stuck our heads into Pekko's frozen yogurt store. Pekko and I began dating, if that's what to call it, and he was enraged when he found out that I'd slept with Denny, that Denny wasn't just a young friend I counseled and helped. "Aren't you the one who did a little manipulating in that department?" he said now.

"I mean his death, Pekko," I said quietly. I hadn't mentioned what Charlotte had told me a few weeks ago. I'd been saving it. Now it would let me put together this conference in peace. Maybe. "When he died, you told me he broke into the store."

"And he did."

"You didn't tell me he was in the habit of breaking in. That he broke in every night. That he lived there."

"How did you know that?" said Pekko, rising, troubled; his face changed. How can I put it? His beard was suddenly sticking out at a different angle or something. "How did you know that?"

He had kept it a secret, and I knew he'd mind that I knew. He likes his secrets. "You're not the only one in this city who hears things and knows things," I said. "And I wish you'd leave me alone to act on what I know. To try and make sense of what I know."

He left the room. He barely spoke to me for days, but then he said nothing more about the conference.

⚘

I wrote the above and then walked around the house for an hour, picking things up and putting them down, trying to remember exactly what I knew about Denny in the months before his death, years before that conversation with Pekko. Why didn't I know then that he was living in the store? If I had known, would I have considered it a problem to be solved, or just one more charming fact about that youngster, that dangerous child? I loved him for his unpredictability, his strangeness, his madness. He needed social workers and agencies, and I provided sex, talk, and an appreciation of his imagination, in his last months. Once, he rang the doorbell of my apartment at six in the morning. Pekko and I were seeing each other a few times a week then, but not living together. I'd sworn to Pekko I had nothing to do with Denny, and often I didn't. I never knew when I'd see him. That time, I was furious at being awakened, then interested in being lured out so early. He didn't want sex that day, just a walk in the dawn and breakfast out—which I could pay for—as soon as someplace opened. I don't remember asking where he'd spent the night. If I had, he'd have lied. But if he hadn't lied—

if he'd told me he spent it in the back of Pekko's store—I might have thought sleeping there regularly was a good plan for this mercurial person. Maybe it *was* a good plan. If Denny had lived, settled down, and become, say, a drug counselor—or settled down still further and finished college—we'd consider the period when he lived in Pekko's store a helpful transition. Pekko would be a benefactor because he let it happen, pretending he didn't know. Which is surely what he thought at the time. The day Denny woke me at six, he wanted to look at birds: it must have been spring, when itinerant songbirds pass through East Rock Park. "I didn't know you were a bird-watcher," I said.

"Birder," said Denny. "Let's find the black-crowned night heron."

"Where is it on its way to?"

"Oh, it lives here." But we couldn't find it that morning, and Denny got hungry before long.

⚘

For TheaDora's grown-up dress, Muriel and I went to Horowitz Brothers, where we first examined tall rolls of African cottons, tables of velvet and corduroy remnants, patterned upholstery fabrics rolled on long cardboard tubes. "I have to see what's new," Muriel said, moving with her usual abruptness from table to table, then stopping to grasp silk in her hands—briskly, as if she considered steel. Now that it was summer, Muriel's purple jacket was gone and she wore a purple tunic with her jeans. Her hair still stuck out in all directions. She had told me she worked as a crossing guard when her children were young, and that notion was so right I wondered if I'd ever driven past her corner. I could almost say I remembered a somewhat younger Muriel making the cars stop in every direction, holding them with her taut stance, her swiftly raised hands, while children scurried. Muriel and I bought eleven yards of a dark blue muted cotton print, and two yards of white piqué for trim. I had favored red and yellow, but Muriel talked me out of it. The dress would have long, roomy sleeves with French cuffs. Elastic at her wrists, Muriel said, would make TheaDora look like a rag doll or a child.

I thought French cuffs would be too hard, but Muriel scoffed. "Interfacing to give them shape," she said. She leaned on a counter near men's suitings, where it was quiet, and drew diagrams. Both of us avoided telling the salespeople what we were doing. We chose thread and zippers—two neckline zippers and one huge one, intended for upholstery—and half a dozen big white buttons.

Muriel had come to Horowitz Brothers by bus, so I drove her home, to a small brick house in Hamden. "Do you have time to work on it now?" I said, when we drew up to the curb. "Can I stay?" It was about five.

"I figured you'd help."

Inside, we had a glass of water, standing in her kitchen—which looked more conventional than I'd have expected—then moved to her daughter's old bedroom, with matching maple furniture I didn't care for. In a hurry to begin, Muriel spread the fabric on the desk, then began cutting out the sleeves, measuring on her own arm, snipping and tearing the cloth. "Sleeves are the part I've done before," she said. "Sleeves are like any sleeves." Then she said, "But roomier. Dolls don't have to move."

She made the French cuffs, and I hemmed them into place, once she'd approved of my hemming. I started moving toward the door after that was done, but Muriel said, "You stay while I think this bodice. I have to think aloud." She didn't give me another job for a while, except listening. The phone rang, and she closed the bedroom door. I could hear her voice raised. She was flustered when she returned, and almost stumbled, snatching at a chair back. I went for Chinese takeout, and we ate a quick supper in her kitchen, which was full of appliance covers appliquéd with apples. Other than that, I sat on the bed with my shoes off and watched.

The sleeves waited, draped on a chair back. Spreading the dark blue fabric on her daughter's old desk, cutting and pinning, pressing every seam on an ironing board, Muriel made two fronts with deep bust darts and sewed them together. A line of white buttons would run down the front of the bodice, but the dress would open in back, with the upholstery zipper. The waist could be nipped in a bit, even though there would be two of us, because TheaDora would have such wide shoulders. Muriel had me sew on the buttons, checking to make sure I spaced them evenly. "Did that phone call upset you?" I asked.

She stopped and looked at me, her glasses flashing in the light so she suddenly looked older, almost an old lady. "Family."

She cut two wide pieces for the back, swiftly positioning her shears and gliding them boldly through the fabric. Then she stitched the big zipper in place. She pinned the front to the back, turned it inside out, brought a plate from her kitchen, and traced two evenly spaced necklines between the shoulders. "Our heads have to be far enough apart so we don't get our earrings tangled," she said, as if she was sure she and I would wear the dress. Muriel wore big hoop earrings, and I like dangling ones. She took her big shears and cut two arcs, then slashed straight lines down the back below each neckhole. "For the zippers."

At last we crowded in front of the dresser mirror and put our heads through. Muriel had placed the holes correctly, and we could turn our heads, standing side by side with our inner arms not quite touching, our earrings in no danger.

"We're the same height," I said. I discovered that I wanted badly to be Thea or Dora. I liked the look of Muriel and me in the mirror, our black and white faces—both bossy, but each in a different way—her poky, graying hair and my longer, blond hair. We backed up carefully and began to laugh at the discovery that, because the row of white buttons marked a middle, we did look like one person. We looked like a woman with two heads.

"Now I can finish alone," said Muriel, and for a second I felt the kind of desolation I supposed Thea or Dora would feel if the other said that. But it was close to midnight. I'd have stayed up all night to be the first to see the whole dress, but along with the rest of the cast I saw it finished a few days later, at the rehearsal. Muriel arrived slightly late, carrying a garment bag from which she drew the blue dress, holding it high and fluffing it. We laughed and cheered. She'd made two demure white collars at the necklines, she'd sewed in the neckline zippers, attached the sleeves, and sewed the side seams. The skirt was lightly gathered from a dropped waist. It fell to the floor with a deep, tightly gathered flounce to conceal four shoes.

All the adults tried the dress on—all possible pairs, even men— while Justine and Mo watched quietly and Cindy instructed everybody. Two by two, we carefully unzipped the big back zipper so as to climb in. We clutched each other and took care not to step on the fabric. As each pair took it off, the next two would withdraw a bit, turn aside, give each other advice, and put on the dress. Someone would run over and zip them up. Then we'd watch, and they'd walk toward us.

The men seemed tense but excited at being in the dress, and the women loved it. It was a dress out of a child's daydream, a daydream of being grown-up in a distant time, when women flounced and were glamorous. But being a two-headed person felt right, too, like something we dimly recollected from before birth. Were human beings once two-headed? Would a two-headed skeleton in a cave be the next discovery of some paleontologist?

For those not wearing the dress, perception suddenly changed, over and over. Two people were lost, laughing, in a swirl of cloth. And then a two-headed woman—a great big two-headed lady, with white buttons down her front—would stride across the room toward us. Over and over, we'd clutch ourselves, as if to make sure that, sitting there, we continued to retain the uncertain status we'd thought, until now, was inevitable—the privilege and doom of being one.

❦

When my mother had a cold, around that time, she asked me to substitute for her at the soup kitchen, and there I found Daphne, who explained that she still owed some hours of community service. She happened to be standing between two fat people, behind a big vat of salad, and she looked tiny. But Daphne was tough, quick to refuse requests for extra tomatoes, shaking her head side to side so her light brown hair swung. I stood between her and a woman serving spaghetti. I handed out spoonfuls of canned peas, which many turned down. Daphne seemed just like Cindy, with Cindy's pointy roughness, like a tree that remains stubbornly twiggy and unleafed, deep into spring. I realized how intimately I'd come to know Cindy, her quick speech and hard little elbows, her body bumping into me as we all sprawled on the floor or scrambled to our feet. But I rather liked Cindy, while Daphne unnerved me. As before, her face when she wasn't speaking was defended, a little too flat. She concentrated on serving. "You got four pieces of tomato. You have nothing to complain about, Frank."

The line speeded up, then slowed. I had time to look over the room, where a few dozen people, mostly men, ate their supper, some in conversation with those around them at the long tables, others looking down at their aluminum trays. As always, I noticed the incongruities—the people who didn't look to me like street people— and as always I sensed calm in that room, a shared noncommittal glance that did not make judgments, at least about feeling—that let me, for one, feel what I liked, though I always feel what I like. What I liked feeling that day was desire for Gordon.

At Daphne's left, a tall, gray-haired black man served bread and pastries. I'd seen him each time I was there, and once he told me he was a retired school custodian and now volunteered at the soup kitchen several times a week. "So how are you doing, Miss Daphne?" he asked, when the line subsided.

"Can't complain," Daphne said, and then both said in chorus, "But I do!"

He laughed silently, and I wondered if the joke was his or hers or even my mother's. "You know my mom?" I asked him. "Her name is Roz."

"Gabby," said Daphne.

"Oh, sure, Gabby. We call her Gabby," said the man. "She claims she's older than I am."

There followed boring joviality about my mother's age, my age, and so on. Daphne said she was forty-four. Then she said, "Your mom isn't the easiest lady I ever worked for."

"No?" I said.

"The easiest lady I ever worked for," she said, "wasn't a lady at all. She was a transvestite. I was supposed to think she was a lady. That was the only hard part."

"You mean a man?" said my neighbor on the other side.

"What did you do for her?" I said.

"I cleaned, but she didn't care, she just wanted to talk. Your mom likes to talk, too, but she's mad if I don't get anything done."

"What do you talk about?"

"Regular girl stuff. Men."

"I didn't think my mother had much to say about men."

"You'd be surprised. We talk about Pekko a lot, of course. You can always talk about Pekko. She tries to figure him out. I gave up long ago." She seemed to think I'd take it for granted that Pekko had been her lover.

I was furious. I was supposed to agree that figuring out Pekko is a challenging pastime, but I couldn't and wouldn't make friends with her, and certainly not over that. I had to say something, so I said, "He says you're a good carpenter."

Daphne had repaired and refinished that staircase in Pekko's single-room-occupancy building, and had now moved on to other projects there. Pekko said she was doing a decent job, and cleaning up after herself, unlike her predecessors. My mother complained that Daphne was slow.

"I'm great," she said. "I know how to make joints and every-thing. These jobs don't use half of what I know."

"Why don't you work for a cabinetmaker?"

"Cabinetmakers are particular," Daphne said. "I don't do well with particular people."

Suppertime was almost over, and soon we carried the remaining food into the kitchen. I found myself standing near Daphne again as we scrubbed a tabletop. The room had emptied. "Pekko's hitting on me," she said, squeezing out a rag in a bucket of hot water. "I thought you should know."

"What's that supposed to mean?" I said.

"You know what I mean."

"Well, you'll have to deal with it," I said, moving toward the kitchen.

Daphne spoke a little louder. I moved closer to her again, so she'd quiet down. "He's trying to buy me off," she said. "If I get good sex, I'm not going to mind having roaches in my kitchen and a leaky bathtub. Maybe that was me ten years ago, but now I've got kids. And I'm sorry to say this about your husband, but he's not as attrac-tive as he once was."

"And I suppose you're getting prettier every year," I said. Yet she was ten years younger than I. I wasn't going to cry, and I wasn't so angry I'd scream, but I was hurt, hurt for my husband—and for myself. I glanced at my watch, said, "Have to leave," before Daphne could answer me, waved a good-bye to the people who ran the place, and left the building. In the last weeks I'd sometimes imagined Gordon, Pekko, and me as a lighthearted movie trio, an unlikely but blessed grouping that would never saunter together down a street in Paris or New York but should. But in my mind now, interesting

Gordon stepped confidently on along the sidewalk, while Pekko and I remained behind—old, clumsy, undignified.

❦

It wasn't Daphne's opinion of Pekko that hurt, I understood the next afternoon. It was that she considered me so weak that she could wound me with a sentence or two. Lying in Gordon's bed, I had a sudden nostalgia for the day, not long ago, when I'd planned to sleep with him only once more, and had even thought I might stop where I was and just save that last time. If I still had that choice, I thought illogically, Daphne couldn't hurt me.

"What are you thinking, lover?" said Gordon from his postcoital position next to me, under the thick, ivory-colored sheet. Now he propped himself up on his elbow as if to see which lover I might be, his straight, gray hair flopping down on his forehead, his blue eyes studying me.

"Do you have more than one lover?" I said.

"Naturally," he said. "I'm not going to remain faithful to my married lover, am I?"

"Naturally not," I said. "I was thinking about something that happened yesterday, at the soup kitchen."

"The soup kitchen? What were you doing there?"

I explained.

"Soup kitchens exist for the benefit of the beneficent," said Gordon, from his elbow. I reached my hand up to trace the line of his black, pointed eyebrows. Daphne would think I was powerful if she knew I was in the bed of a man with eyebrows like that, agreeing with him that he needn't be faithful.

"Hungry people do eat there," I said.

"People who like spooning out porridge serve it to people who like lining up for their porridge. 'Come and be humiliated!' 'Oh, thanks, I love being humiliated.' "

"Not true."

"I used to date a woman who ate in a soup kitchen off and on for a year, though she had plenty of resources. She was in medical school."

"A doctor?"

"Now she's a gynecologist."

I was silent. I wondered how old she was. "Look, that was years ago," he said. "I'm dating someone else now, but I'm not thinking of her when I'm with you."

"Well, I'm not thinking of my husband when I'm with you," I said. "I'm not quarreling with you about women. I don't understand fidelity. I never have."

A gynecologist, I told myself, wouldn't give him AIDS. At least he was a snob. But a gynecologist who ate in soup kitchens might have been a complicated gynecologist. Dismissing the question of whether I was risking my life with Gordon, I tried to decide whether I had to defend the soup kitchen. He began kissing my neck, hard, and for a moment I was happy, because the intensity felt needy. "Did you think I'd break up with you if you mentioned another woman?" I said.

"No. You're not stupid—and I don't think."

But he said it fast. Maybe we were equally needy. I took his bony head in my hands and kissed him girlishly, the way a woman in a blue print dress with long sleeves, a flounce, and white buttons down the front might kiss. Gordon pushed me aside so as to kiss my neck some more, aiming for the indentation in the front, thrusting his rough head at my throat, kissing. His hair was prickly against my skin. He kissed his way down until he was driving his head at my crotch, kissing and licking till he was breathless and I'd come recklessly, hither and thither on the bed. "Right this second, you're the only woman in the world," he said, but a second doesn't last long.

☙

For years, while Charlotte stayed faithfully married, I kept starting over with a new man. She'd had lovers before she met Philip, and hadn't forgotten the patterns of love affairs. With brief, sardonic laughter, we'd note "the day he talks about his childhood," "the day you go to the grocery store," or "the day he criticizes your clothes." Then there was "the day he tells you he's seeing someone else." I'd lived through that day several times in the long years when I had boyfriends who overlapped with others, who had girl-friends who overlapped with me. Charlotte and I distinguished between the early announcement—"Before we start this, you should know there's someone else"—and the late one, when he was seeing someone else because he'd decided you wouldn't do. "Don't go hiking," Charlotte would say, when I'd begin to be tense about a man, because twice I'd heard about another woman on a hike in the woods.

But the process was surely different if you were married and he knew. I had no intention of telling Charlotte anything about sex

with Gordon, but it was she I phoned—when I couldn't stop thinking about Gordon's other women or woman, whether that made
sense or not—a few days later, in the middle of July. We met for
lunch on a working day, although I'd rather see Charlotte at some
other time. On weekdays she can't dismiss the inward, professional
woman, and is perhaps too conscientious about looking steadily and
speaking plainly. For most of the morning I'd been sorting books
and papers—speaking toughly, to little avail—in Ellen's dining
room, and I was so glad to be in the instant comfort of an air-
conditioned restaurant that I almost said, "Charlotte, I'm having an
affair." I heard myself think it. I'd told no one about Gordon, and
there was no danger. Yet Charlotte heard me, or heard something.
"Did you just sneeze?" she said, as a waitress handed us menus. We
were at Atticus, a big, brightly lit bookstore with a café. I'm fond of
their gazpacho in summer. "I have the feeling I was thinking so
hard just now I missed something."

"No."

"God bless you, anyway," said Charlotte.

"Same to you," I said. "What were you thinking about?"

I've always considered Charlotte beautiful. Now she's a grandmother, but I still love to look at her pale blue eyes. For a moment
she stared, as if she was surprised that I'd want to hear what she was
thinking, then took me at my word. She'd been thinking about
scheduling a long weekend away with Philip, a topic slightly more
interesting than it might have been because it concerned Olivia,
who might or might not have a day off, and might or might not visit
her parents if they were home. "Boring," she said, stopping herself
from a full analysis of this subject. "Are you still working with the
man who doesn't believe in foster care?"

"I'm putting on a conference with him." That interested Charlotte, and I told her more about it.

"Is he still obnoxious?" she said.

"He's never exactly been obnoxious. He's opinionated, certainly."

I knew what I wanted to eat, but Charlotte had to read the menu and consider, so I had time to observe myself and know that something sad was occurring. The reasons not to tell her Gordon was my lover were clear to me, perhaps not reasonable reasons but my reasons. I said nothing more about him as we ordered and ate our lunch. But we talked about uninteresting subjects, then looked at our watches, signaled the busy waitress, and waited with too much attention, glancing over our shoulders, for the check. I took our money to the register and gave Charlotte her change, which she stuck into her skirt pocket instead of taking out her wallet. It's a habit; sometimes we've bought treats with money she finds in her pockets, as if she thinks fairies left it there. Remembering one of those times—ice cream cones after Charlotte reached for a tissue and came up with a five-dollar bill—I wished I had treated her to lunch. Maybe a gift would have kept her quiet. As we left the store, she turned the way I did, though her office was in a different direction, and said, scurrying slightly as if she thought I'd bolt, "When I don't have a good time with you, I know you've got a secret. I'm tired of your secrets, Daisy."

I stared without answering, and after a while she turned and walked the other way. At first I shrugged and walked on toward my car, parked a block farther down Chapel Street. I like what's unresolved. Trouble to be sorted out captures my attention, and in the past I've taken new interest in a diminishing friendship or love affair when I've sensed resistance. So I walked away, promising myself that Charlotte's censure would be worth it, because we'd have such a good time, not quite yet, arguing and fixing our friendship again.

Waiting in the heat for a traffic light to change, eyeing the Yale summer school students in shorts; the street people, always dressed for cooler weather than we had (some were in coats and watch caps); the office workers looking uncomfortable in jackets—I admitted to myself that irresolution with Charlotte was not fun. A sense of desolation claimed me, and when I got into my car, instead of driving the few blocks to Gordon's office, I drove onto the highway and all the way to Hammonasset Beach State Park on Long Island Sound, not far from where he lived in Madison. My red bathing suit was in my bag in case Gordon had wanted an afternoon together. Now, driving, I worsened my mood on purpose, imagining him on the phone—since I wasn't there—with a woman in another Yale office, jauntily proposing an afternoon swimming near his house, and some time in his bed. I was angry with Charlotte. What sort of friendship could exist without secrets? Had she no secrets from me? I'd be boring without secrets.

That evening I told Pekko about my afternoon at Hammonasset. "I should do it more often," I said. "It was too hot to work." It's a long, wild stretch of beach, with skinny, rocky peninsulas, and I told Pekko that going there had been a terrific idea. It's crowded on weekends, but on that weekday afternoon I saw mostly suburban women with kids. Pekko nodded noncommittally; he doesn't like to swim. But I was no more persuaded than he was. I had thought my afternoon at the beach would soothe and comfort me, but it didn't, and I began to feel a sense of irresolution that made it impossible to sit still, or do anything useful. All I wanted to do was phone

Gordon. And then I did, while Pekko walked Arthur. Gordon wasn't home, and I left a message: "Don't call me, I just wanted to say hello." I regretted leaving any message as soon as I'd done it, as if I'd left something of value he might alter to his own purposes. What would prove Charlotte wrong would be a happy affair, the one I'd described to Arthur in that walk at the river. I'd stayed away from Gordon that afternoon so as to prove to myself I was free, to prove the affair was fun.

The next day I went to his office, and after I'd sat tensely for a while, trying to work as Gordon had incomprehensible phone conversations, I walked past him to the bathroom, and when I returned he followed me into the archive, talking in his light voice about the heat ("Can't think, can't *think* . . ."), then grabbing my arm, then becoming quieter and gentler, but no less insistent, as his gestures became caresses. But as I was chiding myself inwardly for my nerves—and wondering what I'd do for a bathing suit, since I'd forgotten to return the red one to my bag—he dropped his arms at his sides, shook his head, and said, "Not a good plan today. Another day."

"Okay," I said lightly, but I minded. As usual, his shirt—short-sleeved, striped blue and white—had worked its way free from his pants, and he stuffed it back where it belonged, and returned to his desk.

In some ways the weeks that followed, through July and into August, were better than the start of the affair—just because I *do* like irresolution. Gordon made me as uncertain as an adolescent, needy for the phone or the touch of a hand. The last person who could make me wait that way was Bruce Andalusia. Gordon didn't ordinarily call me, because we couldn't talk much—and anyway, he

didn't see any point in discussing sex—but now and then he'd have a
professional question, and I anticipated those times too intently. I
experienced anew the convalescent feeling (when he *did* want to
leave the office with me, when he *did* phone) that makes minor illness such a pleasure for the young: pain succeeded by euphoria when
pain goes. Identifying to myself what made me happy now, I recalled
with pleasure even menstrual cramps, because of the moment when
after hours of pain enough pills loosened the body into sleep, sleep
and comfort. Postmenopausal, in July I became a connoisseur of pain
that will dissipate, postponing even glasses of water in the heat,
aspirin for headache, until I could no longer bear waiting for pleasure. I didn't want Gordon to swivel his chair around and start up
with me at work, because I wanted to prolong hoping he would.

I couldn't stop suggesting afternoon encounters, but I was no
longer natural about it. I'd lost my sense of rhythm. I always wanted
to do it, and twice he said no and didn't change his mind. Then one
afternoon, his back to me, Gordon said from his desk, "Can you go
away for a weekend?"

"Me?"

"Who else?"

"Sure," I said, before trying to figure out how that might be possible. Eventually I decided to tell Pekko I wanted some time alone,
away. Pekko likes cool-weather vacations in cities with lots of jazz.
He wouldn't want to come.

"New York?" said Gordon.

"Not the country?"

"I live in the country."

New York in summer wouldn't have been my first choice, but
Gordon said, "Hotels are air-conditioned." I told Pekko I wanted

to sleep alone in an air-conditioned hotel for a couple of nights, visit my brother, and see a drawing show in SoHo I'd read about. My plans didn't sound quite plausible to me, but he made no objection.

❦

Our weekend took place a couple of weeks after we first discussed it. In the interval, one hot afternoon Ellen lured me into her backyard with iced tea. She talked about her married boyfriend. "It would be simpler to have this out of my life," she said. "I picture having picnics in the park with the children. Of course I could do that whether I'm seeing Lou or not—I don't see him every day—but I know I won't."

I didn't say anything.

"If I go on a picnic, something terrible will happen to the children. A punishment for dating a married man. I'll take them to the top of East Rock, and they'll fall off the cliff and get killed."

"The monument on top of East Rock," I said, "looks like an erect, circumcised penis. With a woman on top of it."

"That's true, it does," said Ellen. Then she continued, "Remember when I told you my neighbor saw you going into my house with Gordon Skeetling, and you explained how he loves houses and wanted to see the shape of my dining room?"

"Yes," I said, startled that she'd remembered Gordon's name. I swallowed some tea. Maybe now I could get her to come inside and work.

"I didn't say so at the time," Ellen said, "but she saw you go in with him twice."

I said, "What do you want, Ellen?"

"You're going to tell me about it sooner or later, so why not now?"

"I don't have time," I said. "Sorry." I put down my glass and left by the driveway, without returning to the house.

That night or maybe the next, Daphne called when Pekko was out. "I called to talk to him," she said. "Some of the neighbors are pretty impatient. But there's something I've been meaning to tell you, too. Your mom feels bad about you. She keeps telling me she's worried because you haven't dropped in. She thinks there's something wrong that you're not telling her."

I called my mother and yelled at her for talking to Daphne about me. "I don't tell her any secrets," my mother said. "I don't know any secrets."

I never told my mother secrets, because I told so many people the history of my progress in and out of men's beds that *secret* wasn't the word, but my mother was one of the people I told. I don't think I talked about Denny to anyone but Charlotte, and I lied to her, minimizing the affair, but I talked about everyone else. As for Roz, she was never great at the comforting remark, but in my single days I did like dazzling her with a carefree tale of my recent exploits, reassuring myself as well that *carefree* was the right word. I'd point out to myself that if I were in love—meaning needy and at risk—I wouldn't talk to Roz. Now I hung up without persuading her she shouldn't have talked to Daphne. I might have been in her kitchen, bending my legs around her table leg, drinking iced tea or iced coffee (preferably iced coffee, but she didn't make it on purpose; she had it only when there was leftover morning coffee), and talking, giving myself daughter points for being there. I missed that happy woman, that me.

၆

Muriel and I got the part of TheaDora, though we were older than the other women, older than TheaDora. But we were the same height, and finally everybody thought that mattered most, as it did with the children. In the dress we looked most like one person. Cindy, now TheaDora's little sister, Hydrangea, tormented her. Cindy chanted, "You have two he-ads, you have two he-ads."

"So what?" I said. I was Dora.

"Now, Hydrangea, honey," said Thea, "I want you to think about what you just said. How do you think I feel?"

"We'll be late for work," Dora snapped.

Thea kept talking, but in practice, if I hurried, she fell into step. Dora's consciousness ruled. "We have to go to the bathroom," I said once, just to see what would happen.

"You think I don't *know* that?" said Thea.

TheaDora worked as a carpenter. Invited by Ellen, Daphne came in from the corridor, where she lurked, to provide technical advice. Ellen was a brisk assistant director, quite different from the Ellen I knew at home. She wanted the play to be "right," as she put it.

"I'm more interested in spontaneity," Katya said.

"Up to a point," said Ellen. As TheaDora staggered around the stage, enormous in her blue dress, the others tended to pair off and shout back and forth.

All but Hydrangea, a loner. "You're *always* late to work. Why should today be any different?"

Daphne listed carpentry terms for us to use. "One-by-four. Mortise and tenon."

TheaDora was hired by Jonah, a foreman on a construction project who advocated affirmative action and was delighted to see her. "You are not only a woman," he said, "you are of mixed race!"

"We are two women," I said as Dora.

"No, dear, we are a woman," said Thea.

We took our place in a line of people hammering. Jonah hammered, David hammered, and I hammered with my right hand while Thea held the nail with Muriel's left hand. As we hammered, Jonah said, "Well, you certainly are a pretty girl!" and Dora said, "It's nice of you to notice, although we're two girls," but Thea didn't answer.

"What do *you* think, Thea?" called Ellen.

"He's fresh," Thea said. Thea liked David, but Dora liked Jonah.

"We need a little more going on in this story, not just love and work," said Ellen, as Muriel and I climbed out of the dress at the end of rehearsal.

"TheaDora could witness a murder," I said, since murder was always on my mind these days. "One head sees it, the other doesn't."

Denise offered to murder Hydrangea.

"I don't want to be murdered. Then I can't say anything," said Cindy.

"You'll say plenty before you're murdered," Katya said.

"Can I die slowly?"

"We'll think about it."

❦

When we went to New York, Gordon insisted on driving— that is, he didn't merely insist on going to the city by car instead of by train, he insisted on taking his own car, which he'd

drive. I protested, then left my car at home. It was a Friday afternoon, and I took a cab to Gordon's office. I found myself trying to
decide what I'd do if he wasn't there, but Gordon was answering
e-mail. I waited in his extra chair rather than start up some project
of my own. I hated waiting. At last he picked up a briefcase and an
overnight bag. He looked different. He was wearing glasses, the
glasses we'd chosen together. The frames were darker than I
remembered. "You're wearing your glasses."

"Sometimes the contacts bother me, so I don't use them for a few
days."

"Are you bringing work?" I said.

"Laptop."

"Why?"

"Didn't you?" he said.

"No. I thought this was a lovers' tryst, not a business meeting."

"Sex makes me want to work, and I expect to spend a lot of time
on sex this weekend. And the hotel is expensive. If I do a little work
I can take it off my taxes." He'd made a reservation at the SoHo
Grand, after I'd mentioned the drawing show.

Now we got into his Saab. Again he turned down my offer to
drive. The traffic was bad all the way to New York. Gordon kept
NPR on. We reached the city so late I was starving. I'd imagined
falling into bed, but we checked into the hotel, washed our faces,
and looked for a restaurant where we wouldn't need a reservation.
We ate at a little Italian place in the West Village. Good salad. I had
looked forward to unlimited conversation but—oddly shy—couldn't
think of a subject. I talked about salad.

Then he said, "Want to see a show tomorrow night?"

"I'd like that."

"Maybe we can get tickets. We should have planned."

"You said we'd just be going to bed and working on your laptop."

"Sorry, sorry. I don't like the theater," he said. "Not true. I only like what's extremely good, and I don't like taking risks. Maybe that's why I didn't suggest it."

"You don't like the theater?" I said, picturing our grubby troupe of amateurs, our endless conspiracy about the implications of the headline I'd first seen in Gordon's office. "You know," I said, "it's time I told you something."

"What's that, you're an actress?"

"In a sense," I said. I ordered a second glass of Cabernet. "You may not remember this," I continued. "The day we met, you showed me your favorite headline."

"My favorite headline? I have a favorite headline?" He looked at me, knife and fork poised above his plate, ready to disagree and be amused and amusing. I couldn't get used to his glasses.

"Two-Headed Woman . . ."

"Oh, *that.*"

And so I told him about Katya, the players, and huge TheaDora in her blue dress with white buttons. When I'd told Charlotte, she'd listened with increasing glee, and I was proud of myself for getting involved in such a mess—such a quintessentially New Haven mess, both naïve and sophisticated. Its ethnic variety, as always in New Haven, was in part self-conscious and in part too ordinary to notice. I was proud of the play, too, as an effort of the imagination. I hadn't believed in it, but then I did. Not all the time. Sometimes I thought it was stupid.

I finished my story and leaned back in my chair, reaching for my wineglass, examining Gordon's face for signs of admiration, looking into his eyes through the glasses. Just then the waiter asked if everything was all right. Was I still working on that? I was.

"Not as good as you expected?" said Gordon.

"The play?"

"No, the shrimp."

"The shrimp are all right."

"Oh, you want me to say something about the play. Well, better you than me." He smiled. Gordon had a jaunty smile, and when he'd smile at me, I'd calm down.

"You don't mind that I appropriated your headline?" I said.

"Of course not. I don't own it. I didn't write it. Of course, there never was a two-headed woman."

"Did you ever read the article? Was it just a hoax?"

"What else could it be?" He shrugged. "Are you done now?" He signaled the waiter for the check.

I felt buoyant from wine, but I knew we'd need to return to this conversation. Not now. Then I didn't wait. "What's wrong with my play?"

"Well ... it's not really a play, is it? I mean, you're not playwrights. You don't have a dramaturge, a director ..."

"We have a director." We had two.

"Putting on a play that an audience will sit through isn't easy, even for professionals," said Gordon. He replaced his credit card in his wallet. "Tell me if I'm wrong."

"You don't have to pay for me," I said belatedly. "I know it's not *good*, exactly," I then added quickly. "It has its own validity."

"I like paying for you." And we stepped onto the crowded Greenwich Village street on a warm but pleasant Friday evening. Gordon steered me straight back to the hotel, so I thought he was too lustful to wait, and I liked that, but once in our room, he turned on the television.

People in the hotel and in the restaurant had assumed we were married—you can tell when people don't find you worth puzzling over—and like a married couple we fell asleep at different times, though we were spending the night together for the first time. I lay down on the bed in my clothes while he watched an old movie. I fell asleep, not wanting to stay up and pay attention to this weekend, this evening in a luxurious hotel room with the lights of the city outside. I awoke when I felt Gordon get into bed next to me. I rose, showered, and returned to bed, naked. Gordon was naked, too, I found, reaching for him across the unfamiliarly wide bed. He was awake—or he woke up—and he stroked my shoulder with his fingertips and then, shifting closer, my back. He took my face in his hands.

"I'm sorry," he said. "It's been a difficult week. I should have told you."

"What?"

"A woman I'd been seeing ended things."

I drew in breath. We were naked, our knees drawn up, touching, our hands on each other's faces as we lay, our mouths inches apart.

"What was she like?"

"Young." I watched his mouth shape the words, his teeth.

"Were you in love?"

"This isn't fair to you, Daisy. You don't want to know."

"How long have you known her?"

"Oh, a year or so. At first, we were just friends."

"Do you want to get up and talk about it?" I said. "Do you want me to put on the light?"

"No. I want to make love to you."

I drew him to me, feeling old—not just older than a woman for whom there was only one adjective, *young*, but older than Gordon. I *was* older than Gordon, but only two and a half years. Now I felt decades older, my body supple with experience of man after man: supple but leathery, without sensation, like the skin of someone who's been out in so much wind and rain that now no weather stimulates the nerve endings. I thought of getting up and phoning Charlotte on my cell phone, in the bathroom ("I'm going to tell you the whole story"), but I stayed and let him suck my breasts, and then I was aroused, and came before he did.

Saturday was better, at first. From the windows of our room we could see much of downtown, including the World Trade Center. Quick sex, breakfast, tenderness in the still-quiet downtown streets. *Tenderness*. Gordon put his arm around me as we walked and mumbled teasing compliments. "Why, it's Daisy of New Haven, mysterious, sexy Daisy in her tight black pants with her nice little ass . . ." He seemed glad to be where he was. We looked into store windows, walked, returned to the hotel for "more and better sex," he said. We'd been hurried first thing in the morning.

But after sex that never quite concluded, he opened his laptop, still in bed with the covers over his knees. The hotel had an Internet hookup, and he checked his e-mail. Then he dressed hurriedly and left while I was in the shower. And didn't come back. When I stared out the window, the air looked hot, glittery, though the weather had been pleasant earlier. Maybe Gordon was sitting in the lobby, talking on his cell phone. I didn't want to see that, didn't want to see his intent face in those glasses. I dressed, left the hotel without looking left or right, and began walking north. I was hungry. I walked as far as Washington Square Park and sat on a bench, observing a young man managing a small crowd of retarded kids, who'd been walked here and then were walked away. Dogs made me miss Arthur. Old people on the benches talked to me. An old man claimed to remember me from years ago, and I eventually agreed that I'd been in that park before, though not often. "You were a girl. A beautiful girl. You're still a beautiful girl."

Finally I was too hungry to wait any longer but too upset to go someplace and buy food, no matter how many times I ordered myself to do so. I walked back to the hotel, I who rarely walk except with my dog, because walking feels less powerful than driving, and I like to think I am a powerful person. My feet hurt in sandals. My feet felt dirty. I was hot in my tight black pants.

Gordon was in the hotel room. "Where were you?"

"You left, so I left."

"I came back," he said.

"I waited a long time."

"I was back in twenty minutes."

I'd been gone for an hour and a half or longer. "I'm sorry," I said.

"Listen, I have to leave," Gordon said. "It's not what you think. It's not the woman. Or, it is that woman, but it's something else. She and I have broken up—that's clear—but she needs me today, as a friend."

"You don't have to lie," I said.

"Look, I'll tell you. She had an abortion. She's at her parents' place in Westport, and she's bleeding. She doesn't want them to know, and she's scared. I'm going to drive to Westport and take her home, maybe to the hospital. She doesn't have a car—she got there by train."

"How old is she?"

"Oh, for heaven's sake, Daisy. I shouldn't have said she was 'young.' She's not that young, and I didn't mean it the way it came out. She's emotionally young. Not like you and me. Not able to take care of herself."

He had packed his things. He was checking the closet and the bathroom. Then he said, "I wish you hadn't gone wandering around Greenwich Village like a fifties beatnik. I didn't want to leave you a note, and I've just been getting tense, waiting. The room is paid for. You can find something to do in New York, I'm sure, and go home on Metro-North. I love you, I want to be with you—but I can't. It's our weekend. I know that. I should have canceled when I heard the abortion was this week, but that didn't seem right either. I'm sorry."

"Gordon, don't go," I said, though I don't say things like that.

"Please, Daisy."

"Never mind. I'm sorry. Of course, go. I'll be fine."

"You don't mind taking the train home, do you?" And he kissed me and was gone.

I lay on the bed with my eyes closed. Then I called room service. Then I called my brother and got his machine. I'd visit my brother. I'd go to the movies. I'd spend a night by myself in this fancy hotel. I happen to like going to the movies alone. I happen to like being alone. Gordon had said he loved me. I saw *Pollock*. I bought a book for the train. I ate ice cream in the New York streets. After many hours I came back to find a message from my brother, who invited me to lunch on Sunday. I called him back—awakening his wife— and accepted. Then I went to bed and couldn't sleep. Among other events, I remembered Gordon not believing in the play, Gordon persuasively dismissing the play from behind his glasses, as if nobody could take it seriously.

෫

When I called Stephen, he insisted that I take the subway to Queens but promised to meet me at the station. I felt elderly, unattractive, and not sufficiently in charge. Arriving at my brother's in a taxi might have helped, but he said, "A taxi will cost you a million dollars, and the subway is faster. I'm leaving now for the subway station. I'll wait there all day if you don't come." My overnight bag bumped into me on the subway stairs. I inwardly blamed my brother but also felt obscurely and sentimentally grateful that someone else was making decisions. Gordon had said his girlfriend was emotionally young, unlike him and me, and I wanted to be emotionally young.

I even had to change trains, but Stephen was right; it wasn't a bad trip. Still, as I stood in the second quiet station, waiting for the oncoming roar, I felt desolate. Pekko didn't miss me or wonder what I was doing. Charlotte was angry. Gordon was with the woman who had aborted his child. It had to be his child. He would be thinking of me as someone who cavorted around making up nonsense, who didn't know the difference between nonsense and a play. I was too selfish and trivial to grieve for the loss of his only chance, ever, to father a child. I wanted to be a triumphant woman visiting her brother, not someone who'd been left alone in a hotel by a man with more urgent plans involving worthier people. I wanted to be the one with urgent business. My brother in Queens, with his hushed museum job, is just a little bit like a loser, and I prefer seeing him at good moments in my own life.

Stephen was waiting just where he said he'd be, outside the turnstile, looking thin and dark, ironic, as if standing in a subway station was an inherently foolish activity. He took my bag and kissed my cheek. "You look well, Daisy," he said.

"So do you." He looked slightly uncomfortable, but he always does.

We climbed the stairs, and he pointed to where he'd parked, at a not quite legal spot near a corner. We climbed into his Toyota. "Marlene's having lunch with some people." His wife.

"What about Leah?" His daughter.

"Away for the summer. She's working at a hotel in the Adirondacks."

"That sounds good."

"Maybe." There has long been something sad about Stephen. He made Leah's summer job sound as if it had just the remote possibility of tragedy, as if his only source of information about the Adirondacks was Theodore Dreiser. The terrorist attacks of September 11, a month later, didn't change Stephen, though he can't stop talking about them. For him, everything that happens successfully does so by an unlikely accident. I've fought and argued with him on that subject much of my life, but that day in August, settling into his car, for a moment I gave up trying to be the successful sister and wished I'd shared his almost Eastern European pessimism all along. I could say, "I'm having my heart broken, but hearts are often broken." Instead I was Daisy Busy, with my calendar full of foolish plans and projects—connections that existed, apparently, to hurt me.

But being me, I soon began, a little defensively, to tell Stephen what I'd been up to. I described working for Gordon, and the conference—the aspect of Gordon that was going reasonably well. "Off and on all summer," I said as we parked in his driveway and went into his little brick house with its patch of grass, "I've been quarreling with Skeetling about Malik Jones." I explained who Jones was—the young black man killed by an East Haven cop in a car chase. "Skeetling says it isn't murder, but plenty of people think it's almost as bad." I told Stephen about the police report I'd read. There had been a report of reckless driving, and the officer had pursued two boys (both high on drugs, one out on bail) into New Haven, where he cornered them in a vacant lot. Jones backed the car toward the cop when he approached on foot. So the cop fired. All the witnesses said he had to fire—once things had come to that point— but nobody thought the chase made sense.

"I know it's not murder, technically," I said. "I don't know why I'm so interested."

We went inside. I hadn't been there in years. Usually I saw Stephen in New Haven, and now and then we'd met in the city. As a clutter professional, I was struck by clutter's absence. Gray or brown chairs stood with space around them, as if they made do for larger pieces. Stephen had bought food for our lunch: Dr. Brown's black cherry soda, bagels, lox, and cream cheese. He set about feeding me.

"Usually, when there's a murder," I said, returning to my subject, while Stephen unwrapped lox and forked it onto a plate, "it's all over and nobody can reconstruct it, not really, not even the killer. But Malik's death was witnessed. The death was not yet, and not yet, and not yet—and then it was. Everyone had time to become afraid, but it happened anyway."

I imagined Gordon saying, "Fuzzy thinking,"

"It had to happen," said Stephen, "and it also couldn't happen. Most events have just one of those characteristics."

The phone rang, and we were distracted. Then we ate. Stephen told me a long story about the woman who supervised him at work. It took a while, because he wanted to complain but also to be scrupulously fair. I tried to care. After lunch we went out to the backyard—a bit of untended grass with bushes around it—and he dragged two plastic chairs into a shady corner. (If I show him what I'm writing, he'll read this. Last night he phoned and again asked to read it. But, Stephen, don't be offended, because the point is not that you were a loser but that I was. And you were brilliant. I'd forgotten about our initial conversation, but you hadn't. He hadn't.) After a pause, during which I felt sorry for myself just for being where I was instead of with Gordon, someplace else—how different Queens is from Manhattan!—Stephen said, "When I cut up a bagel, I could do it or not do it. No big deal, either way. We could eat the bagel, or decide to go for dim sum instead. I considered that. There are great Chinese restaurants in Flushing. It's all Chinese now, did you know that?"

"No."

"Some things, the whole universe cooperates in making them happen. You visit here, you leave. I don't mean I'm eager for you to go, but your whole life prepares you to go back home, and mine prepares me to show you to the door."

"But?" I said. I plucked blades of grass.

"But a killing—when somebody kills someone else, or kills himself, or herself—"

Which was when I realized he was thinking of his old girlfriend, the suicide.

"Herself—then everything is keeping it from happening—this is not natural—but also, everything has to cooperate to make it happen. It's so unnatural, how could it take place otherwise? It's a different kind of action."

"Is that why I want to think about murder? Explain me, Stephen. You hang around art all week. You must have learned wisdom."

"I hang around reproductions of art, in that store, but, yes. I think you are interested in a kind of choice, a very intense kind of choice that makes such a difference, that's so risky, that nobody could do it—except people do. And when they do, they don't seem to choose at all, it seems to happen. When Michaela died—"

"Yes?"

"When Michaela died, I was positive it wasn't going to happen, because it just couldn't happen. Certain things just can't happen, or that's what I thought when I was a boy."

"Did you know, Stephen?" He'd told the police, over and over, that he knew nothing.

"Oh, she'd been talking about it for weeks. I was so ashamed, when she really did it. I had no idea people could actually do such a thing."

"Do you mean, when I doubted you, I had guessed *right*?" I wrote and rewrote that piece, again and again and again, explaining those doubts.

"I didn't kill her."

"I know, I know," I said. "But it wasn't the way you said it was."

"No," he said. He paused. "Michaela's been dead almost forty years," he said. "I've been in therapy. I've talked about the truth, finally—not much to Marlene. She's sick of it. This woman who died years before I met her, who had the same first initial. I don't blame her."

"Then my argument didn't make sense," I said.

"It made sense. It was based on a mistake, but it made sense."

I didn't answer. Then he said, "People who die young miss a lot of days."

"Maybe you'd still be together if she'd lived."

"Oh, probably not."

"It's true," I said then. "Killing is so definite. Like stuffing an heirloom into a garbage can. What I do for a living."

Marlene arrived then, as Stephen laughed, and we spoke of other subjects. Stephen hadn't asked me why I was in New York. He wanted to drive me back to the subway, but this time I insisted. I thanked him and hugged them both, then called a cab and settled into its backseat. The driver didn't speak.

❦

By the time I paid my fare and climbed out at Grand Central Station, I was convinced that Gordon had invented the woman with the abortion, that he'd left to spend time in bed with still another woman or, likelier, simply left because he found me boring and stupid, me with my penchant for earthy community dramatics. I considered renting a car. I couldn't think of anything that might make me feel better except fast driving, but there I was at the train station, where a train was departing for New Haven in fifteen minutes.

It was starting to fill up, and I walked past one car, in which every window seat was taken. I wanted to sit alone if possible. The next car looked less crowded, so I entered and made my way down the aisle. "What are *you* doing here?" came an insistent voice, and I looked down into Muriel's still face, lit now by passing amusement at seeing me here.

She was sitting in a window seat. On one side of a Metro-North car, there are seats for two; on the other, seats for three. Muriel was sitting in a seat for two, and she had a dilapidated tote bag with red handles next to her and a purse on her lap. She was in jeans as usual, but she wore a denim blazer with a white T-shirt visible under it. She stared up at me as if I was a tourist attraction, her hair sticking out in all directions. After her initial smile vanished, she looked alert, with that look of hers that resembled anger. "Been having a good time in the city?"

"I went to visit my brother," I said evenly.

"Lucky you."

"What did *you* do?" I said.

"I saw my mom in Brooklyn."

"I forgot your mother lives in Brooklyn." I stood in the aisle, my purse and overnight bag hanging awkwardly at my side. I wasn't sure I wanted to spend almost two hours alone with Muriel, but I couldn't endure one more dismissal. "May I sit here?"

"Of course." She pointed up, and I took the tote bag, put it on the overhead rack, put my own bag there as well, and sat down.

"I didn't know you were waiting for an engraved invitation," said Muriel.

"Polite people don't keep their luggage on the seat," I countered. We sounded like Thea and Dora, and I was tempted to tell her the story of my weekend, just to hear her defend the play.

As soon as I sat down, I was sorry. I could have greeted her cheerfully and gone to the next car, where I'd have been alone. Just to make myself feel even worse, I'd bought a novel that seemed to be about love with a bad ending, and I could have been indulging in that misery, shutting out the glaring fluorescent lights and the conductor's repetitive announcements. Now we'd have to talk for almost two hours. I was uncomfortable with Muriel's apparent bad mood. Maybe she also would rather read a book than talk. I felt what I hadn't felt before with Muriel—that because she was black, I was too nervously conscious of what I was doing, and that my nervous consciousness, which made it impossible to know what might feel natural, was racist. And of course it was. Race wasn't an issue when we were inside that blue dress, but somehow on Metro-North it was.

At first, we talked about the play. "We haven't figured out enough," she said.

"You want a meaning, like Jonah? I don't think that makes sense," I said, too quickly.

"No. It's just, how long is this play?" she said. "I think someone putting on a play should know how long it is. Are we at the intermission yet?"

"You mean we don't know what we're doing," I said, laughing. "Yeah, a friend of mine was pointing that out to me yesterday."

"A friend in the city? You didn't just see your brother."

"That's right."

"An old friend from your single days? Well, I don't have a problem with *that*," she said, and I didn't set her straight. I didn't want to ask how much of my story she'd intuited from the slope of my shoulders and the way my eyes looked, but I rested for a moment, silently, in her scrutiny.

"What's your mother like?" I said then.

"She was never a nice lady, and she's not one now," said Muriel. "But she's glad to have me come and take her out for lunch on a Sunday."

"Are you an only child?"

"I have a brother. I had a sister, but she died."

"I'm sorry."

"A long time ago." Muriel was silent for a while. "A long time ago, but my mom's still angry that she lost her little churchgoer, and kept her little whore."

"Oh, is that how it goes?" I said.

Her big, serious head turned in my direction, and suddenly there came from her a laugh like a bark, startling enough that someone in the seat in front of us glanced behind him. "I am still suffering from those early days you find so interesting," Muriel said, in a voice that sounded subdued, more refined than Muriel usually sounded, as if she'd picked up, that afternoon, delicacy from her churchgoing mother, who perhaps knew how to murmur. "I am still suffering for the way I lived, and I can tell you that you may think I'm cool, making whore dolls and giving speeches, talking on the radio, but my mother and my brother do not think it's so cool."

"They want you to keep it a secret?"

"They believe I should pray over my shame in private. And just now it's especially bad. And maybe I've said enough. Did you bring a book?"

So I stood and took the novel I'd bought from my overnight case. "Do you want anything from your bag?" I said.

"No, thank you. I might take a nap. That might be quite welcome." Muriel tilted her big head against the window and slept, breathing quietly like a girl, and I tried to concentrate on my book. Eventually we arrived at Stamford, the first stop after 125th Street in New York. After that the stops come frequently, and the announcers give repetitious instructions for each station. "Southport next. The head three cars will have to walk back. The head three cars will not platform at Southport."

At Bridgeport, Muriel woke up. "My niece," she said then, as if there'd been no interruption. "My niece, my brother's daughter, is an unusually beautiful and bright child, with brown eyes like candles. She is my darling, but the last time I saw her—six months ago—she was dead in the eyes. Do you know what I mean?"

"How old is she?"

"Seventeen. Honor student until a few months ago. Now they can't control her. They hear stories in the neighborhood, the teacher calls. Daisy, I spent the entire afternoon arguing with my mother and my brother—he came over—to let me see LaShonda, and they will not let me near her because I am not a respectable person. My brother is sorry he *ever* let her get near me. He blames me. She used to stay with me, sometimes. She is a bright child, a lovely child."

And as I said, "Oh, Muriel, Muriel, that's so bad," my friend snatched at my arm, my shoulder—as if she was suddenly blinded and couldn't find them—and then lowered her head and cried inaudibly, her shoulders shaking, into her own crossed arms. I couldn't move or speak, watching her cry. "Is there anything I can do?" I said at last.

"Like call up my brother and tell him I'm hanging around with a crazy white lady in a big blue dress? No, thank you."

"Is that my trouble? I'm crazy?"

"No, you're not crazy. I'm all right."

I offered to share a taxi when we reached New Haven, but Muriel was being picked up by her son, and she insisted they'd drop me off. We waited a few minutes outside the train station, and a big, dark car drew up. I got into the backseat while Muriel got in front and said to the driver, "Hello from Grandma. Who wonders is she ever going to see you again."

"Why, she dying?"

"No sign of that."

"Then I'll wait a couple of weeks," said the son, whom she now introduced to me. His name was Howard, and he turned and smiled at me, then reached over the backseat to shake hands. "Your friend don't recognize me," he said to his mother.

I couldn't see his face clearly in the dim car—it was twilight— but he didn't look familiar. He pulled away from the curb, and I began to tell him where I lived. "I know where you live," he said, and laughed. "Should I make you guess? I am your substitute mail carrier. Last week you told me your dog did not bite, and I told you I'd been told that before."

"Oh, my goodness, you're right, I'm sorry," I said. One more failure. I pointed out to myself that I'd seen him only once. But as far as I knew, he'd seen me only once. Now I remembered a mailman who made a joke about Arthur when I happened to come out as he sorted mail on our steps. I'd gone home in the middle of the day to get my bathing suit, just in case, though in the end I didn't need it that day.

I'd had my red suit crushed in my hand, and my keys in my other hand. Embarrassed, I stuffed the bathing suit into my bag and took the mail. Arthur barked from the house.

"Thanks, Howard. I'll remember you next time," I said when he drew to the curb. I hoped it was true. I felt guilty and racist and silly, too self-involved to pay attention when someone spoke to me. I squeezed Muriel's shoulder as I climbed awkwardly out of the car, bumping myself with my bag. She had said nothing from the time she'd introduced me, as if that act of civility had used up the last of her will.

ॐ

My house looked pretty in the summer dusk. I hoped Pekko wasn't home. I was sure he'd read the whole bad story from my face: how I'd lied to him, hurrying to New York in a naïve, stupid fantasy of love, how I had not been pretty and interesting enough to keep Gordon Skeetling to myself for two days in the city, and even how I had not been able to help or comfort my friend in her trouble—the size of which reminded me of the pettiness of mine, without making me feel any better. I was ashamed of my stupid grief, but no less grief-stricken. I kept reminding myself that Gordon had not broken up with me. Probably he would, any day, and I'd blame myself then for this hysteria. After all, nothing was wrong yet.

I fitted my key in the lock and heard voices in the kitchen as I opened the door. Arthur came skidding and cavorting toward me, so I had to put my two bags on the floor and sink down to have my face licked, to grasp his muscular body.

"Daisy?" came Pekko's voice. He sounded surprised. He must have assumed I'd have dinner in the city.

"I'm here," I said.

"Should I go?" I heard a man say.

"Of course not."

I picked up my possessions and walked into the kitchen, where Pekko and a man I didn't know were drinking O'Doul's from bottles. Pekko thinks nonalcoholic beer is pointless, so he must have thought well of this plump, middle-aged man if he'd picked up a six-pack. Or the man had brought it. He stood, a man in his forties, black hair slicked back, in a white shirt, open at the neck, and dark pants you'd wear to work. He had an eager look, a readiness to smile, as if he loved jokes but couldn't remember any, and depended on others to tell them. "This is Edmund," said Pekko. "My wife, Daisy."

We shook hands. "I'm sorry," I said. "I'm just back from New York." I felt unpresentable, my makeup old and my clothes wrinkled.

"How was your weekend?" said Pekko.

"It was good," I said. "I went to see Stephen. He gave me lunch."

"How's Stephen?"

"He's fine. Thinking deep thoughts," I said.

"He does that," Pekko said.

Edmund offered me an O'Doul's. I wanted a glass of wine. I hesitated, not sure if bringing out the bottle would be rude. Then I was too tired to look after this person of whom I knew nothing. If he was a recovering alcoholic who suffered when he saw others drink, he'd just have to suffer. I did everything wrong anyway. I might as well do that wrong too. "What I need is Chardonnay," I said, "and I think we've got some." I opened the refrigerator, found the bottle and a glass.

Then I took my wine and said, "I need to change my shoes." I thought I'd go to bed with my Chardonnay and stay until this man left, though I hated being in one more situation in which I couldn't or didn't take charge. I went upstairs, unpacked my bag, washed my face and repaired my makeup, changed my clothes. I felt unreasoning rage at Pekko for bringing home a stranger, unreasoning rage at the stranger. He looked nice, foolish and nice—just the sort of boring person Gordon might expect me to hang out with.

I didn't want to go to bed after all. I wanted to do something to somebody, and if nobody else was available, I could demoralize this innocent former drinker by drinking. So I went back to the kitchen. As I came down, Pekko was telling Edmund about his troubles with the former contractors.

"Edmund was my assistant, when I had the bike store," he said to me. That went back a long time. Edmund must have been a young assistant.

I poured another glass, then sat on the faded green sofa. "Do you still bike?" I said. "Pekko doesn't."

"Now and then," he said. He didn't look like an active man.

"We were thinking of going out for a pizza," Pekko said. "Did you eat?"

I had had nothing since Stephen's bagel. I went along with them and drank more wine at Modern Apizza. Edmund seemed unperturbed. He discovered I had a mother who lived near me and expressed envy. His parents were in New Haven, he said, and that was why he came back here from where he lived—somewhere a couple of hours away, apparently—but he didn't see them often enough, and they weren't doing well.

"Did you grow up here?" I said.

"We moved away when I was in high school, but my parents came back when they retired."

I told him my mother had moved to be near me when she retired.

"That's great. But she must be a worry, too."

"My mother's just fine," I said truculently. "She has more energy than I do."

"My mother's not too bad," he said, "but my father's losing ground pretty quickly. Forgetful. I've just come from arguing with them about giving up the house." As we waited for our pizza, I felt sorrier and sorrier for myself, listening to this man, who had come from an intergenerational fight about whether the old people were too feeble to continue their lives and couldn't make them interesting. Charlotte would have made the story exciting. She often talked about the peculiarities and obstinacies of the old people she worked with, scrupulously omitting identifying details. But I didn't like thinking about Charlotte. When I thought of her disapproval, I imagined her laughing at me, though Charlotte isn't like that. I excused myself and left, looking for a phone. I found one, phoned Gordon, and got his machine. I didn't leave a message but returned to Pekko and Edmund, and slid into the booth next to Pekko. He patted my thigh.

"Now, how could he say he's a perfectly safe driver, after something like that?" Edmund was asking Pekko, who shook his head solemnly. Pekko is never bored.

"What do you do for a living?" I asked Edmund.

"I'm assistant principal of a middle school in Worcester, Massachusetts," Edmund said, and I almost laughed, he seemed so like the assistant principals of my youth.

"He counts paper clips," said Pekko.

"I once told your husband that one of my responsibilities is supplies," Edmund said, "but I assure you, I spend plenty of time counting children, too. I was telling my mother," he continued, "I don't have trouble with the mischief makers, but sometimes good kids need attention, too, and I'm less sure of myself with them."

"What do you do?" I said. We had meatball pizza, and I'd eaten two or three slices. I wondered if I wanted another.

"I ask them to help me count paper clips!" he said triumphantly, and as I laughed, I began to see why Pekko liked this man. "That is, I find something useful for them to do, and I hang around and start talking about some problem of my own. That gets them started. I'm not too bright, and the smart ones see I'm not too bright, but sometimes they trust me anyway, because they need someone to trust so badly."

He paused, then said, "Nobody *ever* has an easy time," in a slightly admonitory tone, as if I was a shy child in his office, too shy to be bad but in need nonetheless. I was not too shy to be bad but I was in need. "Children's anxieties are as bad as those of adults," Edmund continued, "but it's worse, because when it's the first time, they don't know it's ever happened before. No boy has ever disappointed a father before. No girl has ever lost her boyfriend."

"Does *anybody* learn that it's not the first time?" I said, quieted.

I minded Gordon's departure from New York as much as if nothing had ever happened to me.

"Maybe not," Edmund said, and I found myself taking unforeseen comfort from a counter of paper clips. The waitress brought our check. "Maybe nobody ever does."

Curled sycamore leaves—faded green with brown edges—lay at the curb on Temple Street on the Thursday after the weekend in New York. It had been hot and humid all week. Would we still be lovers in the fall? I hadn't seen Gordon since he walked out of the hotel room. I'd done little, making appointments and breaking them. I considered phoning Charlotte and didn't; I wanted to go to Gordon's office and didn't, though there was work to be done. By Thursday I'd stopped hoping he'd phone. I figured out when to arrive at his office, leaving time for work plus swimming and sex. I spotted his Saab as I hurried along the street, but when I went inside he was standing, gathering papers hastily.

"How are you?" I said, standing in his doorway, my arms around a big, stuffed loose-leaf binder in which I carried everything I needed for work on the conference. The office wasn't air-conditioned—Yale took Gordon seriously, but only up to a point.

"Hi, Daisy. Awful weather. I'd have called you, but I have a feeling it isn't a good idea to call you. Tell me if I'm wrong. How was the drawing show?"

"I went to the movies. I visited my brother."

"Stephen."

"You could have called me," I said. I'd waited at home all day. Pekko wasn't home during the day. "Are you leaving?"

"I'm meeting with that guy in city planning about the project in Schenectady." I couldn't remember what Gordon was doing for Schenectady. "I said to him—your place. He has air-conditioning."

I should have continued through his office and begun work. I'd been making calls from home about printing the brochure for the conference, but now I had to call the speakers to confirm their time slots. It was almost time to mail the brochures. I'd been compiling a mailing list and making labels. The printer would do the mailing, which would arrive just after Labor Day, when with any luck the weather would be cool and people would be energetic, looking for something to do, a reason to leave home. I'd lure them to New Haven. By the end of the conference, in October, everybody else would have learned what they learned. As for me, I'd know something more about killing, how it can become the next event in a series, how an action that wasn't going to happen becomes an action that has happened.

But I stood in Gordon's office, twisting my hair like Cindy. If he didn't say something now to renew the affair, it was not quite— surely not quite—the same as if he'd ended it, but almost as bad, as though we were lovers day by day, like travelers in a hotel who must inform the proprietor if they wish to extend their stay. I wanted a lease. It crossed my mind that Gordon—like me at the start—might

have decided we'd go to bed a fixed number of times. "Thirty-two,"
I imagined him thinking, climbing out of bed at the SoHo Grand.
"That's it."

"Did you choose the design?" he said. I'd had a couple of mock-
ups of the brochure.

"I don't have to let them know until I give them the copy, and I
can't do that until I talk to a few more people."

"People are away. They're hard to reach."

"Don't worry." I'd had long conversations and lively e-mail
exchanges with my proposed speakers. Everyone who'd promised to
speak would come to my conference.

"Gordon, let's pick a time to go to your place, okay?" I said then.
I couldn't help it. "If not now, whenever."

"I'd rather keep it spontaneous," he said.

I forced myself to pass through his office into the archive and get
on the phone. Before leaving he interrupted me, coming to my
doorway. "Have you talked to the man who's going to speak about
Marie Valenti?" he said. "When is that scheduled for?"

"The last morning." I hadn't been able to think of a good enough
reason to cancel that discussion. Gordon was right—it was a little
bit of reality inserted in a theoretical few days: Who killed Marie
Valenti? I'd pretend Pekko had never spoken.

As I sat there, not turning to look at him while he stood in my
doorway and asked two more quick, impersonal questions, I remembered Pekko's friend Edmund, his kind eyes ready to hear something funny. His eyes had met mine as we both reached for the same
slice of pizza at the same moment. We laughed, and he pulled his
hand back. I pictured that hand—a little pudgy, quite pale. Now the

thought of it, the hand of a man I wasn't attracted to sexually and had never touched, comforted me as Gordon also left without touching me.

I worked for a while, not well, then found myself thinking of a reason to go to Ellen's house despite the heat. She'd probably be home, and wouldn't mind my coming without an appointment. She didn't want to be away from New Haven while her lover was here, and he wouldn't be here much longer. I drove to her house and rang the bell. I was businesslike, and within a few minutes, though she'd proposed drinking iced tea instead of working, we were going through a closet together. I heard the children's voices from the backyard. A heavy coat in her arms, Ellen suddenly turned and let it fall to the floor. She held out her practiced hands. "What?" she said. "What?" I pictured myself falling into her arms, but I said, "Some of this could join the pile upstairs." That's how we'd taken to working at her house—I colluded with her. We didn't throw anything away, but we organized everything into ever more precisely defined piles. Her children both now hopped from room to room, which wasn't strictly necessary but made the point. She and I walked demurely in narrow paths like ladies with parasols.

She shook her head and smiled. As we worked it started to thunder, and I left, so as to drive in the rain. I took a long drive, just to be driving, before I went home. My hands, aching for Gordon's body, squeezed the hard steering wheel. When I came home at last, Pekko was sitting in the living room, patting the dog and watching the storm. He seemed larger than usual. His knees were spread, and he leaned forward, his elbows on his knees, listening as if to distinguish mood and tone in the thunder. He opened his left arm, and I nodded, then busied myself for a few minutes, too restless to settle. I went to the bathroom and washed my face. I drank a glass of water and stroked the dog, who had come forward, quieter than usual, when I entered, and now followed me expectantly. I looked at the mail. Then I returned to the living room and sat down, leaning back against Pekko's arm. He put his hand on my shoulder. It was five days and some hours since Gordon had touched me. I began to cry, though I never cry. I cried with the sheer exhaustion of wanting. Pekko didn't ask questions but rocked me forward and back and pulled me closer.

The storm lasted a long time. When I thought of wine and went for a glass, the air had cooled so quickly that opening the cupboard door released distinctly hot air. I brought Pekko a glass of ginger ale, and I drank some Chardonnay. Then he put his arm around me, and we walked upstairs to the bedroom, where he undressed me and we lay until we were chilly before turning to each other, thrusting our tongues into each other's mouths. I didn't care that he was he and not Gordon—I'd always liked both.

As we lay naked, satisfied, in the new, cool air, I thought again of Edmund reaching for the pizza and pulling his hand back. "Did Edmund kill Marie Valenti?" I said. "Is he the one?"

"Let's not talk about that." Pekko climbed out of bed, and I heard him pad to the bathroom, piss, flush the toilet, and return. I wanted Pekko to get back into bed with me, and he did. We lay in silence. So Edmund, who could pull his hand back from a slice of pizza, had stabbed a woman he loved to death. Was it true? What did I learn, knowing Edmund, knowing that about him?

At length Pekko said, "I might have been wrong about Daphne, all those years ago. I thought it didn't matter much to her." All right, we would change the subject.

"It mattered," I said.

"I'm not Cindy's father."

"I know that," I said. "But what does she want now?"

He sat up, turned away from me, and put his feet on the floor, so his wide hips and big thighs were what I saw, not his face. "Just to make trouble."

"She says you hit on her."

"She can't imagine decency," Pekko said. "She thought I gave her a break with the rent so she'd go to bed with me."

"Is that what it was like before?"

"Oh, no," Pekko said. "Nothing like that. No, it was good before. It was good but she was married. And screwed up."

I touched the side of his hip.

"She wants different paint," he said, "I buy her different paint. I don't know what I'll do with the paint I already bought. If she scraped properly, she wouldn't need different paint."

Daphne was working in a second building now, stripping and refinishing a different staircase and stairwell. "You think it's easy, an apartment house, somebody constantly working on the staircase?" Daphne resisted what Pekko told her to do, claiming her instructor had taught her something else. Meanwhile she and her neighbors complained about their house. There were bugs despite fumigation. The plumbing needed work. "Well, of course," Pekko said. "You can't replace plumbing just like that." A tenant with small children claimed there was lead paint in her apartment. Daphne had called a newspaper reporter about that, and then called in the fire marshal, who gave Pekko a summons for a blocked hallway, just because he'd allowed tenants to leave things.

"Why didn't you tell me all this?" I said.

"It's boring."

"What does she *want?*" I said again.

"Oh, she's sincere. She's bringing about justice."

"She's not doing this because she's mad at you?"

"I guess she was mad at me to start with. She acted friendly, but I guess she never got over all that, way back. But right now she's on a crusade. She's saving the poor by living among them." He had stood up, somewhere along here, and slowly begun to put on his clothes. We went to Basement Thai. I was glad Gordon lived in Madison, but people in Madison may spend an evening in New Haven. As we left the restaurant, I thought I saw his Saab pass, with two people inside. A woman in the passenger seat with long, dark hair had turned sideways. I could not see her face, which looked toward the driver.

❦

My mother kept calling, and at last I suggested we meet for lunch downtown.

"Clark's Pizza?" she said.

"All right." Gordon might come in. But surely not with a woman, unless it was a business lunch, and maybe I could stand that. I agreed because I hoped he'd come in, but he didn't.

"I know what the trouble is," Roz said, peering out from under her white curls as soon as we'd put down our menus. This was a Thursday, one week after the day I'd seen him. I'd been in the office several times, alone.

"What trouble?"

"Daphne's been hinting at this all summer. I have to tell you. She's in love with Pekko."

"No, she's not, she's trying to ruin him."

"People are complicated, Daisy. But I am sure you're not going to lose him."

"To Daphne? Of course not."

She glanced in both directions, but the booths near us were empty. "But it's been worrying you," she said. "I know it's been worrying you."

"No, Mom, it hasn't."

"Then what?" I could have insisted I was fine—but I couldn't insist I was fine, so I told a truth that was less humiliating than the exact truth. "Oh, you know me. There's someone I like. That didn't stop just because I got married."

"With you, I assume there's always somebody. I hope you can keep it within reasonable limits."

"You mean, stay out of bed?"

"Or at least be careful."

"That's my mom. To tell you the truth, it happened, a little, it's over, and I'm fine."

"You got it out of your system."

"Maybe," I said. "Did Daphne finish your kitchen cabinets?"

"She never gets around to the last coat of varnish. She's one of those people who doesn't do the last thing, so you can't pay them and end things. But I don't want her to stop coming to see me."

"She's interesting," I said.

"To be fair, with the humid weather, it didn't make sense to put that coat of varnish on. But now she should do it. It's almost fall. Schools are open. It's cool today—I wish I had a sweater." It was cool, though it was still August.

I asked my mother if she'd like to help with publicity for the play, and she had a couple of ideas immediately. We had a small budget, and I gave her Katya's number. I'd eaten as much lettuce from my Greek salad as I wanted—as had happened once, I thought I remembered, with Gordon—and I was finishing olives and feta cheese as she enumerated all she might do, sounding like me. Cool weather had brought on list making in her, and as I listened, I began to make my own inward lists, of all I had to do for the conference. List making was a comfort. Enough lists, perhaps, and I could manage this affair.

"She's more sensible than she seems, that Daphne," my mother said, after a silence. "At first I thought she had to be exaggerating, because I know Pekko is a good landlord. But now I'm not so sure. Reporters are interested—newspaper and radio."

"She's crazy," I said.

"Have you ever seen the building?"

"I don't even know the address," I said.

"Oh, I know the address," said my mother and reached into her bag. "It's in Fair Haven. I dropped Daphne off once. It looked all right, but she says that's deceiving. Here it is." She handed me a piece of paper. "What I wanted to say, honey—you're going to keep him, but you'd better pay attention."

When we separated, I couldn't imagine why I wanted to drive straight to Daphne's house and look it over, and then I did know why, and I did drive there. Of course, it was what Roz intended. She was saving my marriage, somehow, by making me find out about that house, what was or wasn't wrong there. My father died many years ago, but the expression I imagined on my own face now was one I'd seen on my mother's during his lifetime, a tolerant alertness for the peculiarities of men. You loved them, you trusted them, but you kept an eye on them.

But I wasn't thinking about Pekko twenty-three hours a day, I was thinking about Gordon. I had to see if Pekko's building was a wreck, because I had to know it wasn't, so Gordon wouldn't think even less of me if he ever found out—wouldn't think I was married to a slumlord. I was fighting the image I'd had when Daphne was so difficult at the soup kitchen: Daisy and Pekko, a couple of old fools. I was discovering something marriage does: it defines you, in part, as the sort of person who'd marry whoever your spouse is.

The building was on a quiet street full of two- or three-family wooden houses, most covered with aluminum siding. Fair Haven is a neighborhood much like my own but older, with bigger trees, and poorer, with vacant lots and, lately, buildings here and there being briskly put to rights by some community-minded effort. Pekko's building was a rickety, red three-story frame house with two doors: two attached three-family houses. It needed painting. I didn't think all the apartments were floor-throughs, so quite a number of people lived there. I parked and went up on the porch. A wall of tidy steel mailboxes was inside a locked front door. I hurried back to my car, unsure what I'd learned, but before I could reach it, another car parked and Daphne got out, shaking her limp, tan hair from her eyes, looking like a teenager who'd borrowed her mother's car. She'd obviously seen me, but before she spoke she locked the car deliberately and deposited her keys in a tiny black purse on a long cord, which she hung from her shoulder. Then she said, "What are *you* doing here?"

"My mother gave me the address. I wanted to see if it was so bad."

"I'll show you."

Her apartment was not attractive—a dark kitchen; ugly green appliances—but I didn't see anything to interest a newspaper reporter. The bathroom was worse. Daphne invited me to press my hands on the broken tiles in the shower, and I could tell that the wall behind them was porous, crumbling. Tiles had fallen, more would fall. Some were stained from leaks. Most convincing was the smelly basement, full of junk, dangerous to children. Traps were set for rats and roaches.

We climbed the stairs. "You see?" she said. "I don't know what he's trying to do. Bribe me to keep silent by being nice to me? He gives me a break with the rent, he gives me fatherly pats on the shoulder..."

"You said he made a pass at you."

"One day it seemed like that..."

"Well, which do you mean?" I said. "He's giving you the apartment so you'll go to bed with him, or he's offering to take you to bed to shut you up? Is bed a treat or not?"

"How should I know?" Daphne said. Pekko was nice to her because he's nice. He might have gone to bed if she wanted it, except that she was too unpredictable. He didn't take that kind of risk. Or maybe he believed in fidelity. I found I didn't know if he did. Maybe he did. Probably, come to think of it, he did. I thanked her for the tour and drove away, thinking of Pekko for once—Pekko who had acquired too many properties and bestowed too many favors, so he couldn't care for his holdings as he should. With stubborn goodwill and stubborn cynicism, he thought it was better to house ten people under some kind of roof than five under a roof that didn't leak. Pekko didn't believe good could be done neatly. He had an instant suspicion of anything that wasn't for profit—some profit to someone. I'd hoped to find out, in my tour, whose side I was on—Daphne's or Pekko's. I hadn't been married to Pekko long enough to side with him without an investigation, or maybe I'm the kind who could never do that. Now I thought he was laying himself open to trouble, doing too many favors for mixed-up people who could turn on him. Certainly there was enough wrong with the place to satisfy someone who wanted trouble. What I saw made me angry with Pekko.

As I signaled to turn at the corner, a man came walking around it, and I was startled, because I knew him but couldn't place him for a second. Then I recognized him: Edmund, the man we'd had pizza with, the man who'd looked at me sadly and kindly when he sensed I was troubled—the man who had probably killed Marie Valenti. He walked with his head slightly tipped back and that same eager expression on his face: as he walked down the street, even a stranger might tell him a joke. He didn't notice me as I drove around the corner.

❦

The sight of Edmund made me remember I'm a curious person, someone who likes to know, who likes to do. I was pleased to be the kind of person who glances from her car and spots someone with an interesting secret—which I knew. I still had the list-making energy I'd felt when my mother and I talked about the play, and propelled by that energy, maybe I could work at Gordon's office without feeling the risk I'd felt there lately. I walked in energetically. Gordon sat at his desk, large and floppy-haired. "How're you doing?" I said and walked past him, still feeling all right.

"You?" Gordon said.

"Fine."

I had seven phone messages. Speakers needed information. Caterers responded to my questions. We'd serve food—muffins and coffee in the mornings, and lunch one day.

I hung up the phone after several calls to see Gordon leaning Gordon-like in my doorway, one hand exploring the top of the frame as it had done many times, all that summer. His arm rose from the short sleeve of his shirt. His palm measured the depth of the molding in the frame, then one finger at a time stroked it, perhaps feeling the paint for tiny imperfections—not as Pekko would, so as to evaluate the paint job, but as a tactile accompaniment to his thought, as if he brushed a drumstick over the surface of a drum, just barely shaping a series of notes.

"Who's going to talk about Malik Jones?" he said.

"A retired New Haven cop and a black sociologist."

"Do they claim it was murder?"

"There's some notion of wrongful death. His mother's suing for wrongful death."

"I still think it blurs your argument to include it. And it takes away from other topics."

"Like Marie Valenti."

"Oh, Marie Valenti. That might have been a mistake. The guy from the state bores me on the phone. These unsolved cases—when you first come across them they seem exciting, but there are an awful lot of them. I think it's the exception when they do get solved, and maybe after a certain time it never happens."

I grunted. Wanting him while talking of other things made me tired, but I was stunned with tenderness, despite myself, for the unimpeded space in Gordon's mind, the roominess of a head—and he did have a large, roomy head—so uncluttered with memory, association, and the workings of the imagination that thoughts could pass through it with the freedom of a hang glider leaping from a mountainside into the empty air above a treeless valley. That's how I wanted my clients to be, once I was finished with them: thinking without impediment in unblocked air, after they wrote me a check and ushered me out the door. But nobody except Gordon could think that freely. He didn't even know that he'd changed his mind. He didn't imagine my memory of the old idea.

"Let's get iced coffee," he said.

"Why not?" I said, though I didn't have time.

We walked up Temple and through an alleyway, past the Bryn Mawr bookshop and onto Whitney Avenue, where we were stopped by someone I'd often seen, a woman who offered to recite Shakespeare for money. She was thin, imperious, a graduate of the Yale School of Drama who had found a way to act despite illness and trouble. Gordon looked impatient—mystified—but I nodded, and this time she spoke not Shakespeare but a speech from Euripides' *Medea*. Her voice was rich, and her black eyes moved with authority and sanity in a dark-skinned face with strong cheekbones. I teared up as I took in her pain, Medea's pain, my own. I thought Gordon would hurry away and say something disparaging, but to my surprise he handed her a dollar. Then he took my elbow and steered me down Audubon Street to Koffee? which is usually full of students staring at nothing, then typing on laptops, then staring again. Now it was almost empty, with summer school over and the fall term just beginning. We bought iced coffee and sat at a table in the back, looking at a small, grassy park, a self-conscious urban amenity but a good one. Across from us, in the back window of the Foundry Bookstore, a hand-lettered sign, which has been there for years and years, read, YOU COULD BE DRINKING KOFFEE? AND READING NOW IF YOU HAD BOUGHT A BOOK HERE FIRST.

"Iced coffee season's almost over," I said.

"I drink it year-round," said Gordon. In the long years of my single life, I'd sometimes seduced a man with a touch, perhaps to his hair or his wrist. Once I did it by unbuttoning a man's cuff as he sat next to me. But most often I simply asked, and either he'd been wondering or the question itself was enough to evoke desire and will. This time it was no game, and I didn't know how to make Gordon go to bed with me again, now that he seemed to have let the habit lapse: it was almost two weeks since New York. I could all but hear a woman breathing behind him, a woman with long, dark hair, for whom I couldn't design a face. As I looked past him into the Park of the Arts, filled with frisky teenagers, I thought that if he didn't invite me to his house, his white bed, that afternoon, I'd be helpless to continue moving through the complicated life I'd succeeded in arranging for myself, which I had thought was mine.

I'd just given the final schedule to the printer. Gordon talked about the layout skills of the woman who'd designed the brochure, about one thing we might have done differently. "It's fine," I said. "It's clear, and it states the days of the week as well as the dates. That's all that matters."

He still thought he'd have done one thing differently.

Gordon didn't imagine, so I couldn't try to make him imagine taking me to bed. Lately, asking seemed to arouse resistance. Syllogistic reasoning did not come naturally to me. If I could stop thinking it was over, I'd be fine, but I couldn't stop thinking he wanted it to be over.

"Do you want to stop being my lover?" I finally said, playing with my straw, regretting my words.

"No. Why, have you had enough?"

"No."

"It's a busy time," he said.

"How's your friend? The woman who had the abortion."

"Fine. We're not in close touch."

"That must have been hard," I said.

"For her?"

"And for you."

"Well!" He shrugged. Then he said, "What's excellent about you, Daisy-love, is directness," and I was fine for three seconds. "You must be a nuisance in the cast of that play, though."

"Oh, everyone in that group is outspoken."

"But from the way you described the group, you're the only one who might, well, bring to it a more ambitious awareness."

"I'm not ambitious."

"Of course you are."

"Not about the play," I said.

"Ambition doesn't make distinctions. People like us—we need everything we do to achieve a certain level."

"I suppose that's so," I said.

"If I did want to stop," he said then, "stop our—afternoons—or stop for a while, would you mind?"

"Of course I'd mind!"

"You're not in love, surely?" he said. "Because I love you, but I'm not in love with you."

"I'm not in love," I lied. "But I want to give you a present."

"What sort of present?"

I'd had an idea, and then I'd had a different idea. The first idea was that Gordon would think better of me if I could surprise him with some fact he'd like to know, and the fact was that I knew who murdered Marie Valenti. I could tell him what I knew, making him promise not to tell—or even not making him promise. I didn't even know Edmund's last name. Nothing could come of my knowledge. I had no idea why Edmund was living in an apartment Pekko had rented him, or sometimes living there. I was powerless. Maybe that was the lesson I'd needed to learn about myself. I had thought of myself as a woman who could make events happen, but maybe I was a woman who gazed at events as they took shape before me. It would be unfair to Pekko to tell, but since it would do no harm, it would be no more wrong than the wrongs I committed against him whenever Gordon did invite me into the bed with the fluffy white comforter.

That was the first idea, and it made the second one possible. I didn't need to tell Gordon about Edmund. Knowing I could made it unnecessary. He was attracted to me. He loved being my lover. We didn't need to have this competitive conversation, hurting each other with nonsense about being in love or loving, whatever that meant. It meant nothing. Anything I did that shifted his attention even a trifle would work, I now knew. So I'd buy a book, as the sign I faced suggested. I told Gordon that I'd seen birds I couldn't identify at the shore near his house, and that I knew there was a new bird guide. "Maybe the Foundry has it," I said. "I'll buy it for you."

"I'd like that," Gordon said, and for some reason I thought of my young self turning down a Marimekko dress—which I'd have loved to own and wouldn't have bought for myself.

We bused our table, as instructed by a sign on the wall, then walked around the corner and down a short flight of stairs into the bookstore, which is below ground, as if to suggest that reading is private, that reading's a secret vice. Henry, the proprietor, who's known for plaid shirts and suspenders, was in long sleeves for fall. "Hi, Daisy," he said. "Hi, Gordon. Didn't know you two knew each other."

Henry had the book, and Gordon watched quietly while I paid for it. Outside on the sidewalk again, holding the book between us, we turned the pages, looking for shorebirds. Our hands pushed against each other as we each tried to control the book and our investigation of it. I made a joke, just because I felt so much better—for no reason. Then I said I ought to get back to work. I knew he'd invite me home, and he did. We took two cars. I kept seeing his on the highway, changing lanes just ahead of me.

It was too cool to swim, and too late in the day. We hustled into the house and into bed, as we had the first time, ignoring birds. His hands were all over me. I said, "Shall I get on top of you?" and he murmured no and pushed my shoulders down, vaulting on top of me. Then he thrust himself into me from above. I couldn't remember why I had thought he wanted to end it, but I also imagined it might be the last time, as if affairs never persisted from summer to fall.

After he'd withdrawn from me, Gordon put his hand on my belly, and we lay silently for a long time. His hand was warm and heavy. I wanted to get up and pee, but I had to stay and keep his hand there. "I know who killed Marie Valenti," I said.

"What do you mean?" I didn't have his full attention yet.

"A high school friend who'd moved away. He came back that night. They'd dated, but so briefly nobody thought of him. Pekko's known all along. A school administrator in Massachusetts. His name is Edmund. I've met him."

Gordon's hand stayed on my belly for a few moments longer. Then he took it away and sat up. "No shit," he said.

When I left, alone in my car, I didn't dare imagine being in bed with Gordon again. I imagined the conference, the discussion of Marie Valenti's murder—boring for others, interesting for Gordon and me, who I pictured on opposite sides of the room, taking it in and saying nothing, each knowing exactly what the other was thinking.

❦

Early in September, Katya said we'd begin rehearsing twice a week, and after discussing everyone's elaborate schedules, we held an extra rehearsal on the evening of Sunday, September 9. Ellen asked me to drive her and Justine because her car had been unreliable, but I thought she wanted the time with me, and I was glad. I had no intention of telling her about Gordon, but in my mind I told her the whole story many times: receptive Ellen, Ellen the receptacle. When I picked her up it was almost dark. Justine was waiting on their deeply shadowed porch as I drove up, and she called into the house, then climbed into the backseat of the Jetta. "Mom's talking to the sitter."

Ellen got into the car next to me, fluttering and hesitating. "I wanted to say," she said, "the dalliance ended."

"I know what you mean, in case you're talking that way for my benefit" came Justine's voice from behind us.

"If you know what I mean I don't want to know it," said Ellen.

"You don't seem too upset," I said.

"I ended it."

"Why?"

"Scruples."

But when we reached the theater—we were now rehearsing where we'd perform—she sent Justine in, then turned and burst into tears. "Of course I'm upset. It was the best thing in my life, other than the kids."

"What kind of scruples?"

"Not scruples," she said. "Fear."

"I know about that," I said.

"I figured you did."

※

TheaDora went hiking in the forest in her big blue dress, accompanied by her younger sister, Hydrangea. Some discussion about the proper route. Katya offered a piece of paper they could hold and look at, and Daphne promised to provide a map. TheaDora's hands snatched the paper, one hand trying to position it so Thea could take a good look, one hand favoring Dora. They could go nowhere until both heads agreed, so it made sense to follow Hydrangea, who scampered back and forth across the stage. "I'll make trees," Daphne called. "Plywood trees."

"We take the left fork," called Thea.

"We already *took* the left fork," said Dora.

"That wasn't a fork."

"Of course it was."

At that moment a scream was heard, and Denise ran across the stage in front of us, followed by Chantal. Thea studied the map and looked to the left, ignoring Denise, but Dora looked directly at her, and Chantal raised her arm, imaginary knife in hand, and stabbed Denise, who fell dead. Dora began to scream, "Police! Police!"

"What happened?" cried Hydrangea, who had run ahead and seen nothing.

"Murder! Murder!"

"What?" said Thea. "What happened?"

Chantal had fled through the woods. Now, after weeping over the body of this stranger, TheaDora and Hydrangea began hiking back for help—crossing and recrossing the stage.

Chantal returned. Alone on the stage, she said, "Killing her was easy. I brought the knife just to scare her. Then she said something bitchy. I knew it was sharp. I moved it toward a place on her arm between two freckles. They showed me a place to go. I thrust the knife between those freckles, and then she was bleeding and screaming, running away from me. She ran, I followed, and when I reached her, I pushed it as hard as I could into her body."

Jonah appeared, chased Chantal, and caught her. He led her off-stage, and the next scene was the trial.

Denise was the judge, Jonah was the prosecutor, and David was the defense attorney. Chantal was the defendant. TheaDora was the witness.

"Do you recognize the defendant?" said the prosecutor.

"I do," said Dora.

"Well, I don't!" said Thea.

"See," said Jonah. "She does."

"Objection!" called the defense attorney. "Half of her doesn't!"

"Where were you at the time of the murder?" the prosecutor asked.

"I was right there," said Thea. "I was looking at the map. But I'd have seen a murder. I didn't see anything."

"But we have the body," said the judge. "The question is, Is the defendant the person who killed her?"

"Couldn't say," said Thea.

"Yes!" said Dora.

"I have a confession to make," said the defendant.

"So do I," said the judge.

The defendant confessed to the murder. She had never intended to do it, and would never get over it. She was prepared to spend her life in prison, where she would dedicate herself to the welfare of her fellow prisoners.

"Now it's my turn," the judge said. "I used to be a doctor. I quit and went to law school, and later I became a judge. The reason I quit was that I was the doctor who delivered TheaDora. TheaDora, I didn't think. Later I was sorry, and I tried to find you, but your parents had moved."

"What are you sorry about?" said the defense attorney.

"I said you were one baby, but I was wrong. The more I thought about it, the more I knew that two people can live in one body. Thea and Dora, you're twins!" The judge banged her gavel on a table we'd set before her.

"In that case, we can both marry her. Marry them," said David. He explained that law was a second career for the prosecutor and him as well. "We were the carpenters who fell in love with you. It was an intolerable situation. To distract us, we quit carpentry and went to law school."

Thea had been in love with David all this time, and Dora in love with Jonah.

"Doc says she's twins," said Hydrangea.

§

Living in New Haven, one is never alone—though not in the way Thea and Dora were never alone. Wallace Stevens writes about the difference between "New Haven before and after one arrives," and I think he means that New Haven is in your mind before you get there; when you do, there's the real New Haven and the imagined one as well. But I think "New Haven before and after one arrives" also means we change it by arriving, because it's just small enough that everyone matters—or seems to—though not as in a small town in which you can keep track. It's a city, but not an anonymous one. If you cry on a street corner, someone you know will drive by, or walk past, looking. On vacation, I like going to a place where I know nobody.

Daphne had left the rehearsal early. Ellen said Cindy was sleeping over at her house and added her to our group. As we were walking to the car, a little sweaty, Ellen said quietly, "It's all right not to tell me. I like secrets—I mean, secrets I don't know. I know you have a secret, and I'll help you own it, even though you don't want to talk to me about it. You can lie to me, too, you know. I don't mind lies."

"My friend Charlotte can't stand it when I lie." I laughed and looked at her more frankly than I had in the past.

"That kind of friend is useful too," she said.

I dropped them off and drove home. Arthur met me at the door. As I had the night I came home from New York, I heard voices, but these were the voices of a man and a woman. Daphne and Pekko were sitting in our kitchen, Daphne looking small and accused on the big sofa, clutching a glass of what looked like water, Pekko at the table with his own glass. "I'm sorry," Daphne said when she saw me. "I meant to be gone by the time you got home. How was the rest of the rehearsal?"

"Okay, I guess."

"It better be okay. The performance is in a month."

"More than a month." Mid-October, after the conference.

Daphne stood. "I guess we've said all we have to say, Pekko," she said.

Pekko stood too but said nothing. I stood in the doorway, my hand playing with Arthur's curls. I took a step toward the hook where the leash hung. I'd walk him, so I wouldn't have to find out what Daphne and Pekko had been discussing, and so I could be alone for the first time in hours, persuading myself that more times with Gordon would come.

So I reached toward the leash, and Arthur was starting to wag, when Pekko said, "Wait." He raised his hand and let it fall. "Wait, Daisy."

"What?" I said, and he didn't answer.

Daphne said, "I tried to be fair. But he's not listening." She wore a skimpy tank top that wrinkled over her flat chest, and shorts that were quite short, though the weather was cool. Daphne never wore bright colors, and her clothes often seemed chosen to match her no-color hair, yet there was something appealing about her. "I want results," she said. "I want results that already happened."

"You want what nobody can give you, Daphne," Pekko said. "Free rent—"

"I *said* I'd earn it."

"You can't earn it. You think you know what you're doing, but you don't."

"Look, I'm going," Daphne said. "That isn't the important part, anyway. The important part is the condition of the building."

She walked toward the door, and neither of us followed her. Then she turned and said, "Just so you know, Daisy. We're having a rent strike, starting tomorrow. Nobody's paid the September rent, and nobody's going to. We'll be picketing this house in the morning. The *Register*'s covering it, and maybe the *Advocate* and Channel 8."

Arthur saw her to the door. She left it open, and I followed her to close it, then returned to Pekko in the kitchen. He was still sitting, drawn up to the table as if to eat a meal. As so often, I was looking at his back. "I'm sorry," I said.

"I'm a slumlord. That's what they're going to say. All over the paper."

"You're not."

"Of course I'm not."

I sat down and put my hand on his big, muscular arm with its gray hairs. "But, Pekko," I said. "What she wants— Can't you do some of what she wants?"

"Which puts her in the driver's seat. Which lets her say I *admit* I'm a slumlord."

"Nobody will take it that seriously. There's a lot wrong with that building. You could send in a crew tomorrow. There's bad plumbing. Bugs."

"I'm not a slumlord, Daisy."

"I know what you're doing. You're stretching yourself thin so you can take care of all these people. Daphne. Edmund. Is Edmund living in that building?"

"He just needs a base there, so he can help his parents. Please don't tell anybody. Did Daphne tell you?"

"I happened to see him there."

"You were there?"

"Yes," I said. "I was there. I wanted to see for myself."

He pushed his chair back, so he was farther away from me. "And what did you think?"

I stood up. There were a few dishes on the drainboard, and I began putting them in the cupboard to give my hands something to do. "I didn't like what I saw. You're not a slumlord, but you seem like one. How do you expect people to understand what you're doing? You make no effort to explain yourself. And I think you could do a little better. You don't have a lot of money, but you can fix the place up a little better than that."

He didn't say anything. There was a tiny nod, as if to acknowledge the answer to a question. "She's organized my other buildings," he said.

"I don't even know how many buildings you own," I said then.

"You don't?"

"No."

"Well, four. You didn't know it was four?"

"I suppose I could have figured it out."

"You don't seem like my wife, Daisy," he said. He stood up, slapped his knees, and began to leave the room.

I was enraged. "I don't seem like your wife! How can I sympathize with you? You never say anything. You are secrets piled upon secrets. You know who committed a murder twenty-five years ago, and you don't go to the cops—you have no—"

"You're not going to the cops, are you?" He turned faster than I'd have thought he could move.

"Of course not. Of course not—if you don't—" I said. "But why is it a secret he lives in your house? If he does? If nobody knows, why can't he just stay anywhere, like anybody?"

"I don't know," he said. "I know it's important to him."

"I don't believe that's the whole story," I said.

"Sometimes you have to trust me. Why did you marry me," he said, "if you don't trust me?"

I stopped shouting. I put the plate in my hand on the table, as if I were setting the table, and then I sat down at my place and said nothing more.

Never being alone means you are part of what you didn't agree to and responsible for what you didn't do. I knew why I married Pekko. I'd always liked sex with him. I recognized his goodness. I was titillated by his mysteries. I felt huge affection for him, when I wasn't exasperated. But I didn't marry him in the way my mother married my father. I didn't open a joint account with him—not at the bank, not metaphorically either. After a while I stopped sitting there and went to bed. I didn't walk Arthur, but Pekko did. He came in late, and I woke for only a moment when he got into bed.

In the morning, Pekko was not in bed. I lay listening. When I came downstairs in my robe, he was filling the coffeepot. "Are they here?" I said.

"They're here." He was dressed and had brought in the *Times*.

I went to the window. In front of our narrow Goatville house, on our undistinguished street, three women—one small white woman who, when she turned, was Daphne, two black women, one big, one small—walked wearily back and forth on the sidewalk. Daphne held a poster in her hands. I couldn't make out the words.

"They look tired already," I said.

"They got up early."

"How long have they been here?"

"Six or so."

"What are you going to do?"

"There's nothing to do."

While we ate breakfast, a reporter called. I answered the phone and handed it to Pekko, then listened as he refused to comment.

"I can't stand that," I said, as he hung up.

"What?"

"You want me to behave like your wife. All right. As your wife, I object to your saying nothing."

"If I don't want to be quoted, it's a good idea to say nothing."

"They'll say you refused to talk. Call her back and say *something*."

"What? What do you want me to say?" he said, pushing away his coffee cup and standing. "I'm going to the office."

"Are they picketing that, too?"

"I suppose."

All I wanted then was to stop him. I put down my bagel and cup of coffee, and stood, putting my arms around him, holding him so he couldn't leave.

"What is it?" he said.

"I love you."

"I know," said Pekko. "I love you, too. But let me do what I have to do."

"What do you have to do?"

He wrested himself from my arms. "Look. In a city like this, if all the apartments are beautiful, a lot of folks will be homeless. I do what I can."

"Can't you tell them *that*?"

"No. I can't. Partly because I don't want anybody looking over my books—and partly because I don't want anybody looking at Edmund, thinking about Edmund, noticing Edmund."

"But why should they?"

"I don't know, but I'm sorry I told you about him, and I'm not going to talk to any media people and take any more chances, whether that makes sense to you or not."

Pekko drummed his knuckles on the table vigorously, and Arthur thrust his head into his lap. "Daisy," he finally said, his voice sounding odd, with less resonance than usual, "will you come with me?"

I almost said no. I had two appointments that morning, and I had hoped to get through them quickly so as to go to Gordon's office, because I had plenty to do, and because I was always hoping for more with Gordon—more sex, more fighting, more disappointment, more anything. And I don't believe in agreeing to do what you don't want to do. I could make lengthy arguments having to do with the uselessness of unwilling sacrifice, even when it's small. And there's my habit of doing right every other time. Or, better, my belief that I'm half good. I thought Pekko should fix up his houses. I thought he probably should have gone to the police about Edmund, so even if it happened to be one of my good moments, I wasn't sure I should stand by his side in this instance. I didn't quite respect his decisions, even when I didn't think them morally suspect. I thought he could limit the charity and look after his image.

But sometimes one is given a little extra breath, and that time, air filled my lungs. "Of course," I said, and we grabbed each other. I ran upstairs and dressed quickly. Leaving the breakfast things on the table, though I knew Arthur would nose them for crumbs, possibly until they fell and shattered, we went outside, avoiding the pickets, and got into my car (I wasn't going to be a passenger, even now) and drove—mostly silently—to Pekko's office on Whalley Avenue. I passed it, looking for a parking place, and saw three men walking back and forth outside, clutching hand-lettered poster board. SLUMLORD read their placards. A few people had stopped to look at the men. We parked a block away and walked back. "Will Henrietta be there?" I asked. His secretary often opened the office.

"I called her last night and told her to take the day off."

I hadn't been in Pekko's storefront realty office for a long time and noticed that it had been improved, with plants in the windows. Most of his income-producing business was in renting low- to middle-rent apartments owned and managed by others. He also managed several buildings. The ones he owned, though they seemed to receive most of his attention, didn't take up most of his time. Only now did I think about the harm Daphne and her buddies could do him. People in the neighborhood would think he was preying on the poor. Landlords would be less likely to list with him, tenants less

likely to inquire. He could lose management contracts. Pekko served
on the boards of a soup kitchen and a drug treatment facility. He was
what Charlotte once called "a noble businessman." He snarled when
praised for charity of any sort, but he valued his good reputation.

Now he ignored the pickets and ignored the stir that occurred
when he took his keys from his pocket and picked up the newspaper.
We opened the building. It was cool inside, cooler than outdoors—it
was one of those September days that would become warmer and
warmer, until the afternoon was pretty hot. Indoors, you'd want a
long-sleeved shirt all day. "What are we going to do?" I said.

"There's plenty. I thought maybe you'd answer the phone."

"So you want to act as if those people aren't there?"

"What else could I do?"

"We could talk to them. We could negotiate. We could call up the
press and give our side. We could arrange for repairs."

"I've got a schedule for repairs. I get to them when I can."

"And if they put you out of business?"

"There are other businesses. People who know me, know what
I'm like."

"You're just talking tough," I said. "You're not going to like what
happens. You wouldn't have asked me to come if you didn't want me
to make a difference. If I'm going to be here, I want work that will
make some difference."

Pekko shrugged. He had sat down at his desk and was looking at
a paper on it. He didn't seem to have heard me. Then he said, "Do
whatever you want."

So I started making phone calls, which is what I like. I called
everybody I could think of. I called Gordon. "This is Daisy."

"Yes."

"What would you do if you wanted a favorable newspaper story?"

"What does this have to do with?"

"Pekko's business."

"Such as it is. I'd do something that could be photographed." The pickets were doing that already. The buildings themselves could be photographed. I tried to stop myself from thinking about "such as it is." I was glad I'd called him because what he said was smart, but I was sorry I called because it wasn't helpful, and I'd taken a risk.

I called Charlotte at work. "Are you speaking to me?"

"Of course! Wait." She could be heard excusing herself. "What is it?"

I told her the story, and she was aghast to hear of picket lines. "He's not a slumlord. This is idiotic." I didn't tell her I couldn't summon quite so much loyalty as that. She'd scold again. She offered to put together a second line of positive pickets. "Do whatever you want," I said, repeating Pekko's words. But she couldn't do it for a day or two.

I went on calling friends and acquaintances, almost anyone at all. In between calls I watered the plants and picked off withered leaves. Then I'd think of someone else to call and do that. Everyone was interested, but nobody made an offer except Charlotte, who couldn't help right away.

"How long can you last without rent?" I said at one point.

"I need it to pay the mortgages," Pekko said. "I don't have money lying around."

I did answer a few calls that morning, but of course I didn't know what to say, so I'd immediately put Pekko on the line. What I most wanted to do—invite the pickets inside, find out exactly what they were demanding, and figure out how to do some of it—was not allowed.

I know what I'm like when I'm not accomplishing anything, and after an hour I began to recognize that woman—Daisy Pointless, she was called. It was too early to offer to go for sandwiches. Pekko stayed on the phone, giving orders having to do with garbage pickup, somebody's check, and a maintenance man's days off. "Pretty good," he said over and over—his invariable answer to "How are you?"

I couldn't think. I'd never worked in a storefront office, and I'd have felt exposed to the street even if pickets condemning my husband—the same three bored-looking gentlemen—had not been walking back and forth on the sidewalk. They ignored us, but passersby looked in curiously. Pekko was obviously used to scratching his nose and hitching up his pants in public.

Pekko's and Henrietta's desks faced the street on either side of the room, while several chairs, against each side wall, made up an informal waiting room. Behind the desks were file cabinets and odds and ends that I supposed came from houses Pekko owned or cared for: a lawn mower, a battered bank of mailboxes, several ladders and paint rollers. I'd been here, meeting Pekko or stopping with him to get something, but I'd never spent time here. I walked to the back of the building. A narrow corridor in the middle of the back wall led to a small bathroom, a closet full of leases, receipt forms, and other papers, and then a storeroom at the back. In the storeroom was some dilapidated furniture—a few kitchen chairs, a TV stand— and I sat down. A back window looked out on a Dumpster.

I was sure I could feel Pekko's relief when I left the room. The air in the building circulated more freely. Would he be better off with-out me, altogether? I had continued to love and want Pekko all spring and summer—I hadn't wanted to leave him—and I didn't that morning either. But I thought maybe I ought to. I speculated whether this rent strike was just some large expression of sexual tension between him and Daphne, and I tried to decide whether the solution was simply for them to crawl into a bed somewhere.

But the night before, Pekko had wanted me, not Daphne, in the house and in the room with him. He had asked me not to walk Arthur, to stay. And this morning, he'd asked me to come with him. I just needed to know what I was supposed to do for him now. The room I was in had a back door as well, and I opened it and stepped outside into the warm air. There was nothing to do behind a Whal-ley Avenue building surrounded by similar backs of buildings. I walked back and forth, now thinking not of Pekko but of Gordon, who had sniffed at the idea that Pekko had a business at all. When I thought of Pekko again, I wondered if what I owed him was a con-fession, and I almost laughed at that idea. The last thing he needed was the pain of learning what I'd done and hoped to continue to do. You need to be a lot purer than I to achieve anything by confessing. I decided at last that all I could do for Pekko was to be present—that was what he'd requested—and it was an odd decision for me. I assume I'm useless as I am but useful for what I do. Pekko seemed to need me to be useful as I am.

I returned the way I'd come, locking the door. Pekko looked up and looked down again when I came in. I began making phone calls having to do with my own work. I'd just do it there. An hour passed, a peaceful hour in its way. Then a woman came in, asking about an apartment. She didn't notice or didn't care about the pickets. Pekko wanted to take her to see the apartment, so I said, "I'll drive you both to your car," and the three of us locked up the office and departed. The woman talked about her own problems as we drove. I pulled up to the curb as soon as I turned the corner onto our street. I could see the pickets in the middle of the block, but we wouldn't have to encounter them. Pekko's car was near the corner, and I parked behind it. Pekko and I kissed lightly as he and the woman got out. Then I left my keys in the ignition and ran after him. I seized him around the waist, and he turned. Then we had the longest nonsexual hug of our life together. He kissed me heartily, and I kissed him back. "It'll work out," I said. What a wife would say.

"Oh, I know," he said and stolidly led his new tenant to his car, while I didn't immediately return to mine but walked the other way, to say, a bit hysterically, to Daphne, "You're half right, but so what?"

"I don't mean anything personal, Daisy," she called, "especially to you."

I got into my car and drove to Gordon's office, stopping to pick up a sandwich.

"What did you mean 'such as it is'?" I said.

"I assume Pekko's business is not entirely legitimate," Gordon said.

"You think he's a crook?"

"I've always thought Pekko Roberts was a crook."

"Well, he's not."

"I admire your loyalty." I sat down in the archive to figure out what to think, what to say, and the phone rang. While I spoke, he waved and left. It was all I could do not to drop the receiver and chase him. He—or he and I—had brought me to a sense of power-lessness such as I do not remember experiencing before in my life.

"I'm sorry, I'll call you back," I said to the person on the line and hung up, then sat down on the floor, leaning against the wall with my arms around my knees, the way Denise used to sit in rehearsals, when she seemed to want to keep herself quiet. I prevented myself from doing the only thing I knew how to do—following Gordon, running and grabbing someone who'd prefer to be left alone. When I let myself stand up, I could no longer think of anything important to do.

The next day, September 11, terrorists flew three hijacked airplanes into the World Trade Center and the Pentagon, and a fourth hijacked plane crashed before reaching a target. Pekko and I found out when we turned on the news to see if he was on it. There hadn't been anything about the rent strike the night before, and now there never would be. We watched for hours, seeing repeated films of the planes striking the towers, the towers falling. Once or twice, Pekko cried.

The *New Haven Register* ran a short piece about the rent strike that morning (quite short, because the big news in New Haven that day was supposed to be a mayoral primary). By September 12 nobody was thinking of Pekko the alleged slumlord. The Wednesday rehearsal was canceled—Katya said she couldn't do it—and I assumed, in those early days in which nothing seemed to be as it had been, that we'd cancel the play. Guiltily, I felt some relief. With guilty relief as well, I discovered as this public catastrophe claimed my attention that Gordon no longer could hurt me; I didn't care whether we continued our affair.

When the cast gathered on Sunday, everyone but me insisted the play should take place as planned. Denise said, "The president says we should lead our regular lives." David said, "We can't let those criminals stop us." I felt like saying, "Better to cancel," but didn't. We spent more time that night discussing September 11 than the life of TheaDora. When Muriel called me the next morning, she and I discussed September 11 for another twenty minutes. Finally, Muriel asked if I had any money around that might pay for TheaDora's bridal gown. We'd gone over budget. Katya had suggested a bedsheet. "A bedsheet will look like a bedsheet," Muriel said.

I said I'd pay. Neither of us felt like making a wedding dress, but we agreed to meet at Horowitz Brothers a few days later. In the meantime, days were passing, and on some of them I spent time at Gordon's office—more time than usual, because the conference was approaching. I had trouble believing that in a few weeks people would be thinking of murder in small cities instead of world terrorism, but I'd accepted money to put on this conference, and put it on I would. And my fall rush was delayed. When the weather turns cool, people decide it's time to straighten up, but not in the fall of 2001, or not for a few weeks. It seemed irrelevant to sit in Gordon's office, contemplating individual murders. Our criminals—I now felt oddly protective, almost indulgent, of the murderers our conference would consider—had believed what they did was momentous, and society had corroborated that belief.

I told Gordon I was afraid of nuclear war, but he scoffed. "You think you're the only person who doesn't want obliteration?" he said. "Or maybe you do want it. All this professional throwing away you do. All this snooping about killing."

He said that in bed. My indifference to our affair lasted less than a week. The first time I worked in his office after September 11, Gordon was absent. The next time he was there, and he was the first person I saw with whom I didn't immediately have a conversation about what had happened. He had questions about the conference, which he wanted answered as soon as he saw me. Then he came from his office into my room and put his hands on my breasts. I put mine on top of his and moved his.

"What's wrong?"

For a moment I thought that I could end the affair or not, that I was in charge. But I wanted his hands on my breasts, I just wanted the necessary ceremonies first. With everyone else, there had been the necessary ceremonies. Living close to New York, I kept hearing stories of people who barely escaped death. "Did anybody you know die?" I said.

"Yes," Gordon said.

"Oh, my God. Who?"

"A college classmate."

"How do you know he's dead?"

"A dozen e-mails. Now may I touch your breasts?"

"Okay." I felt happy and free for a few seconds, happy and free and guilty, enjoying the sensation of hands on my breasts—soon, under my shirt and bra—despite the death of Gordon's classmate. Then we agreed to drive in separate cars, as usual, to Gordon's house near the water, and as I drove, I began to feel bad again: incomplete, unfinished. I found myself in an imaginary conversation with Gordon, in which he made fun of Pekko the slumlord.

Bed was fine, but then we talked again about September 11. "Do you constantly imagine your friend jumping from the tower?" I said. "I wonder if he jumped."

"He wasn't a friend, and you know I don't imagine."

"Is that actually true, Gordon, or do you just say it?"

"It's true. My inner life is not pictorial."

"No wonder you don't like theater," I said.

"I do like theater, I just don't like bad theater, and good theater is rare. I don't have to imagine the play, however. I can see it."

"But you have to imagine that the stage is a living room."

"Oh, I can do that. I can pretend." He turned playful. "I shall pretend that Lazy Daisy is my lover, and I want to kiss her in as many locations as possible."

"Lazy Daisy?"

"Just a good rhyme. Although if you don't get that conference pulled together . . ."

"I'm doing it," I said.

"Interrupted by theater. Sort of theater." It was true that we were now holding three rehearsals a week, and once I'd rushed out of Gordon's office so as not to be late. The conference would take place two weeks before the play; by the time of the performance, this job would be done.

"Moments in the play are quite interesting," I said, wondering if Gordon and I would still be lovers after the conference.

"No good play was ever written by committee. Tell me if I'm wrong." He got out of bed, and in a moment I heard him in the shower, washing me off. I was still lying under the comforter in his chilly bedroom when he returned. "Hurry up, Lazy Daisy, I need to leave," he said.

❦

Charlotte and I had the requisite twenty-minute conversation about September 11. Then I said, "One of these days, I want to tell you the whole story."

"I might not like the whole story."

"There's that risk."

"Are you going to tell me now?"

"No."

❦

I wanted a wedding dress for Thea and Dora, though I had not wanted one for myself. (That's what my two weddings had in common: I wore what I had around.) I met Muriel at the fabric store and put more than a hundred dollars on my credit card for satin and netting, figuring in a discount from the store because we were a theater group and planned to donate ticket proceeds to the soup kitchen. (One of Roz's ideas. It gave us publicity. I said there would be no ticket proceeds, but she said of course there would.) It was pleasant to think about the likes of cloth and thread; had I believed that September 11 somehow destroyed everything minor? I wanted to see Muriel cut cloth recklessly again, this time with expensive satin between the blades of her shears. She hesitated when I proposed going home with her but then agreed. Again, we drank glasses of water in her kitchen with its silly appliqués, again I later went for Chinese takeout. The waiters wore T-shirts with American flags. At Muriel's house, we planned and cut and I followed instructions. The dress was just like the blue one, with a few improvements she'd thought up. It was easier this time, because we had the other dress to measure against. But as we worked, I was uneasy. Muriel looked angry when I happened to glance at her face in repose. I thought her talk was excessively patriotic. "So you think the United States should just destroy something quickly, and you don't care what?" I said.

"That's not what I think," said Muriel. She was in a chair at the desk, her back to me as I sat on the bed and hemmed with white thread. Muriel didn't approve of machine hemming. Now she turned her big head to look at me. "You're pretty quick to jump to conclusions, Miss Daisy."

"I'm sorry," I said. "Tell me again."

"Oh, I think what everybody thinks. I think what if it was my son, sitting at his computer, and that plane coming closer and closer."

"I don't think that, because I don't have kids," I said. "I think, What if it was me?"

"How come you never had kids?" Muriel said after a pause.

"It never happened."

"But you could have made it happen."

"I wanted kids," I said. "But always in the future. Like wanting to live in Paris someday."

"Fantasy kids."

"How many kids do you have, Muriel?"

"Just the two. LaShonda was almost like mine, for a while. My niece."

"How's that going?"

"Nice of you to ask," she said, but I thought she meant I should have asked before this. "I want my brother to bring her to the play, but he says that's just more of my craziness. He says the play will teach wildness. Even the play."

"The play doesn't teach wildness," I said.

"Of course not! We're doing it in a bunch of schools. Those schools wouldn't let us in if it taught kids bad stuff."

"What schools?" I said, putting down my needle. "I thought we were doing just the one performance."

"I don't know what schools. Some schools. Didn't Katya tell you?" She'd gone back to a complicated pinning and clipping operation at the desk.

"No."

"She's going to announce it at the rehearsal. I talked to her this morning. She's getting all kinds of calls. Schools. Public access TV."

"But I don't want to be on TV!" I said. I pictured Gordon flipping channels, suddenly hearing my voice shouting nonsense about two heads. "It's not that kind of play," I said. "It's fun, but we're amateurs. We don't know how to make up a play, and we don't know how to act."

"Oh, you're a ham," Muriel said, rising to find another task. "You have a fine time acting!" She worked faster than I did, and her hand didn't stop to gesture when she spoke. I was waving my needle in the air. "You do just fine," she said.

I said, "Katya can't sign us up without consulting us."

"She's consulting us," said Muriel. "She didn't give them definite dates."

"I don't want to do it."

"If you're so sure it's no good, how come you're buying satin? How come you're always pushing me around?"

The play, I now understood, was stupid. Gordon was right. I'd liked the friendship that had formed among the cast, the recurring thought that we wouldn't have known one another except for this odd project, the tension and laughter at rehearsals, our arguments, our stubborn different notions about two-headedness. I liked being in a dress with Muriel, learning not to trip when we walked and learning how to gesture so we looked as if our two outer arms belonged to the same body. I was titillated by the claustrophobia I couldn't help feeling when we were in the dress, by the intimate smell of Muriel's sweat and breath, the touch of her solid body when we collided. It was like an affair in some ways, like my intimacy with Gordon, someone else whose body I knew better than his mind. As we sat there, I wanted to climb into the new dress with Muriel. But the play wasn't professional, and Daisy Andalusia did nothing in public that wasn't at a professional level. And the play had nothing to do with the terrorist attacks. It wasn't inappropriate in the way a sex farce might be, but it was beside the point. Who would care, now—if anyone ever could have—about the wedding of a two-headed woman?

"I don't have time for a lot of performances," I said.

"You already put in the time. It would be a shame to do it only once."

"I don't want to do it," I said. "I don't want to do it."

"You're just a worrier. You'll be fine. It'll be fine."

"Muriel," I said, "I might not do it at all. I just realized that."

"Don't be silly," she said. "You're tired. I'll finish the hem. Go home."

And she hustled me out of there.

I didn't think about the play much in the next few days. For a while, my default mental topic had been September 11, but now, when my mind was not specifically occupied, it returned, as it had all summer, to Gordon: sometimes I remembered, sometimes I imagined good times, most often I imagined rejection or disapproval—disappointment in what I'd turned out to be. In my mind, we talked back and forth. He seemed to supervise my life now, and I'd imagine him commenting as I fed Arthur or did my laundry.

I hated the next rehearsal. I'd been trying to ignore uneasiness since we'd moved to the Little Theater; now I let myself feel it. Being in a real hall revealed shortcomings I hadn't noticed in the room where we'd worked before. Some of us sounded stilted, some moved sloppily. Our method of working made me frantic. By now, we had scripts in our laps (and of course some of us couldn't memorize), but many speeches were not yet fixed. Katya had explained how she worked, and her method was reasonable. She listened to the tapes, transcribing what moved the story along or struck her as worth keeping, skipping chitchat and inconclusive arguing. Then she rearranged what she had. She wasn't confident enough, though, so at every rehearsal she handed us not just the play to date but a sheaf of alternate speeches, about which we argued for too long. Jonah wanted to add abstract, preachy language. Denise tried to tone down conflict. I complained about wasting time but took up time fixing subtle grammatical errors and logical lapses that bothered nobody but me.

Now we were trying to run through the whole play at each

rehearsal. It was repetitious. There were too many scenes in which people chased each other around the stage, too many spats. "Stop putting your hands on your hips," I said to Chantal, who played TheaDora's mother. At least we'd figured out who would play whom.

"Maybe you're not the director," Chantal said.

"Sorry." But I was angry.

"Well, Daisy's right," said Katya. "But maybe everybody should leave the directing to me."

"Direct, then!" I said, but so quietly that nobody heard me except Muriel. We were lying on the dirty floor, playing pregnant women at the childbirth preparation class, and she reached over and pinched my arm. I thought Katya should point out that Chantal gave all speeches the same rhythm, that Denise always looked to the right when she spoke, that David talked too fast. Sometimes Ellen might whisper to Katya, or pass her a note, and then Katya might say something.

"How do you keep from getting angry?" I asked Ellen on our way out of the building.

"Why would I be angry?"

"You think this is working out?" I said.

"You don't?"

"No, I don't." Of course, her child was in it. She was applying the standards of a parent. We'd reached her car, and she put her hand on the door, turning back to note Justine and Cindy approaching. "I should get going," she said.

I felt outnumbered as I walked alone to my car, which was parked two blocks away. It was dark and shadowy under the still, thick leaves, and Afghanistan—which our country would be bombing shortly; a horrifying thought—seemed extremely far away. It was raining lightly. I loved my quiet city in the rain, loved not being afraid, though some might consider it risky for a woman to walk alone in a city at night. A few months earlier, I'd have used the couple of blocks of solitude to think about Gordon as if he was a sour ball I'd unwrapped and popped into my mouth. Now I struggled not to hear him, in my mind, pointing out that Denise always looked to the right, that David talked too fast.

❦

ut have they paid the rent?" I thought to ask Pekko. I was talking to him through the bathroom door. He'd just turned off the shower.

"Some have, some haven't."

He'd left the door unlocked, so I went in. He was drying his thick, compact body, jerking a towel back and forth across his behind. "Are you going to start eviction proceedings?" I said, closing the door behind me to keep the cooler air out. It was fall now, and chilly.

"That's not my style." Pekko rubbed his head and his beard.

"So your idea is that eventually they'll feel guilty and pay?"

"I don't care if they feel guilty. Eventually they'll pay. People do. Or they don't. If I can't pay the mortgage, I lose the building. But I won't starve."

"We won't starve."

"We won't starve." He dropped the towel and kissed me. His body was warm and steamy as he drew me closer, and I put my hands on his backside and felt aroused. We walked to the bedroom and lay down. Being with him temporarily soothed the pain in my mind over Gordon, who hadn't touched me all week.

☙

My mother dropped in on a Saturday, and I gave her coffee. "The rent strike might have been my fault," she said, leaning forward in the empty house with conspiratorial enthusiasm. Pekko was out, finishing repairs Daphne had never completed. "But it might have been worth it," she went on.

"All right, what?" I said.

"I said to Daphne, 'You may not wreck my daughter's marriage.'"

"Daphne wasn't wrecking my marriage," I said.

"So you tell me, but I saw how you were all summer."

"Mom, it was something else. I told you it was something else."

"Maybe it was something else, but it was also this. That girl wanted Pekko. She was going to lure him away. I talked her out of it, but of course that made her mad. She had to find a way to get back at him."

"Do you want a cookie?"

"Sure."

"It was a guy bothering me." I put the package of cookies on the table and sat down opposite her. "I told you."

"But you're married. That comes first, even if you don't want it to."

"It was a guy." My mother looked up at me, cookie in hand, one bite missing. I saw her consider understanding me. Then she chose against it. "Maybe you *thought* it was a guy," she said.

"Did you talk to the paper about the play?" I said.

"I'm working on it. I forgot all about it, that week."

"Of course. Nobody did anything, that week." But then I continued. "Listen, do me a favor and don't talk to the paper."

"Why not?"

"The play's not very good," I said. "If there's no audience, that might be better."

"If the rehearsals aren't good, the play will be great. That's a famous thing about the theater. Don't you know that?"

❦

In the past, when a man was upsetting me I'd tell Charlotte or my mother, and we'd have one of the two traditional talks women have: Relax, he's crazy about you, or Forget him, you're worth a dozen of him. This time I didn't tell anyone the whole story. Though every morning I read biographies in the *Times* of people who'd died on September 11, my selfishness thrived and I felt terrible about my own small trouble. I smoked for the first time in years, only in my car—not in the clean, pleasant house I shared with Pekko and Arthur. I didn't want Arthur breathing secondhand smoke. Toward Pekko I felt a brutal recklessness, mixed with tenderness. I cherished Pekko with a new fondness, unrelated to sex. But at the same time I felt dangerous and bad, an outlaw who cared scrupulously for her buddy or her horse but put them at risk by holding up the stagecoach at gunpoint. Gordon proposed sex once or twice during those weeks, and I agreed, and it was good, but I never stopped scrutinizing him—looking for evidence of another woman, other women—and that hint of a dismissive laugh was never completely absent when he spoke to me.

With the crash of the towers, New Haven murders had become quaint, the mischief of kindergartners, and at times, those weeks, the mail didn't work. I claimed nobody would come to the conference, but Gordon was confident. "E-mail's working," he said.

"I might drop out," I said to Muriel, again, at the next rehearsal. That night I couldn't endure being enclosed in that dress with her. I wanted to burst its seams and escape. I am half good, I reminded myself. I pictured myself throwing the play—a little package containing Katya, Jonah, David, Chantal, Denise, and Muriel, clutching one another in a bunch—over my shoulder. Then throwing the dress. I said, "I just don't have time." The clutter business had picked up again; I really didn't have time. Ellen and I had decided to draw up a written plan to deal with what she'd created, her household of frequently vacuumed artifacts, now arranged in categories her kids took pleasure in modifying and modifying again. Ellen's house was a weird but colorful museum, and mostly she and I toured it at our weekly appointments. After September 11 she created shrines all over the place—drawings by the children, postcards and souvenirs from New York. We'd look and talk and write things down. Working with her wasn't time-consuming, but my jobs added up. I was loyal to the conference, and loyal to my clutter business. I wouldn't throw paid work over my shoulder because I was unhappy about a man, but I might throw the play. "I might drop out."

"Daisy, this isn't you," said Muriel. "Why are you telling me this?"

"It might be what I want."

ordon had no complaints as I worked on the conference, but I thought he forgot about me when I wasn't there. He was right that registrations happened. We'd had a good response to the brochure. People who had always been interested in crime in small cities were still thinking about the subject, or were thinking again after a few days' break, and every day more of them e-mailed, faxed, or mailed in their forms. We had room for eighty. I'd planned to feel successful when we reached sixty-five, but one day we went from sixty-three to seventy all at once.

When we weren't making love, Gordon and I spoke as if we never did. We were generally alone but talked as if a stranger were present. Once I heard him on the phone, making a date with a woman. Maybe it was business. I blamed him for talking in my presence as if we weren't lovers, but I did it too. Within that context, he was friendly and full of warnings, advice, jokes, and the usual assurances that I needn't pay attention to his opinions.

"Six was too many for a panel discussion anyway," he said one morning, when I told him a speaker had canceled. "Five is fine. Make the fifth guy the moderator, and use the moderator someplace else. Who's the moderator for that one? Oh—me. Okay, put me on that afternoon session that nobody's signing up for, with the lady from Baltimore. Then you'll get her following plus my following."

"What will you do together?" I said, already jealous of the lady from Baltimore.

"You'll figure something out."

He was standing and I was sitting, and he grinned down at me almost lewdly, as if what I'd figure out would be pornographic, and as if he was taking a liberty, acting lewd with me, someone with whom he'd never been lewd. It was almost noon. With some unexpected free time, I'd gone to his office. Gordon wasn't there when I arrived. He came in as I was reading my e-mail, and the sound of his quick feet elated and frightened me. Now he said, "I've been thinking about Marie Valenti. That panel will be fine."

"I shouldn't have told you what Pekko told me."

"Why not?"

"You don't see why not?" I said. "I had no right to tell you, even though I know I can trust you."

"Trust me to do what?"

"To keep quiet, of course," I said.

"Don't worry," said Gordon. He walked to the window and adjusted the Venetian blind. The sun was strong. "I'd like to kiss you," he said, "but not go further."

"You mean ever?"

"No, just today."

I stood and met him at the window. Maybe that was why he'd closed the blind, though I didn't know who could see us. We kissed, and his tongue explored my mouth for a long time. I put my hand on his pants.

"I have some good ideas about what we could do now, but there isn't time," said Gordon. Then he said abruptly, "Shall I come to your play, Daisy?"

"No."

"If you weren't ashamed of it, you'd want me to come."

He seized me and kissed me even longer than before. "Could we maybe have a quick time somewhere, after all?" he said, looking around the office, which contained no soft furniture. "I have a meeting at one. We can't go to my house."

So I took him to mine, for the first time, feeling as if I'd lost a contest. He didn't like Arthur, who barked at him. "You're jealous," I said.

"Possibly."

We lay in the bed I shared with Pekko. I felt bad, but it was quick. We dressed, then Gordon held me tightly and I pressed my face into his chest. Hugs are metaphors for attachment, but we stepped apart, and he left me standing in the bedroom while he let himself out of the house. I was alone, at an hour I'm rarely home. I didn't feel like lunch. I checked my e-mail. I played solitaire. I had nothing to do for an hour. I left a message on Katya's answering machine, withdrawing from the cast of the play.

What were you doing when you paid for that fabric, buying your way out?" Muriel shouted on the phone. "You think all we want is your money? You pay for that cloth, you can just go?"

"No. It had nothing to do with that."

"Are you one of those white people who think if they just hand over some money, that's all they have to do to fix the world?"

"That play isn't fixing the world, Muriel," I said. "Did you see the schedule Katya sent? I don't have that kind of time, and I don't think the play is interesting enough to take up the time of all those audiences."

"So you're going to leave the rest of us to do it without you—so it's even worse?"

"It'll be fine. Ellen will play Dora."

"She is not you."

"Of course she's not me, but she has more experience acting than I do. She'll be great."

"She is not you. This is not right, Daisy."

"The play is not right," I said. "We should all drop out and forget about it. It was fun rehearsing, we learned a lot, and that's enough of an accomplishment."

"You don't mean that, and I don't want to hear you say it," Muriel said. "I'm not going to talk to you anymore. I got plenty of trouble today, and I don't need more. I called because I just didn't believe it when Katya called me."

"What kind of trouble?"

"LaShonda was arrested. I got to go, Daisy."

෴

No, Daisy," said Ellen. "I'm *not* glad. I'll make an adequate Dora, but I'd prefer not to do it."

"Is Justine mad?" I said.

"Of course. She says I've been conspiring to crowd her out. She says between Cindy and me, nobody notices her. It's not true, because she looks so strange, but she can't know that."

"I'm sorry to dump it on you, Ellen." I wouldn't have said Justine looked *strange*. Well, maybe.

"That's what people do. They dump things on me."

"I was supposed to help you with that problem," I said.

"That's right."

"You still want to know what's been going on with me, don't you?"

"I think you'd do better to tell me, Daisy."

We were on the phone. It was late at night. She'd called me. I lay on the bed in the dark. Pekko wasn't home. I delayed and changed the subject three or four times, and then I said I was tired and hung up.

🐿

I dropped out of the play," I said to Gordon. We were in the office. "Then I can cross it off my calendar."

"You were planning to go?"

"Only to see you."

"I decided you were right. It's not very good. I wish they'd just give it up."

"Are they angry with you for dropping out?"

"Very angry."

He picked up a notebook as my phone rang. We were in the office. "Meeting," he said, pointing to the door as I reached for the receiver. Hearing his quick footsteps on the stairs outside, I was angry with myself for expecting to be praised for dropping out. The person on the phone was the caterer, with a question about tables and another about muffins.

But even while being distracted by practical questions and by Gordon himself, I had not lost interest in the subject matter of the conference. I kept saying it was about small cities, but the city I cared about was New Haven, and I wanted something for me from

our three days of talk. I wanted to learn that New Haven was, somehow, despite everything, all right. I wanted confirmation that I was
correct when I sensed neighborliness and health, up to a point,
whenever I arrived in New Haven from another place. I didn't want
the conference to make fun of my faith in one small, grubby city; I
didn't want it proved that I should adopt Gordon's unsurprised
shrug, his cynical certainty that he wouldn't be impressed. Pekko
was a complicated character, but in some ways his faith was entire
and childlike. In the contest between naïveté and knowingness,
Pekko was naïve, and I wanted him to win. I wanted the smart, pessimistic speakers we'd invited and the smart, pessimistic audience to
conclude that we in New Haven were managing, that we weren't
killing one another as often as we might have, or behaving with fla-
grant injustice on every occasion when a killing occurred. I wanted
Pekko to hear about the conference, and to understand that I was
not irresponsibly trying to bring trouble to the city in which he
lived and did his work.

৳

The conference—Murder in Small Cities: Who, How, Why?—
was well-attended, and reporters showed up for some sessions,
but we don't get the *Register* at home, and if Pekko read the article
headlined SCHOLARS DEBATE VALUE OF PRISON, which recounted a discussion about the efficacy of long prison sentences in preventing
murder, he didn't mention it. I had listened, inward questions unan-
swered, then left the room when my cell phone vibrated.

The session on Malik Jones was impassioned. The main speaker, a
black sociologist, repeated what those of us who lived in town had

long known—that the issue was not the shooting as much as the
pointless police chase leading to it. I had expected that a Boston
police detective, speaking next, would disagree, but he concurred,
which made the hour satisfying in a sense but repetitious. Yet, sitting in a dark corner of the auditorium, away from the participants,
who quarreled and praised and questioned their way through the
days—real persons in jackets and ties or jeans or pantsuits, who'd
replaced the theoretical audience I'd been working with for
months—I felt, during the question period, something large. A
remark by one of the speakers—I wasn't even sure which—made
me imagine Malik Jones's death in a way I never had before: his
young, scared, defiant vitality, and then, when the adults wouldn't
give up—and he couldn't—his ceasing to be. I stood, trembling a
bit, feeling nothing but the terrible fact that human beings die, and
some too soon, that nature doesn't care—there are enough left to
continue to populate the earth—and also that each loss is as bad as
anything could be, that the death of young people is something to
weep for, over and over again. Gordon waited for me in the aisle, and
we walked together to the back of the auditorium, an old-fashioned,
particularly Yale-like setting, with mullioned windows and scarred
old furniture. I almost didn't want to be with him. I wanted to be
alone, to think of what I'd just thought, to imagine murder.

"I didn't think it would fit, and it didn't," Gordon said.

I didn't answer. Finally I said, "It needed to be talked about."

"You've said that, Daisy," he said and briefly put his arm around
my shoulders. I couldn't help but lean into him, like a child—or a
lover—and my body flared with erotic pain. Gordon pulled me
tighter yet while the participants, who'd been gathering their folders and interrupting one another's progress toward the exits, began

to walk toward us. Then he dropped his arm. I stumbled and recovered. Nobody looked surprised at our awkward embrace, if anyone saw it. It was a collegial gesture, what friendly cohosts do all the time. Maybe people thought we hugged clumsily because we were so professional and shy that we'd never touched before. Someone came up to me to ask about restaurants. I didn't cry out as Gordon waved and departed before she and I had finished speaking.

ॐ

That night Pekko and I went out to eat. We went to Amato's on State Street, a plain Italian restaurant where there was always a table of cops in the corner. I drank red wine and pleated my paper place mat with its map of Italy, and Pekko had two birch beers with his eggplant parmigiana. We talked about the conference. I had my cell phone, but it didn't ring. I enumerated all the calls I might get. The next morning—I didn't say this—we'd be holding the last session, the one on Marie Valenti's murder. I talked about our decision to serve fruit salad along with muffins and coffee, though it required plates and spoons. I talked about Gordon's quick, funny introductions of speakers.

Pekko was quiet for a long time, eating. Then he said, "You think you know about murder in New Haven."

He hadn't criticized the conference in a long time.

"I think I know how to order fruit salad and muffins."

"These murders you're talking about," he said—and I wondered if he'd somehow seen a schedule and knew we'd be discussing Marie Valenti in the morning—"these are the showcase murders, the fancy murders that get all the attention."

"You mean when black people murder other blacks, that doesn't get attention," I said. "We had quite a discussion about that yesterday afternoon."

"It doesn't have to do with race. You think everything has to do with race. You don't know who gets murdered in this town, who doesn't—it's not always in the paper. It happens, and nobody knows, or a few people know, but nobody says."

"But *you* know," I said with some irritation. I was tired.

"Sometimes I know," he said. "Your little Denny Ring, the supposed druggie. He was murdered."

"Denny was murdered?" I said.

"Dennis Ring was murdered. I can't prove it, but I know it. He was not taking drugs—not then. He did not inject himself with an overdose. People knew he was living in the store, and he talked too much. He was a courier who knew names and talked a lot, and somebody decided to inject him with an overdose. That's how he died."

"How do you know?"

"I knew before it happened. I tried to stop it. I went to people who knew and tried to stop it."

"So what is your point?" I said through sobs. "Why are you telling me this? You know about every murder in the city of New Haven forever? You go around with all these secrets, just to make yourself feel good?"

"Nobody could prove it. There was no reason to ruin *my* life, talking about it. I'm sorry I made you cry, Daisy. My point is that it's more complicated than you know—more complicated than Skeetling knows."

I pushed my plate of meatballs aside and dropped my head on

my arms to cry. I'd done nothing to help Denny, all those years ago. I could do nothing for anyone. I cried for his solitude, alone with a murderer. Denny was almost always alone. That was why he was irresistible. He told me no secrets—though he talked all the time— and I told him none. I never had a phone number for him. He didn't even clutter my address book. "My conference isn't bad," I said finally, "even if the people talking don't know everything. Even then."

"Let's go home and walk Arthur," Pekko said. "I'm sorry. I should have told you years ago, or kept my mouth shut."

The leaves were turning and falling now, and our feet crushed leaves as we walked, with Arthur pulling to the left and right, sniffing, pissing on piles of leaves. The night was breezy, and the leaves on the trees were dry enough now to rustle. I had put on a heavy sweater when we stopped at the house for Arthur, and I pulled the sleeves down over my hands. We walked through Goatville to East Rock Park, and along the path at the edge of College Woods. The moon was out, and it was easy to see. We didn't talk. I thought of Denny, times I'd been in this park with him. He liked to sit on the swings. He liked what he called "kid things." When I too sat on the swings one night, Denny said, "You're like a kid in some ways, Daisy, but not in my way."

"How am I like a kid?" I said.

"You're by yourself."

"Kids aren't by themselves," I protested. "They're surrounded. Family, teachers . . ."

"You felt surrounded because you were all by yourself," Denny said as we swung—sometimes parallel, sometimes one up, one

down or one forward, one back. "When I was a kid, I didn't feel surrounded. I felt *with* people."

"But now you're alone."

"Not the way you are."

"You're the most alone person I know!" I said, all those years ago.

Now Pekko and I sat down on a bench. A few years ago, workers took out trees and installed two benches at a place on the path
where the river turns. The view is surprisingly grand—even in
the dark—as the river comes toward you. We sat until I was cold.
Pekko talked about a dog he'd had as a boy, who ran away. He
stroked Arthur, who wouldn't have run away but was firmly
attached to his leash. We stood up. "I shouldn't have told you,
lovey," he said.

"I'm not perfect, either," I said but gave no details.

When we got home, it was too late for the news—we'd have to
trust that there was nothing new and big—not in New York, Washington, or Afghanistan—and we went to bed quickly. I fell asleep
while Pekko was still brushing his teeth.

♋

So I slept late and had to hurry in the morning, but it's only a
short drive from my house to the Yale building where the conference was held. I glanced at the *Times;* although people were worried about anthrax cases in Florida and New York, nothing
significant had happened since the day before. I heard a weather
forecast and one song while driving to the conference. When I
reached the lobby of the building where we'd held most of our ses-

sions, the caterer was setting out rows of muffins on trays, and a few early participants, talking together with cups of coffee in their hands, were eyeing them. A man squatted near the wall, the *Times* open in front of him.

I answered a question the caterer put to me. The door crashed open behind me, and I knew it was Gordon from the urgency of the sound. When I turned he was standing still, squinting in the dim light, but then he came toward me swiftly. He had a newspaper under his arm, and I could see that it was the *New Haven Register,* a paper he ordinarily bypassed. "Guilty to making it happen. Not guilty to making it happen today," he said. He seemed excited—happy—but a little uncomfortable.

"What?"

"Haven't you seen the paper?"

I tried to remember if I'd seen a headline on my way over. I hadn't passed a box. He handed it to me. I still was more interested in the moment his hand touched mine as he thrust the newspaper at me than in what he wanted to show me. Yet I also felt a peculiar, new discomfort—noting his discomfort—and some fear: had something unbearable happened, too late for the *Times?* Then I had a sudden crazy thought that a decade late the newspaper was reporting the murder of Dennis Ring, young, white non–drug user, living in a frozen yogurt store that hadn't existed for years and years.

The headline announced the arrest of a suspect—Edmund Doyle, said the first sentence of the article—in the ancient Marie Valenti murder case.

"I didn't make it happen this way on purpose," Gordon was saying. "It's going to look like a cheap trick. Are you too busy counting muffins to talk for a minute about how we can work it in *without* making it seem cheap? Of course we have to include it. The worst thing—do you agree? Tell me if I'm wrong—would be to lead up to it and then announce it as a surprise. And I suppose it would backfire—somebody would have seen the paper and would bring it up too early."

"You went to the police?"

"Well, of course I did. I don't know why you didn't. I don't know why Pekko didn't, long ago. Well, I suppose there was a certain loyalty there, but he could have made it happen without doing it himself. Maybe that's why he told you. Maybe that's what he wanted to do—make it happen without making it happen."

"No," I said. I don't think I've ever been less able to speak and make sense, but Gordon wasn't listening. I didn't ask myself whether somebody should have turned Edmund in. At the time all I took in was the difference I had made. What I had said—what *had* I said?—had made it possible for Edmund to be arrested.

"But I didn't know his last name," I said.

"Oh, that was easy. My contact said they had a list of everybody who'd been in school with her. But there was no reason to connect him, no more than any of the others. I guess there weren't many Edmunds. Finding him was easy, once they knew."

The arrest had been made on the basis of fingerprints, which they had kept, of course. Edmund had been fingerprinted ten years ago for a job. That was long after the active search had ended.

We'd walked through the corridor and into a stairwell. Time was passing. "So," said Gordon, "I'm sorry if this isn't what you had in mind. But I think the main thing right now is the morning session. What do you think?"

"Did you mention Pekko?" I said. "Is Pekko going to be arrested?"

"I did not mention Pekko. I said I had a friend who had a friend. I refused to give names, other than mine. Pekko won't have to be a witness—unless he chooses to, of course."

I thought of Daphne's house. If she recognized Edmund's picture, she could turn Pekko in. Pekko had been Edmund's teacher. It would be easy for the police to prove that Pekko knew Edmund, and not too hard to prove that he was sheltering Edmund. I didn't know what the penalties were for obstructing justice, but I understood at last that because of what I had done, and because of Pekko's unique notions of right and wrong, not only could Edmund go to prison but maybe Pekko could as well.

"But Edmund was doing good work. It was a single, terrible moment in his life. There was no point in ruining it now. What good will it do? Will it bring her back?"

"Oh, Daisy, that's nonsense, of course I had to turn him in. You're proposing a totally chaotic legal system, in which everybody has his own philosophy and that's how we make decisions."

"But didn't you think of what it will be like for him, for his parents?"

"I don't think that way." I stepped away from him, from his gray, floppy hair and his pointed, black eyebrows.

"I have to leave," I said.

"We're putting on an event here," said Gordon.

"I changed the catering order yesterday, so you'll need a new invoice from her." I touched Gordon's sleeve and pulled my hand away. I gathered myself, my error-prone self. It was over. It was over. How could it be over? It was over. I couldn't. I didn't have to.

"What? What?" Gordon shouted. "Where do you think you're going? Daisy!"

"I'm leaving," I said. I did have to. I could turn around. I could walk.

"And I suppose what we've had is meaningless to you?" he said.

"No, it's not," I said. I turned around and touched the tiled wall, to push myself off, the way a swimmer pushes herself off from the side of the pool. I walked through the door to the lobby, and through the lobby, pretending not to hear a question someone called to me. I watched myself to see if I'd turn again, but I didn't.

Walking to my car, I was thinking of Daphne. I'd have to find Daphne and persuade her to keep her mouth shut. But Daphne was not going to be persuaded, and by talking to her I might let her know there was something to think about. I got into my car and drove through the downtown traffic, up Orange Street on that quiet morning, when nobody was out except women with strollers, old people going to the markets, and kids from Cross High School, with backpacks and baggy pants. I didn't make the turn to my own street. I kept driving. Orange Street passes the high school and goes straight into East Rock Park, straight to the base of the hill—the hill of stones—and if you cross the river and turn left, which I did, passing the trail where I walked with Arthur, you can drive a loopy road under trees—lots of color just then—through woods and around the mountain, up to the top of East Rock, where there's a parking lot, a Civil War monument, a place to look at New Haven and Long Island Sound, and meadows where families picnic on hot days. On a weekday morning in October, nobody was present. I did not jump off the cliff. I parked and sat on a bench and looked at the city below me, the lines of houses and trees, the bigger buildings downtown, the green, the water.

I thought about what I'd learned at the conference. I'd learned that murder is dreadful, disgusting, and real. And appealing. I'd never murder anybody, but I did like to get rid of things, and maybe that was what had given me the nerve to get rid of my affair, which might as well have been stuffed into garbage bags and dropped off at the Salvation Army. My body seemed to have nothing inside it. I drove down the hill and stopped for coffee at Lulu's. It was warm enough to sit outside in the sun, but the morning rush was over, and nobody I knew was there.

☙

As I write on my laptop at our kitchen table in the evening, in the hot, dry summer of 2002, Pekko walks in, coming from a meeting of a neighborhood group he belongs to. "Last month, in this area, no crime of any type was reported," he says, leaning over to stroke Arthur, who has learned not to jump but is frantic with self-discipline and joy, seeing Pekko for the first time in two hours. "This month there were three break-ins. But the murder rate is the lowest in decades."

☙

I drove to Ellen's house. I knew she'd be at work, but I still had a key. I wanted to be in her house, with its intricate arrangement of uselessness. I wanted to walk from room to room and touch things, look at things. Instead of a dreary, cluttered house, it was now a zany, cluttered house. I saw she'd been busy yet again. The shrines to New York were giving way to other shrines, maybe shrines to complexity. A battered end table I hadn't seen before held a collection of old kitchen utensils—ladles, tongs, tea strainers, wooden spoons. A shelf in the hall held more odd pieces of china than I remembered seeing there before. The floors were still mostly impassable. Soon dust would take over. Nobody could keep things clean here.

I heard a key in the lock, and Ellen came in. I stepped forward and said her name, so she wouldn't think I was a prowler. She started anyway. "I thought you were busy all week."

"I walked out of the conference."

"You left the play *and* the conference? What's wrong with you?"

"Different reasons."

"Did you come here today to meet Gordon Skeetling?"

"No. That's over," I said.

She looked doubtful, standing in the archway between the living and dining rooms, her pocketbook over her shoulder, confronting me as if she in her jacket were the visitor and I in my shirtsleeves dwelt there. She took off the jacket and put away the purse. "I came home for lunch, and to do a little crying," she said.

"Over the man?"

"I don't know. I'm still crying about the World Trade Center. Come in the kitchen and I'll make lunch."

Ellen's complicated house now constantly shifted meanings, as she did. As she walked through the rooms, the objects complemented and enlivened her indefiniteness, so I had the sense of someone whose surroundings matched her, but in a somewhat scary way. "Are you tired of living like this?" I said.

"I'm tired of living," said Ellen.

"What should I do?"

"Distract me with your story."

"Is that a suicide threat?"

"No, I'm a mother."

"Some mothers do it."

"Not this one."

"Getting help?"

"Getting help. Not to worry. Distract me, distract me," she said.

She'd distracted me, but now the heft of the morning's events stopped my mouth. She seemed to know my story already, so I told it to her, told her the story I've been telling here, leaving out what she already knew—herself, the play—but including, without details, Pekko's connection to Edmund and what had happened. This time, though I was sure that now I had before me someone I could trust, I swore her to secrecy before saying that Pekko had known all along who killed Marie Valenti. "It's funny," I said. "From the time I first met him, I knew there was a secret. Maybe that's why I married him. I knew he knew something that everyone wanted to know."

"I won't tell," she said, and as far as I know she hasn't, though if Pekko knew I'd told her, I can't imagine what he'd think. Of course, that's not all he doesn't know. Or so I believe.

As I spoke, Ellen took a container of eggs and a bunch of spinach from the refrigerator and made us an omelet, beating the eggs in a bowl she placed on the only bare spot on her counter. "Is Gordon why you gave up the play?" she said. "Because he might phone when you were at a rehearsal? I used to stay home, hoping Lou would call. It's shameful."

"That's an old-fashioned reason. I have a cell phone." But Gordon never used it. He said he hated the sound of cell phones. He said there were gaps in my sentences.

"Or because he thinks the play is stupid?"

"It *is* stupid."

"In fact, it's not," said Ellen. "I wouldn't be in it if it were."

"You let everything happen to you," I said.

I don't remember everything Ellen said about the play, my inextricable connection to the play. She didn't say that I'd be sorry because I'd hate my disloyalty, or that I'd be sorry because I'd miss my friends and their fun. She may have said the connection existed whether I wanted it or not. "Thea can't leave Dora," she may have said. "Dora can't leave Thea." After a while she became tedious. I waved her quiet, and left quickly.

☙

As I entered my house—after driving many miles up I-91, fast, into Massachusetts, then back, fretting against the traffic—I didn't hear anything. I was glad Pekko wasn't there. Arthur came to greet me as usual. I scratched behind his ears and grasped his big, black feet to lower him when he placed his paws on my chest. The mail was on the table. Pekko was home, or had been home. I heard a sound and climbed the stairs. A light was on in the bathroom, but the door was ajar. "Pekko?" I called.

"I'm in the tub. Come in."

The bathtub is against the wall at a right angle to the door, so when I paused in the doorway he was looking straight at me. Uncomfortable—still in a jacket in the warm bathroom—I had to stop myself from reaching to outline the doorjamb with my fingers. Gordon's gesture.

"Did you turn him in, Daisy?" Pekko said. He had filled the tub as full as possible, and his thick limbs and stubby penis shifted and wavered under the water. His beard rested on its surface.

For many miles I'd been planning this conversation. I don't remember what I'd decided, but I told the truth. "No. Gordon Skeetling turned him in. But it was my fault. I told Gordon."

"I thought it was Daphne."

"Daphne knows?" I said.

"I told her ten years ago. I never should have told anybody. I was sure it was Daphne when I saw the paper, but she came to the office to tell me she didn't. She knew he stayed in the house sometimes. She said, 'I know right from wrong.'"

I stood silent for a long time. "So you figured I didn't know right from wrong."

"I didn't know what else to think. Nobody else knew."

"I'm sorry I told Gordon."

I waited for Pekko to ask why I did it—and I don't know what I'd have said—but he didn't. He sat silent in the tub, his arms under the water. He had no washcloth or soap. His face looked sweaty. The water must have been quite hot.

In the car, I'd imagined putting my arms around him and saying "I'm sorry" into his neck, but hugging him when he was in the tub would have been ludicrous. Another woman might have knelt and put out her arms and gotten wet, but I didn't.

"Sending Edmund Doyle to prison accomplishes nothing," he said at last. "It does only harm, no good."

"You could argue that upholding the law accomplishes something," I said, even though it was what Gordon would have said. "You could argue that he did commit murder."

"I don't see things that way," Pekko said.

I left Pekko in the tub and walked downstairs to feed Arthur and start supper. I wondered momentarily if Pekko would leave me. I'd done two wrongs, I thought, as I peeled an onion. I had told Gordon about Edmund, and I'd quit the play for fear of embarrassment. But I'm the woman who's good half the time. I couldn't turn into someone three quarters good. Still, I didn't want to reduce my average. That night I called Katya to ask for my part back. She was glad. Angry but glad. "Ellen and Muriel wasn't a combination that worked," she said, after sounding angry for a while.

We rehearsed almost every night for the final two weeks, and at last we had a play, which most of us memorized. Denise spoke in a singsong when given a script, but Katya was able to get her to improvise over again, so what she said came out slightly different each time but sounded natural. The play was to be performed with no backdrop but with several large, colorful props made by Daphne and friends of hers—cheerfully gnarled trees—and objects borrowed by Ellen, who knew how to get objects. Katya recorded some songs, and the play began with music. There was music as well in between scenes, and of course at the wedding, about which we had some disagreement. Tradition won out: we had Wagner for the processional and Mendelssohn for the recessional. "Definitely traditional," I had said, my first day back. I was instantly full of opinions about the play, once again. I suppose I should have been humble, but I wasn't. When I first walked in, Muriel took my head in her hands and held it so tightly it hurt, for a long time, staring at me. Then she ducked my head roughly into her chest and kissed my hair.

"It's funnier if it's traditional," I persisted, later that same evening.

"Is the wedding supposed to be funny?" said Jonah.

He was upset when he realized that Thea and Dora were having secular weddings. "It needn't be Christian, if that's a problem," he said to me, and I realized that he'd figured out I'm Jewish, the only Jewish cast member. "We could have a rabbi perform the ceremony if you'd rather," he continued. "But I think a religious wedding would be more seemly, don't you?"

"In real life, I've been married twice, both by judges," I said, and Jonah looked disappointed, but the list of characters already included a judge (who was formerly a doctor), and we thought it would be confusing to have Denise play a minister, priest, or rabbi at that point. The cast also included a minister, Jonah, in the baptism scene, but by the time we reached the wedding, Jonah was one of the grooms—mine. We did add a nondenominational prayer, to be spoken by the only adult actor who was not in the wedding, Chantal. Chantal could sing gospel, it turned out, so we added a gospel song at the end of the wedding, just before Mendelssohn. It made me choke up every time, but I didn't have to speak at that point.

Katya had come up with a donation from a printer, and a friend willing to design a poster, and my mother did a good job with publicity. A week before the play, stories ran in the *Register* and the *Advocate*, and posters appeared in store windows all over town. We had eight performances altogether. I knew I wouldn't feel bad about Gordon—not truly bad—until they were all over. It was good to postpone that pain (which, in its time, was considerable). Now I cared only about the play. I had vowed to behave myself, returning, but from the first I was arguing my complicated positions as forcefully as ever and taking people aside to give them hints. Chantal habitually said "flustrated" for "frustrated." She looked hurt when I mentioned it, and at the next rehearsal she still said "flustrated."

"It's not important," whispered Muriel firmly, when I tensed up as that happened. We had just climbed into the blue dress and were pacing back and forth in the back of the theater, feeling our way into the rhythm of our double walk.

"I'm cranky," I said. Then, "Pekko's mad at me." He was distant, not angry. Muriel and I had a little time. Now that the parts were fixed, we weren't needed much at the beginning of the play. Chantal and David played TheaDora's parents, Denise was the doctor and the teacher. Before we got dressed, Muriel and I were extra students in the childbirth preparation class, and neighbors who commented on the two-headed baby.

"What did you do?" Muriel said.

"How do you know I did something?"

"I thought you might have." Pace, pace, pace. We were in sync now, but we seemed to be marching. That evening, we were working on a stroll. Muriel took my hand, underneath the dress, and we strolled together.

A two-headed person would not have told Pekko's secret, I thought. People are supposed to have two heads. I said, "I gave away a secret. It hurt someone."

"That wasn't right, Daisy."

"No." Why wouldn't a two-headed person have told? Because if she simply couldn't keep quiet, she could tell the other head.

"But he'll forgive you," Muriel said.

I tried to keep that, tried to maintain the resolve I formed just then. The rehearsal took a long time. "Forgive," I said to myself, several times, and when I walked into the living room that night, I said, "Please forgive me."

"Daisy," Pekko said, turning off the TV and dropping the remote. Then he started to cry while Arthur greeted me. "If only I'd kept my mouth shut," he said. He stood and sobbed without reaching for a tissue. Finally I brought him the box.

"Maybe they won't send him to prison," I said.

"They'll send him to prison. Look, I have to forgive both of us." He blew his nose. "My friend goes to prison, and I shed a tear and go to bed with my pretty wife," he said. "It's kind of disgusting."

"He did commit murder," I said. I couldn't help it. I can learn, I can change—but only so much.

"He was a boy. He didn't know what he was doing."

"Then it won't be first degree."

"I don't know."

"Pekko, do you want to stop being married?" I said, feeling afraid.

For a long time, he didn't speak. Then he said, "Sometimes it doesn't seem to work."

"So . . ."

"Do you want to end it?" he said.

"No," I said. "No, I never wanted to end it."

"Then we won't," said Pekko.

We did go to bed. It did feel as if we'd been let off easy, though we hadn't committed murder and Edmund had. You may feel—whoever you may be—that I should have taken the opportunity to tell Pekko exactly why I had told Gordon. I did not tell him.

And that's where I stopped writing, about a week ago. Then Stephen called. He called when I stood up to fix myself a cup of coffee after the words "tell him." He was coming to town to see Roz the next day. I told him I'd been writing.

"Oh. That thing you're writing."

"That thing I'm writing."

"I want to see it."

I don't know what I'll do with this thing I'm writing, but at that moment showing it to someone, someone I loved, was enticing. "All right," I said, and the next day I printed out everything I had and dropped it off at Roz's. I saw Stephen for just a little while; I had dinner plans he persuaded me not to break. I think he likes being alone with my mother, whom he takes to a restaurant, lately, when he comes. Roz is a year and a half older than she was at the beginning of this narrative, half a year older than when I began writing, and like a child she is noticeably older, now, each year. It was a warm day. When I arrived, they were on their way into her house. They'd been sitting on chairs they'd carried outside. Roz walked while Stephen hovered over her, turned back to fuss with the chairs, watched to make sure Roz made it up the two steps into her front door before he turned again to retrieve them. I was impatient, and I also thought maybe he was right to watch carefully. I handed him my big package. "What's that?" said Roz.

"Something about that conference I did," I said half truthfully.

After that I didn't add to the narrative for days, and I wondered whether I should have shown it to my brother. He called tonight. "It's interesting," he said.

"I didn't mean you were a loser, Stephen."

"Oh, I am, in a way."

"You read the whole thing?"

"Daisy," he said, "I don't think you understand it. You felt powerless but you had the power, you were the one who had the power. That man wasn't breaking up with you."

"Didn't I say that somewhere? Don't I understand that?"

"But that's what you did wrong," said my brother. "You failed to know you could make things happen. That you could hurt."

"You don't mean Gordon?"

"Edmund Doyle. What happened to Edmund Doyle?"

"The trial hasn't happened yet," I said.

"Why did you tell?" said Stephen. I didn't answer, but I thought, I told the secret to keep everyone away. I was a whore who doesn't know the name of the man in bed, a killer who turns a person to a thing.

❦

The houselights went down to complete darkness, and the audience hushed. Piano music by Schumann: happy-sad. Stage lights.

"Did you sign up for childbirth preparation?" said the husband of the pregnant woman.

"Shut up, I'm cooking."

The doctor was no help. "May I dance? May I eat?" said the woman.

"None of the above."

"Leave me alone," said the wife. "I want to suffer."

"I'm scared I'll kill the baby," said the husband.

The doctor disappeared under the wife's dress and came out holding a two-headed baby. The baby's arms were slightly bent, and her legs were cutely plump. She wore a yellow nightgown. She had one dark head with black hair and staring black eyes, and one fair head with yellow hair and staring blue eyes.

The doctor said, "She's going to die. Better not love the baby."

A neighbor said, "If you nurse only one head, maybe the other will drop off." A minister baptized the baby. "We must examine our thoughts about this child," he said. "We must destroy prejudice in our hearts." An uncle proposed cutting off one head. But the baby grew older and learned to talk. "I don't like being squashed together with somebody," said Thea, a forceful, dark head in a red dress.

"You think I like it?" said Dora, a cool, blond head.

"I don't want you breathing on my face."

"I hate you."

Thea said, "I hate me too. I don't want to be the same person as this white girl! Nobody understands what this is like!"

"We have to go to the bathroom," said Dora, now grown, in a big blue dress with Thea.

"You think I don't know that?" Thea said.

The foreman at the construction project said, "You are not only a woman, you are of mixed race!"

"We are two women," said Dora.

"No, we are a woman," Thea said.

And each fell in love, one with the foreman, one with another worker. They fought and left the job, brokenhearted. As they wandered in a forest, Dora witnessed a murder. The prosecutor and the defense attorney were their old boyfriends. The judge was the old doctor. The doctor said they were twins.

"It's not exactly a happy ending," said Thea, "but at least we can marry two men."

Music by Wagner. A double wedding. "Do all of you promise to live as decently as you can in an extremely tight situation?" asked the judge.

"We do," said the brides and grooms.

"And how about you in the audience?" the judge continued, stepping away from the bridal couples, because in the end, though I still wanted no moral, I was outvoted. "You're also more closely connected than you might want to be. You also can't get away from one another. Do you also promise to live together as decently as you can?"

"We do," said the audience. Mendelssohn. A recessional march, led by the brides and grooms, joined by brave or exhibitionistic members of the audience. Applause. Pekko and Roz watched from a back row, then joined the procession, she smiling, he unsmiling. Charlotte and Philip clapped, too shy to stand up and march. I clutched Muriel's hand, wondering how I'd do without her when the performances were over, fearing I wouldn't keep her. When the music stopped and the audience dispersed, Ellen came to hug us first. Maybe I'd keep Ellen, in the fast approaching future. Muriel's moist body pulsed with excitement next to me. Her hand held mine, then let it go, and in the emptying theater we stood beside each other, tired and hot inside our big, white wedding gown.

Acknowledgments

Warm thanks to Paul Beckman, April Bernard, Susan Bingham, Donald Hall, Susan Holahan, Andrew Mattison, Edward Mattison, Zoe Pagnamenta, Jennifer Pooley, Sandi Kahn Shelton, Lezley TwoBears, and Claire Wachtel. Thanks also to the MacDowell Colony.

All New Haven murder victims in this book are real except Marie Valenti. Everyone else is imaginary except the Shakespeare Lady, who is Margaret Holloway, and Henry Berliner of the unforgettable Foundry Bookstore.

The following books were helpful:

Anthony Griego, Patrol Officer, Department of Police Services, City of New Haven, "...Above and Beyond the Call of Duty: A Brief History of Policemen Who Have Died in the Performance of Their Duties, 1855–1970." Unpublished book in Local History Room, New Haven Public Library.

Rollin G. Osterweis, *Three Centuries of New Haven, 1638–1938.* New Haven: Yale University Press, 1953.

"Shooting Death of Malik Jones on April 14, 1997." Unpublished book in Local History Room, New Haven Public Library.